Pen to **Print**

This book has been produced with assistance from
The London Borough of Barking and Dagenham Library
Service
Pen to Print Creative Writing Project 2017/8
with funding from
The Arts Council, England Grants for the Arts.

Supported using public funding by
**ARTS COUNCIL
ENGLAND**
LOTTERY FUNDED

London Borough of
Barking & Dagenham
lbbd.gov.uk

A Young Man's Game

Paul Blake

 New Generation Publishing

For Helen,

I hope you think this is worth all the nights it took me away from you.

*'Look, you get older. Passion is **a young man's game**, OK? Young people can be passionate. Older people gotta be more wise. I mean, you're around awhile, you leave certain things to the young and you don't try to act like you're young. You could really hurt yourself.'*

- Bob Dylan, 2015

A Young Man's Game

1

The vibration of the phone disturbed Alec Foster from his thoughts; he glanced down at the desk and saw the smiling picture of his niece, Sara, on the screen. He pressed the 'end' button to silence it.

'Anyone important Alec?' Arthur Newbury asked, with rebuke in his voice as the meeting was interrupted.

'Yes… well no, not really, it was just my niece, Sara, she's coming to here on Thursday to see me,' Alec replied. He could have added more to his response, like how Sara was the only family he had left. His younger brother Mark and his wife, Sophie, died in a car crash seven years ago; and how it had been over a year since he had last seen her; and how not letting her down was the only thing keeping him going. But he felt this meeting about the impending visit of the Prime Minister was not the setting.

'Ok, let's carry on then, shall we? Richard, you were saying,' Newbury directed his comments towards Richard Harper, the Berlin Head of Counter-Terrorism for the Secret Intelligence Service or MI6 as it is more commonly known, dismissing Alec for the time being.

'As I was saying, there have been no direct threats to the PM's visit, however…' Harper resumed; as Alec tuned him out.

Terrorism… that's all you ever heard about these days. As if that's the most significant threat we're facing. We're running scared of a bunch of unsophisticated virgins who cannot hurt us as a nation; cannot make us submit to their will. Alec was the head of the Russian section in Berlin and had left fieldwork behind almost ten years ago and was now counting down the days until retirement from behind a desk. At fifty-one he had nearly four years left and was considering leaving the service early and taking a hit on his pension. As far as he knew, they wouldn't be replacing his role when he left; the Russian section would be amalgamated into a general European section. This he felt was a short-sighted mistake considering the increased Russian hacking plots and the alleged meddling in the recent US and UK elections. Unfortunately, since 9/11 it was political suicide to appear to look weak on terrorism, no matter that a nation-state with nuclear weapons was sitting on your windowsill; coveting the furniture and thinking how the room would look so much better in a nice shade of red.

The meeting concluded without further incident, and Alec returned to his office. He was grateful for the privacy his office afforded, as it was getting harder to hide the shakes and hangovers resulting from his predilection for cheap schnapps from his colleagues. Every night he pottered around his lonely apartment; only the dusty, faded paintings on the wall, the always-full decanter on the sideboard and the pictures of Sara, Mark and Sophie to keep him company. Alec was sure he was despised by his colleagues in the cubicles outside, considering him a relic of the Cold War; a grey dinosaur in an ill-fitting suit. *What do they know? They think spying is all about hacking computers and tracking by satellite. They know nothing of the fear of being alone in enemy territory; armed only with a set of false papers and your wits.* His desk phone jolted him out of his thoughts with its loud and penetrating buzz.

'Foster,' Alec answered.

'Hello, Alec, its Jaromir,' *Polyakov, what does he want?* Polyakov was his opposite number in the Russian Foreign Intelligence Service or SVR; formerly the KGB's First Chief Directorate.

'Hi, Jaromir, what's up?' he asked.

'Alec, we need to meet. Urgently,' Polyakov said, straight to the point, which immediately got Alec's attention. Polyakov was renowned for his ability with ambiguity and obfuscation.

'Sounds serious, when and where?'

'Tonight, at nine, Becketts Kopf Bar in Pappelallee,' he replied tersely.

'I know it; I'll be there.'

'Take precautions,' Polyakov warned and ended the call abruptly.

What the hell is this about? Take precautions? He turned on his screen and noted the details about the call in the Contact Log out of habit. *I'd better inform Newbury about this.*

'Jaromir Polyakov?' Newbury queried, 'Did he give any hint what this was about?'

'Not even a little one – he sounded grim,' Alec answered.

'And he told you to take precautions? Do you think you're up for it, Alec? It's been so long since you were in the field.' The concern was evident in his voice. He'd been Alec's ally over the years and was probably the sole reason why Alec still held his position, much to the displeasure of the young, hungry wolves baying for his job.

'I'm not dead yet, Arthur,' Alec replied with a wry

smile. 'It'll be good to get away from the desk for a while.'

***

Alec decided against taking a taxi as the unexpected snowstorm earlier in the day had passed. The cold would be good for clearing his head and the walk for recalling the tradecraft, which once instinctual, was now barely remembered. He left the British Embassy at six, which gave him three hours to make the one-hour journey to the bar. He joined numerous other embassy staff making their way up Wilhelmstraße to the Brandenburger Tor U-bahn, subway station in the late December night. Alec glanced up at the Brandenburg Gate opposite the station, lit up in majestic glory. It evoked memories of that night in 1989 watching the crowds demolish the Berlin Wall in front of the gate, the feeling of history changing in front of him and the fear of what could happen next. The thump thump of deep techno bass from the busker playing to the crowds echoed through the night. Alec found his feet moving in time to the beat.

Alec felt comfortable blending in with the other workers in their long coats, done up tight against the cold; only his thinning grey hair and stooped shoulders standing out. He was a touch under six foot and moved silently amongst the clatter of high heels and leather soles on the hard pavement. He continued past the station; remembering that it had once been called a *Geisterbahnhöfe* or ghost station; when the East German government built the Berlin Wall and closed the station; the Cold War separating East and West Berlin and ending freedom of movement across the city. As he crossed Unter den Linden Boulevard the pungent, meaty aroma of a nearby wurst kiosk made his stomach rumble and his mouth filled with saliva. *I'd better get something to eat; it wouldn't be good to get there with my stomach growling, there's a restaurant along the river that'll suit.*

Alec continued down Wilhelmstraße, wishing he had brought his hat with him as the wintry cold attacked his neck and ears. Mounds of melting snow on the pavement created a stream disappearing behind him as he walked up the slight incline towards the River Spree, following the over ground blue pipes transporting water from the building works at the Brandenburger Tor station to the river. He turned on to Reichstagufer, running alongside the river, twinkling with reflected lights from the nearby buildings, amongst the dark and forbidding water, and walked eastwards for a hundred paces until he reached the Die Eins restaurant. There were empty tables with large umbrellas on the terrace outside, but inside, the restaurant was packed. The warmth and fragrance of the place, however, overcame the noise and Alec entered and stood at the bar, looking outwards towards the river. Remembering how the wurst stall affected him earlier, he ordered currywurst and chips to eat at the bar and a glass of red wine. While he waited for the food to arrive, he began to take a mental note of the people who arrived in the restaurant after him and those walking past the large glass windows: *Large man, grey suit jacket, dark-rimmed glasses...ah, he's meeting a woman already seated... a couple at that table, faces strained, the woman has tears in her eyes, the man is eyeing the door, a breakup in progress... colleagues having a drink after work surrounding the alpha male, look at them vying for his attention...*He was still people-watching when his food arrived. He paid the waiter, so he could leave without waiting for the bill. After the meal, his mouth tingling from the paprika and chilli powder in the curry sauce, and satisfied with the warmth in his stomach, he took a final look at the diners to embed them in his memory and left the restaurant.

Alec was approximately halfway to the bar, on Auguststraße, when his stomach began rebelling from the spices in the currywurst, giving him slight heartburn. *Come on, Alec, you're not in your thirties anymore; you're going to have to try to watch what you put in your body.*

'Oi, mate!' A loud, deep voice from behind Alec suddenly called out.

Alec turned slowly, trying to allow his eyes time to pick out details and assess threats. His heart beat faster, his vision narrowed, and he fought the urge to urinate as adrenaline coursed through his body. He forced himself to take slow, deep breaths. *Six... no, make that seven males; aged late-twenties to mid-thirties; two of them are helping a third walk, his arms around their shoulders, being carried like a walking wounded battlefield casualty. Is that one wearing a dress?*

'*Ja?*' he queried, in German. 'Yes? Can I be of help?' he continued in accented English, correctly judging their origin from the "Oi".

The closest man said, 'Yeah, mate, do you know where the Reaperbarn is? We're on John's stag do,' he pointed at the man in the red dress, 'and, are looking for the strip clubs and brothels. It's tradition,' he concluded, looking at the ground, sheepishly.

'Ah, I see. Not to worry, my friend, I remember being young,' Alec said reassuringly in a perfect German accent.

'However, the *Reeperbahn* is three or four hours away, in Hamburg. You'll be looking for the Kurfürstenstraße; it'll be too far to walk, though.' *This could be useful for me; a group is easier to hide in, and if anyone is looking to pick me up they'll think twice if I'm with my new friends.*

'Crap.'

'It's ok though; if you get the underground, you'll be there in twenty-five minutes. I can take you to the station if you want. It's on my way and only five minutes away. *Ja*? It's not a problem.'

'If you're sure it's no trouble; that'd be great. *Danke*, I'm Peter by the way.'

No, thank you. Alec smiled, 'Nice to meet you, Peter, my name is Stefan,' he replied. Using the cover name he traditionally used in the field. He put his hands in his pockets to hide the tremors as the jolt of adrenaline faded from his system, and slowly exhaled a sigh of relief.

When they reached Senefelderplatz station, Alec, still using his German accent gave them instructions on where to change trains and when to get off. He also advised them, 'Try to get John to *erbrechen*, uh... be sick, before entering the station. *Ja*. It is early still, that will clear room for more drink and prevent the night ending early for all.'

He leaned in conspiratorially to Peter and in a low voice said, 'When you get to Kurfürstenstraße don't go in the first strip bar you see. Go to the third or fourth one. Fewer customers, so the girls will be more desperate; more bang for your buck.' He added a wink for effect, clapped Peter on the shoulder and quickly walked off down a side street. As he was walking he looked at his watch; he still had over an hour to be at the bar, but he wanted to get there early to assess the situation; see if any surprises were waiting for him.

Reaching Pappelallee, the street that Becketts Kopf bar was on, it was quiet with few people around; the tramlines on the broad road glistened in the streetlight. The bar was down the street on the left, so Alec walked alongside the graffiti-marked buildings opposite; the patterns and tags indistinct in the available light. When he reached the bar, he stepped back into a darkened doorway to survey the entrance. He glanced at his watch and was pleased to see he was there half an hour early. He looked across the road at his target; the entrance was unmarked. A hidden Berlin gem, a person would only know of it via word of mouth. There was a portrait of Samuel Beckett, the Irish playwright, for whom the bar was named, in one of the windows, the only indication of its identity.

Alec saw Polyakov pull up in a taxi and enter the bar. He was tall and solidly built, in his early forties, dark hair, a Stalinesque moustache dominating his face, curved and bushy. Alec, having known him for almost twenty years, was amused that he was still sporting the reviled style and knew that it was worn for purely practical purposes as anyone describing him would start and end at the moustache. Although they were rivals, Alec liked Polyakov, as he played fair and was as good as his word. Alec watched the bar entrance for a further fifteen minutes to see if Polyakov had been followed, but nothing untoward struck him. He crossed the road, making sure he avoided tripping over the tramlines and rang the buzzer on the dark, mahogany door in the lighted archway. The door was opened by a waiter who led Alec past the crowded smoking room to the dimly lit non-smoking bar area at the back where he knew Polyakov, who had recently given up smoking, would be. The room was furnished with low leather sofas, facing a long bar with barstools at the front. There was a distinct lack of patrons in this section. *After a few drinks, all the ex-smokers feel the need to reacquaint themselves with their old habit; even if it is just passively.* The walls were covered in poorly finished plasterwork the colour of blood orange, interspersed with garish prints. Alec loved the dark atmosphere of the bar; the dim lighting giving everything a dramatic shadow; the low-level music, audible but designed to allow conversation to flow amongst patrons. As Alec expected, Polyakov was sitting on the end sofa against the far wall, with a glass of whisky on the table and a serious look on his face. Alec ordered the same from the waiter and sat down.

'Good evening, Jaromir,' he said, with a smile. 'It is nice to see you again; I do love this place, it feels so surreptitious.'

'Thank you for coming, Alec,' Polyakov said in heavily accented English. 'Can I get straight down to business?'

'Of course, this is unlike you; it must be serious.'

'It is. We have reason to believe that there is a plot to kill a government minister here in Berlin by the end of the week. And it is being planned by someone in your building.'

Alec sat for a moment, unsure whether to laugh or be outraged, his mouth formed the start of some unknown words and then closed grimly; he shifted his body in the chair as he processed what he had been told.

'How reliable is the information?' He asked finally, knowing the answer.

'Reliable enough for me to seek you out; you're the only one I trust in that building, everyone else is only looking out for themselves. We have been hearing reports from our former Soviet states that an Englishman has been looking for some friends to terminate a leading government minister in Germany this week; we have a description,' Polyakov paused and glanced up, looking past Alec's shoulder.

Alec caught the figure in his peripheral vision, turned and saw the waiter with his drink on a black, round tray. The waiter bent down to put the drink on the table; Alec looked back at Polyakov to continue the conversation when the waiter had left, he saw a ragged bullet hole appear in his friend's forehead and heard the muffled roar and distinctive rattle of a suppressed weapon beside him. Alec spun and faced the waiter; his eyes opened wide as he saw the gun below the tray, a wide can-like suppressor extending the barrel length, as the waiter turned towards him.

2

Alec reached down and in one smooth motion grabbed his glass of whiskey and threw it at the waiter. Alec felt the passage of a bullet speeding past his cheek as the glass struck the man hard in the face, like a punch, the whiskey splashed into his eyes. He staggered back, groping at his face. Alec followed the throw with a vicious kick to his assailants' knee. He fell and dropped the gun, and the tray. Alec thought for a second about his gun, back at the embassy, locked nice and securely away in his office safe, he frowned, aimed a second kick at the man's face and ran.

He ran through the hazy, smoking section towards the exit, barging past groups of drinkers and smokers; spilling drinks and knocking cigarettes and cigars from hands; ignoring the curses and threats behind him, he threw open the door and ran out into the street. *What the hell just happened?* He thought as he looked around deciding which way to go. Pappelallee ran from South-West to North-East; South-West took him closer to the embassy and his apartment, however, he'd be expected to head that way; North-East took him further into what he still considered East-Berlin, where his knowledge of the streets wasn't so good. He heard a commotion coming from the bar behind him, *got to move now!* He looked ahead of him and saw the alcove from earlier, *there*, he decided. He ran across the road as a bright yellow tram came up the road towards him. He was halfway across the road when he heard the bar door slam open with a crash; he spun around ready to defend himself and saw that the tram was blocking anyone's view of him. He hastily turned back around and sprinted to the alcove. When he got there; he slumped to the ground hoping that anyone seeing him would assume he was homeless. Breathing hard, his heart pounding he turned to watch the bar.

In front of it was the waiter, holding a phone to his ear. Alec couldn't see his face, but he could hear part of the conversation, in German, with a Slavic accent:

'… No, he got away. Come pick me up, before the Police get here,' the waiter turned and looked the other way; shadows obscured his face in the night light.

Come on, step closer to the streetlight, Alec willed, *let me see your face, you bastard.* To Alec's immense frustration the waiter stayed where he was. Alec could hear sirens in the far distance, a stream of people left the bar, *they must have discovered Jaromir*, not wanting the rest of their evening spent talking to the Police, and they quickly dispersed.

A car drove up to the bar, headlights blazing, a silver Mercedes C-Class with tinted side windows, Alec tried to see the driver, but from his vantage point, the driver was on the opposite side of the car. The glare of the headlights momentarily exposed the waiter, but too quickly for Alec to register. The car stopped, and the waiter walked around to the passenger side and opened the door. The interior light came on, and this time Alec could clearly see both the driver and the waiter as he got in the car. The driver was looking in Alec's direction when the door opened, he had a wide neck, supporting a large square head, a rough scar leading from his left eyebrow to his hairline, his hair shaved close, in short, dark bristles. Alec hoped his tramp disguise held. The waiter was in profile; he was smaller than the driver, less physically imposing, medium brown wavy hair, swept back by a hair band, a distinctive bump on his long nose, drying blood trailing out of one nostril. The waiter slammed the door shut, the light went off, and the car sped away. Alec tried to read the license plate, but dirt obscured it.

Alec closed his eyes and exhaled deeply, his hands shaking and his heart still playing a drum solo to its audience of one. He heard the distinctive two-tone siren of the Berlin Polizei getting closer. *Come on Alec; sort yourself out, north or south? The nearest underground station is Schönhauser Allee, to the north,* Alec thought, *about ten minutes away, fifteen if I don't head straight there. You must move.* He struggled to his feet using his hands against the wall for support, his legs were like lead, from the cold, concrete floor and the unfamiliar exertion he had put them through. He left the alcove and headed north-east along Pappelallee, hugging the wall as he went to keep away from the glare of the streetlights. He reached Stargarder Strauss, a wide crossroads, and watched as a Police car, siren wailing, blue lights flashing turn into Pappelallee and head towards the bar. As he waited for the lights to change so he could cross, he thought about which way to go. *Left into Stargarder was the quickest and more direct way to the underground, but the Police car had come from that direction and when they radio for assistance at the bar, more will come. They may recognise me from any descriptions given by staff. Caution is better than boldness here, maybe I should go to the next station out, Vinetastraße, it'll be even further, but it's less likely to be being watched.* Alec shook his head, *this is ridiculous, I was never this indecisive in the field. Choose a course and stick with it, none of this dithering, I'm liable to get myself arrested or killed, got to get safe and figure out what the hell just happened.* He decided to go to Vinetastraße station, which was further, but safer. The lights changed, and he moved on to Stahlheimer Straße, leaving the Police, the bar and Jaromir behind.

***

Alec was walking briskly down Neumannstraße, trying to warm himself up, the street was a lot more residential than previous streets, large, grey, four-storey maisonettes flanked him on either side, neatly trimmed, thigh high, hedgerows ran alongside marking the boundary of the properties and the pavement. Alec had settled himself down and was thinking over what had happened. *The waiter's accent fits with what Jaromir said about an Englishman trying to recruit Eastern-European help. Can it be possible? Why would an Englishman be looking to murder a Government Minister in Berlin? Surely, it'd be easier back in England, make it look like an accident or suicide. Mind you, Jaromir didn't say it was an English Minister; it could be a German... Arthur and I will have to figure it out when...* Alec was woken from his thoughts by a silver sedan car in the distance, turning onto Neumannstraße from Eschengraben, slowly coming towards him. *That looks like a Mercedes,* he thought. His stomach flipped, and he looked around for somewhere to hide. There were tall trees in the pavement, every ten to twenty metres, with long, slim trunks providing little cover; there were no alcoves he could hide in this time. By the time he thought about the hedgerow beside him, he could see two male occupants in the car looking at either

14

side of the street. Without further hesitation, he rolled himself over the hedge.

He landed, hard, on his back with a smack, causing his diaphragm to spasm, Alec's eyes bulged as he realised he couldn't breathe, he forgot about the car, the men and their guns, and fought the urge to panic. The memory of prep school: playing pirates among the ancient oak trees in the school grounds, surfaced in his mind. The times he and his friends would fall while climbing the tallest tree, or in their minds, the rigging of the highest mast of a ship, the wind being knocked out of them, lying in agony among the fallen leaves and scattered acorns. It helped him remember that this feeling was temporary and would pass. He calmed himself down and waited for the block of ice in his chest to melt, the paralysis to fade, and the pain to recede. Eventually, it went, like it always had, leaving a dull ache across his shoulders, and a twinge in his spine when he moved. He struggled to his knees, slightly sinking in the damp flowerbed behind the hedge. He listened before raising his head, trying to hear a car, to make out whether they were still there or not. There were no discernible sounds, so he decided to risk a glance. He lifted his head, slowly, over the hedge, being careful not to overbalance and fall forwards into it, looking left and right he could not see any vehicles moving or any people walking down the street. *I suppose it's nearly eleven; most people are in bed by now, as they have work in the morning. At least the U-bahn is still running, it closes at one thirty. I'll be back at the embassy well before then.* With that thought and a loud exhalation he got to his feet, with his soles slipping slightly on the slick grass, he made it to the pavement and continued up Neumannstraße, this time walking a lot closer to the hedge, ready to dive behind it at a moment's

15

notice.

Alec passed the Netto supermarket on his right, with its car park reassuringly empty of silver Mercedes', the building's normal light-yellow façade, a dull grey in the shadows. He continued until he passed a bright pink apartment block and knew he was at the junction with Vinetastraße. His knees and feet were hurting him now, each step felt like needles jabbing away at the soles of his feet. He was sure there was a blister forming. The walk after the shooting, combined with the earlier saunter through the city, was by far the most he had walked in a very long time, and he was suffering for it. *Too many years sat behind a desk, old man, the station is not far, and then you'll be able to sit down. You should have listened to Sara when she visited last year. She said you should have dumped your antique phone and upgraded to a smartphone, you could have got an UberTaxi back on Stahlheimer and been at the embassy, brandy in your hand, warming yourself by Arthur's fire.* Alec pictured Sara's face, the disgust evident as he pulled out his phone to answer a call, then the fireplace in Newbury's office, dark wrought iron, with its blazing logs, their comforting occasional pop and crackle, and the inviting, sweet smell of the burning wood. He shook his head and turned his internal castigation off and concentrated on his surroundings. He had survived this long by being cautious and wasn't going to change now to satisfy *that* nagging voice. He continued down Vinetastraße, slightly limping now, past apartment blocks in varying hues of grey. He resisted the urge to quicken his pace, physically holding himself back, as he saw the end of the road in the distance, the intersection with Berliner Straße. Knowing that the Vinetastraße U-bahn station was just around the corner, that just past the Tchibo coffee shop on the corner, were the subway steps to cross the busy street to reach the underground platform.

A figure stepped out from behind one of the tall trees lining the pavement, approximately four metres separated them. Alec recognised the man by the hair band and the silenced gun he was holding.

'I think that's far enough,' the waiter said in accented English. 'You will come with us now.'

Alec didn't have time to react; the driver of the Mercedes had come up behind him, silently for such a big man, and landed a heavy punch to Alec's back. Alec's knees buckled, and he fell forward towards the waiter, a loud gasp escaped his mouth. He folded up into a ball shape, his head tucked down for protection, anticipating the beating to come.

3

'Come on, get up,' said the waiter, an impatient tone in his voice.

Alec stayed on the ground, trying to recover from the blow, not understanding why they hadn't taken it further.

'Get up, you old bastard.' the driver said, his voice much deeper than his companion. 'This is the guy who got past you in the bar?'

'I wasn't expecting him to throw the glass,' the waiter replied. 'Who would? Look at him.'

'Pathetic.' Alec wasn't sure if the driver was talking about the waiter or him; he hoped it was the latter. If he was underestimated, he could possibly use that to his advantage.

The driver reached down and grabbed Alec's arm, and pulled. Alec lifted off the floor and his legs scrabbled against the ground to gain purchase and relieve the pressure on his arm and shoulder caused by his own body weight. He sorted out his footing and stood, slightly hunched. The driver let go of his arm.

'Don't make us repeat ourselves again,' the driver said. 'Do as we say and this will be easier on you.'

'You're going to kill me,' Alec said, his teeth gritted together. 'How much harder can it get?'

'Shut up and move!'

Alec held up his hands in surrender and started shuffling forward, following the waiter, who was moving backwards, maintaining the initial distance, the gun still pointed at Alec. The driver followed behind; Alec didn't look to see how far back he was, the deep, nasal breathing behind him told him all he needed to know. Alec recognised this from martial art lectures he had attended as warrior breathing, a practice used by US Navy Seals. It is supposed to be more effective in times of stress promoting recovery from adrenaline rush and increasing sharpness. He had always scoffed at the idea during the lectures and had never carried out the exercises to build up his lung capacity. He regretted that decision now. He tried to copy the driver's breathing subtly, but exhale more slowly and silently, increasing the oxygen to his muscles and brain.

'Hurry up; you're too slow,' the driver said. He pushed Alec forwards. He stumbled but retained his footing; he noted that the waiter did not try to maintain the gap this time, reducing it to two and a half, maybe three metres, not close enough for Alec to do anything. Alec continued his slow shuffling pace and waited for another frustrated shove. He could see the silver Mercedes now, twenty-five metres away, parked at the junction of Vinetastraße and Berliner; outside the Bartels Apotheke on the corner the shutters down, a large red 'A' sign protruding out from the wall above the shop.

Still walking backwards, the waiter glanced over his shoulder to make sure there were no obstacles in his way, as he did so, the driver pushed Alec again.

'Come on, old man,' he mocked.

Alec used the momentum of the shove to close the gap on the distracted waiter; the gun had dropped slightly, Alec sprang forward and grabbed the waiter's gun hand and pushed it away from his body. He spun his body round to face the driver, and as he did so, he bent his free arm and launched the elbow at the side of the waiter's head; upon contact, the waiter involuntary squeezed the gun's trigger. Alec felt the bullet pass him, a blast of hot gas following it. He saw the driver stagger and reach for his thigh. The waiter fell to the ground clumsily and did not move, Alec let go of the waiter's arm, and it dropped to the ground limply, the gun left his grip and slid under a parked car. The driver cursed loudly and started towards Alec.

Run! Alec thought and turned and ran. He crossed over the road and ran past the café; he reached the U-bahn subway steps and stumbled down them. He reached the southbound platform and walked to the end; he leaned next to a red, steel pillar and waited for the train to come. His breathing was rapid, he was taking a deep lungful of oxygen with each breath, his heart jackhammered in his chest, and he felt lightheaded and giddy. *Please don't faint*, he pleaded with himself, *or have a heart attack.* He looked around him; the platform was empty.

The bright-yellow train pulled into the platform and squealed to a stop. It was one of the older style trains, boxy in appearance. The green 'open door' button lit up, and Alec waited for the doors to open. The doors hissed apart, and he stepped inside. The carriage was empty, and he sat down eagerly. The doors closed, and the train started moving. Through the carriage window, Alec saw the Mercedes driver hobble down the stairs to the platform, stare at the train pulling away, shout an expletive and punch the stairwell wall.

***

Safely on the train, and still shaken from his experiences, Alec closed his eyes and tried to calm down; his mind whirled, firing questions at him: *How did they know where to find me? Why did they kill Jaromir and try to kill me? How the hell did I get out of that? Will they get me before I reach the embassy, they must know that is where I'm headed?* He tried to think of the last one first as it was the question with the most straightforward answer. He thought about the journey ahead. He usually chose the Becketts Kopf Bar to meet people as it was on the direct U2 U-bahn line to Mohrenstraße station, just south of the embassy, the journey should take under twenty minutes, the walk to the embassy a further six minutes or so after that. The same journey by car was usually a couple of minutes less, depending on traffic, however, the Mercedes driver may not be able to drive properly with a hole in his leg, and the waiter may have concussion, *that may slow them down*, he thought optimistically, *especially if there's traffic on the roads.*

The train stopped at Schönhauser Allee station, the few people on the platform entered other carriages, leaving Alec still alone. His phone rang, he looked at the display and saw Newbury's name showing. Alec flipped open the phone and pressed the button to answer the call.

'Hi Arthur,' he said, his voice calmer than he felt.

'Alec, what the hell is happening?' Newbury said loudly. 'I've just had the Russian SVR call me; they say Polyakov is dead and they're looking for you.'

'Arthur, this line isn't secure,' Alec reminded. 'I know I'm in the shit; I'm coming in, I should be there soon. Did they give the name of the investigating officer?'

'I've got it written down here somewhere, some captain, I didn't recognise the name…here it is… Captain Lukin Olegovich, mean anything to you?'

'Never heard of him, I would have thought this would

warrant a higher rank than a captain-'

Newbury cut him off, 'Alec, I've had the ambassador in here for the past twenty minutes, he hit the roof when we said we didn't know where you were. Where are you?'

'I'm on the U-bahn, I'll be there soon.' Alec repeated.

'Alec.' Newbury said, stressing the name, elongating the letters.

'Arthur, you know me, this isn't anything I've done. I'll tell you all about it when I get there. Jaromir was right; it is very serious.'

'Do you need me to send anyone to meet you? Help you get home?'

Alec knew Arthur meant sending out the embassy guards to escort him back to the embassy. 'No, that's not necessary. They'll only draw attention. A single middle-aged man walking down the street is a lot more anonymous.'

'Ok, then, make sure you come straight to my office when you get here. Speak to no one.'

'Will do, have a brandy waiting for me, I need it.'

'Will do,' Newbury echoed. 'See you soon.'

'See you soon.'

Alec ended the call, he paused and looked at his phone, something was nagging at the back of his mind, he tried, but couldn't retrieve it. *It'll come to me*, he thought. He placed the phone inside his coat pocket. The interior of the carriage was stifling, especially as Alec had been exposed to the frigid air outside for almost five hours. He stood up and removed his coat. He remembered when he bought it: he had been speaking to Newbury the day before and had remarked that he needed to buy a new coat and had said he had seen a smart looking grey, classic style trenchcoat in the Gant store on Friedrichstraße.

'That's a great idea, George Smiley,' Newbury quipped. 'Don't you think that would be too obvious?'

'What do you mean?' Alec had said.

'Are you going to get a fedora and a tatty-looking briefcase too?'

'Oh yes, I see, very funny. People already call me Leamas, you know, from-'

'*The Spy Who Came in from the Cold*, yes, Alec, you may have told me that a few times over the years.' Newbury said, interrupting Alec.

Alec held his hands up in mock surrender, 'I get your point, Arthur, I'll get a different style.'

Alec went back to the Gant store and, with regret, left the trenchcoat on the rack and chose a sleek-looking, navy, mid-length, jacket, which, he thought, would be perfect for wintry Berlin. It was this coat that he had just taken off. He folded it into a bundle, lifted his legs up and stretched them out along the bench. Leaning his body against the veneered partition, he put the coat bundle between his head and the train window. *That's better, he* thought, as the tension left his legs; *do I think I could get away with taking my shoes off too?* The night's stress had taken its toll, and in the hot carriage, Alec's eyes closed. He blinked them open again but couldn't prevent the heavy eyelids from closing a final time.

Alec felt a gentle shaking of his shoulder, and he bolted upright, his legs knocking into the ticket inspector as he swung them off the bench.

'*Es tut uns leid.*' Sorry, said Alec.

'*Fahrkarte bitte?*' The inspector asked for the ticket.

Alec fumbled his wallet out of his coat pocket and

retrieved the *Monatskarte*, monthly pass and produced it for the inspector.

'*Danke.*' Thank you, said the inspector as he looked the ticket over. He handed it back to Alec satisfied and moved on.

Alec shook his head awake and looked around. He saw that the carriage had gained some occupants while he was out, he gave them a quick once over and didn't think any were a threat. The train pulled into the station and Alec looked out the window for the name. He didn't recognise the wall tiles, a random mix of shades of blue and cream. *Ernst-Reuter-Platz?* Alec thought, *I've slept passed my stop and a further eight stations?* He quickly stood up and gathered his coat; he checked to ensure he hadn't left anything behind and walked to the doors. When the train stopped he opened the doors and walked the length of the platform as he headed for the exit to cross to the eastbound platform to head back to Mohrenstraße. He was cursing under his breath; he had tripled his journey. *Arthur is going to go nuts.* He reached the platform as the train pulled into the station and quickly boarded the first carriage, next to the driver's cabin. He decided to stand by the doors, his coat draped over one of his forearms, rather than risk falling asleep again and ending back at Vinetastraße, where he started. He noticed he had some spittle on his chin, *drooling in my sleep too; Alec Leamas has nothing on me*. He smiled at the thought as he rubbed it away. The doors closed, and the train continued its journey.

The train slowed as it entered Bülowstraße station, the station was overground, and instead of the usual tiled walls it had a church-like appearance: high-vaulted ceiling and glass windows, Alec unconsciously scanned the people waiting on the platform, his eyes continually flickering as they focused on each person for barely a second. His mind screamed at him as the train halted. *The waiter and the driver are there, in the middle of the platform, waiting.*

4

Alec took a second or two to put his coat on as he looked in the direction of the pair. The carriages thankfully obscured them; he hoped they hadn't recognised him as he passed them, with any luck they were looking at those sitting down as there were still four stops before he was due to get off at Mohrenstraße. *How did they find me again?*

Alec could hear the hydraulic hiss as the doors of the train carriages opened. He waited a beat or three and peeked his head out of the door looking towards the centre of the platform for the men. It was clear. *They must have boarded.* He stepped down onto the platform and stayed near his carriage. The stairwell leading down to street level was in front of him. *Wait, Alec.* He heard the door closing signal behind and knew the doors would be shutting soon. A few passengers were heading towards the stairwell; they must have been from the middle or the other end of the train. The doors closed, and the train began to move off. Alec quickly covered the ten to the stairwell and descended, head bowed to conceal his identity. He put his hands in his coat pockets to protect them from the cold air coming up the stairwell from the street. He felt his phone, and the troublesome voice in his head started up again. *They must have been following me either by car or train. How would they know I had missed my stop and was heading back to the embassy?* He thought for a second.

They were tracking my phone signal! That damn phone reception on the train and the network on the U-bahn. In Central London it is a dead zone on the tube; only allowing a signal as you head away from the tunnels to the overground stations. *Either they or a controller was guiding them, maybe even before I reached the bar to meet Jaromir. How could I have forgotten that? They must have gone to the middle carriage of the train intending to split up and go through each car. You can't keep relying on luck, you old bastard. Get your head in the game or you'll lose it. Now let's get rid of that phone.*

Alec reached the bottom of the stairwell and stepped out of the station, looking for a waste bin to dump the phone. Swaying towards the stairwell were a couple of young girls chatting happily among themselves, clearly inebriated, their voices louder than they thought, the pitch higher, more strident. Just before they passed him, the one closest to him stumbled as her heel caught between the decorative paving stones. Her stumble brought her friend down with her. Instinctively Alec reached out to catch them and accidentally knocked the first girl's clutch bag from her hands, it fell to the floor popping the clasp and scattering the bag's contents. Alec held up his hands in apology. He crouched to pick up the bag and retrieve the strewn items, as he was doing this he decided this would be an ideal way to get rid of the phone. He slipped it in the bag, redid the clasp, and pushed himself to his feet. He helped the girls to their feet saying sorry and passed the first girl her bag.

'Watch where you are going next time!' She said, in German. 'Come on let's get away from granddad.'

'I'm sorry.' Alec replied, also in German.

The girls stomped up the stairs in disgust. Alec thought

of the men chasing him spending their time tracking down a pair of drunken girls. *I hope they're going to Ruhleben,* the station at the end of the U2 line; just past the Olympiastadion. The girls' condition, stirred something in Alec, *Man, I could use a drink,* he was missing his usual routine, he could feel it gnawing away at him, he checked his watch, just past eleven thirty. *I'd be in my armchair with a glass of schnapps about now; I've just opened a bottle of Schladerer Zwetschgenwasser, which was very satisfying last night and I'm mid-way through that Nick Harkaway book, and it's getting really good.* He pictured his tatty armchair: an old-fashioned upright wingback, with its nicotine stained, paisley pattern, from when he used to smoke. The familiar faded tobacco smell, comforting without giving Alec the same craving and nausea he gets when he smells fresh cigarette smoke. He missed smoking, like an old friend, *it would have made tonight go quicker if I'd had a pack. Measuring the distance between places by the number of cigarettes I'd smoke. The walk from the embassy to the bar, three hours? Probably eight or nine cigarettes.* He coughed at the memory. *I need a drink, and I need to move away from the station.* He searched his memory for nearby bars that: a) would be open and b) he liked to drink in. One advantage of being in Berlin all these years was that Alec had tried almost every bar within a three-mile radius of his apartment. *There are several bars on Potsdamer Straße open late, that's just around the corner from here, but they're a bit too loud and popular. I know, Lebensstern or Life Star is a little further away, but it's worth it, cosy, relaxed and, most importantly, quiet. Yes, that's where I'll go.*

With a destination in mind, Alec walked with a purpose

down Bülowstraße, past the three massive Commerzbank buildings opposite the U2 rail track and turned on to Potsdamer Straße, where three more Commerzbank buildings were, each a different style and size. When he passed the third one he looked to cross the road, looking left for vehicles coming up behind him, crossed the two lanes to the middle of the road and waited for a gap in traffic to cut across to the other side. It didn't take long and soon enough he was walking on the left-hand pavement heading up to the Landwehr canal, which he had walked along many times on a peaceful Sunday afternoon, strolling from his apartment in Neuenburger Straße to the canal and then following it until it met the River Spree in what had once been East Berlin. For a moment he thought about heading to his apartment and locking himself away, like the title of the book he was reading *The Gone-Away World*. Sara had bought the book for him three Christmases ago and constantly nagged him to read it. It was miles away from the typical Russian literature he normally read, and he had kept putting it off and off, but nevertheless, he was enjoying it. *No, can't return to the apartment yet, it's a good hour away, and they'd be looking for me there. Also, I really, really want that drink.*

He reached the junction of Potsdamer Straße and Kurfürstenstraße, the garish blue and pink LSD – Love Sex Dreams – two-storey sex shop dominating the corner and turned left onto Kurfürstenstraße and started walking to the bar. It was only five minutes or so down this road. Every ten or twenty metres down Kurfürstenstraße there were street prostitutes, standing in the road and on the pavement touting for business. Alec was approached quite a few times by different women; he judged them from their accents to be mainly Romanian or Bulgarian, with the occasional Pole and Turk thrown in. *They must be freezing,* he thought to himself, *out on this night, dressed in little skirts and dresses, knee-high boots, and coats. God, how old are you? You sound like your grandmother, even ten years ago this place was a great source of information for you, the stuff men tell these girls to impress them, it never changes, that frail male ego. I wonder how that stag party got on?* Alec smiled, remembering the only bright spot in his night.

He declined all the girls' offers with a gentle smile and a shake of his head and continued to the Life Star bar. He crossed the road as he got closer. Unfortunately, it appeared to the dark-haired woman standing on that side of the road, leaning against a parked car and displaying an impressive cleavage, that he crossed over to speak to her. He got a mouthful of abuse for the misunderstanding, but he apologised. *It seems to be the night for me apologising,* he thought and walked off, the Bulgarian curse words following him. He came to the bar, with the lighted Einstein awnings above the windows. It was a detached building, three storeys, with an iron fence in front. He entered through the gate to the left of the building and went through the front door. He knew he had to walk through the Café Einstein restaurant to get to the bar.

The smells of the food made his stomach grumble, *I'll get some food from the bar*, and once inside the Life Star bar he headed for the comfortable, brown, suede-leather armchairs and waited for the waitress to serve him. He looked around the curved room, cabinets on all walls filled with all manner of spirits and liqueurs, soft up-lights from the top of the cabinets, brightened the dark red walls to the lofty ceilings; the portrait of Henny Porten, Germany's first major film star from way back in the silent film era, and he knew he had made the right decision. The waitress came over, a pretty twenty-something woman, slim with dark hair and he ordered a plum schnapps, 'No, make it two,' he said, 'and a bowl of fries... *bitte*.'

Calm had descended upon him, and while he waited for the drinks and food, he removed his coat and laid it over the arm of the chair next to him. He closed his eyes contently and relaxed; he didn't sleep this time, just let the tension release itself from his body. He had been taught yoga and meditation back in the 80s on a team building weekend and occasionally used the techniques to relax his mind and body, enabling him to think clearer. This was definitely one of those times a clear mind was needed. The waitress brought over his drinks '*Danke*.'

'Your *pommes frites* will be a couple of minutes,' the waitress said and walked back to the bar.

Alec lifted one of the drinks; the glass was dainty in his hands, tall with a mug-like handle low towards the bottom. He lifted the glass, thought of Jaromir and toasted in Russian, quoting from the traditional Russian Orthodox Requiem Mass, 'With thy saints, O Christ, give peace to the soul of thy servant.' Alec downed the drink, feeling the hard burn at the back of his throat and down into his empty stomach, tears came to his eyes, not just from the drink. He coughed and wiped his eyes, *I'm sorry old friend.* The second drink was imbibed only a fraction slower. The waitress brought over the fries, she looked at Alec, and a frown crossed her face.

'Are you ok?' she asked.

'Yes, I'm fine, thank you. I lost a friend today, and I am just drinking to his memory.'

'*Das tut mir leid.*' I'm sorry to hear that, she said.

'*Vielen dank.*' Thank you very much, Alec said, his

31

words matched the smile on his face, given in gratitude at this stranger's concern.

'Can I get you anything else?'

Alec declined, feeling the alcohol already taking affect. *You can have too much of a good thing and now is not the occasion.* The waitress removed the empty glasses and walked away. Alec popped a couple of fries in his mouth. *What to do from here?* He thought. For someone to have been at the bar, as a waiter, they must have been known in advance that Alec and Polyakov would be meeting there. The meeting was only arranged this morning, and the only person Alec had told was Newbury. *I put it in the Contact Log too,* Alec remembered. Alec thought about Newbury, *I've known him since I joined MI6, he joined the year ahead of me. He was my mentor in the first couple of years and helped me out of more than a few sticky situations; especially that incident in East Berlin where the Russian GRU officer opened fire on me and Stefanie, my informant, a secretary in the East German State Security Service, in that café, I returned fire and hit him and managed to return back to the West before I was picked up.*

He shivered at the memory of Stefanie's last moments: it was early evening, late summer, the trees outside were in full bloom, they were flirting over coffee, each hoping the other would step over the unspoken line and announce their feelings. He knew she was in love with him; he had done everything to make her so. He had broken into her flat, and examined her journal, noting her particular tastes and desires, her dreams and her fears. He played up each aspect, becoming her dream partner. While doing so, he had let his guard down and become emotionally attached to her in return. In quiet, alone, moments he admitted to himself that it was love he felt. The tension between them was obvious; passers-by could see it in their eyes. Alec needed her to remain where she was, in her job, on her side of the border, at least for a short while longer. It was important, he told himself, putting his country's wants before his own.

He had promised to facilitate her escape to the West and had hoped when she was there they would marry. A GRU officer, sitting on the other side of the café opposite their table, Alec never found out his name, must have recognised her from the Stasi headquarters on Ruschestraße, near Frankfurter Allee. Stefanie was easily recognisable to most men. She was taller than most East German women, five feet ten in the sensible and functional, black inch-high heels of her profession. Long, slim, nylon clad legs displayed in a knee-length grey skirt and white starched blouse. Her face was oval, with high cheekbones, a permanent blush to the cheeks, a wide smile never far from her lips, even in melancholy East Berlin. Her hair was blonde with a hint of strawberry. Her eyes were grey, almost silver in some lights, wide with long lashes. Alec always remembered her eyes the most, haunting his waking nights and shattering his dreams. The officer must have overheard Stefanie mention her boss's name, Markus Wolf, head of the *Hauptverwaltung Aufklärung*, the foreign intelligence section of the Stasi, to Alec, as he passed their table to get to his own. Once he sat down and saw her, his immediate reaction was that she was a traitor and he had pulled out his gun and shot across the café. The impact sent Stefanie to the floor. Alec stood up and looked for the threat. The officer fired again, his hands shaking so much he missed and shot out the café window behind Alec. Alec reached for the gun he had hidden in his waistband underneath his trenchcoat. The officer's third shot hit the ceiling; dropping chunks of plaster to the floor, Alec, by now had his gun out and shot the officer in the chest, who slumped back down into his seat, his gun dropping from his hand to the floor with a thump. Alec turned back to Stefanie and saw the large entrance wound, just above the heart, *my heart,* her life fading fast. Alec looked into her eyes as the light departed. He closed her eyes with his fingertips, kissed her softly on the lips, and murmured 'I love you.'

He left her in the café; his trenchcoat draped over her face and body and ran to the border. In the warm summer's evening, the lack of a coat wasn't noticed, Alec had reversed his suit jacket to hide her bloodstains and faked a nonchalant air as the border guards checked his papers and he was admitted across. Alec went straight to Newbury, explained what had happened. Newbury managed things to ensure Alec's involvement was never brought to light.

There is no way Arthur is mixed up in this, Alec thought, *he has been in my corner since day one, I was his best man at his marriage to Julia and his two, now grown up, sons' godfather. I helped him through his subsequent divorce, hell; he even stayed in my apartment for three years while he sorted himself out. So, if it wasn't Arthur, who could it have been? It could be anyone at the embassy with access to the log, or access to someone who has access to the log. Not knowing who at the embassy it could be, makes it dangerous to return there.* He thought for a minute, absentmindedly eating the fries. *I need a new phone and, if possible, a gun. My usual channels will have been compromised.* He thought on. *I wonder if Makary Kalinowski is still around.*

Kalinowski was a Polish black-market dealer, Alec had

known him for about twenty years, he specialised in providing under the table products. Alec had used him occasionally when he was in the field. *How will I find him? His number was in my phone, and I don't have that anymore. Is Brigette still working? She'll know. I haven't seen her or Kalinowski for over ten years now.* He reached into the bowl and was surprised to find it was empty. When he'd last seen Brigette, she'd been working around the Nollendorfplatz area, near the Nollendorfplatz U-bahn station. *That's only a couple of minutes away if I cut through Karl-Heinrich-Ulrichs-Straße instead of going back on myself.*

He called for the bill, paid and left.

5

Alec exited the bar onto to Kurfürstenstraße. Opposite the bar was the Lukas Gemeinde Evangelical church, with its large wooden cross on the front of the building, next to the main door. He crossed over the road and made the sign of the cross over his heart for luck, *I'll need all the help I can get*, he thought with a smile. He wasn't religious. Raised Church of England, religion was drummed into him at school with prayers before meals, chapel every morning, trying not to get caught either revising for that day's test or finishing the prep (homework) from the night before. During the sermon he and his friends played 'dead leg screams', where they would punch each other hard on the quadriceps muscle, which had always sounded to Alec as a child like a dinosaur with four arms, hoping to inflict enough pain to make the other scream out and get busted by Mr Crick, the housemaster for talking during chapel. Getting busted in chapel always meant a slippering: five strikes with the heavy, rubber-soled plimsoll during mid-morning break. You'd head back to your House after second lesson and join the line of boys standing to attention in the corridor, silently listening to the whack, whack, whack, whack... whack, coming from the closed door to the Housemaster's office. There always a pause before the last one as the pain from the first four takes a while to set in, the pause let it develop and make itself known before the fifth compounded the agony. Alec saw religion as a distraction, a waste of time.

He continued along Kurfürstenstraße for a minute and came to the junction with Karl-Heinrich-Ulrichs-Straße, he walked past the large SoVD (Sozialverband Deutschland) building on the corner and headed down to Nollendorfplatz. He passed the seven-storey CVJM Jugendgästehaus hostel with the array of shops at its base, each of them closed at this time. Looking at the shops, he checked his watch and saw that it was coming up to one thirty, *better get a move on, if she's there she'll be gone soon.* He reached Nollendorfplatz, a wide thoroughfare, with the Nollendorfplatz U-bahn station in the centre. There were a few girls around. He went over to the closest one: A slim, blonde, maybe in her early 20s, wearing a leather jacket, pink skirt and the obligatory knee-high boots.

'*Entschuldigung,*' excuse me, 'is Brigette working tonight?'

'Why do you want Brigette? She is old. I am better.' She said, her voice had a Romanian accent. To emphasise the point, she swayed her hips seductively.

'She is a friend, not for business.'

The girl pouted and pointed over to the U-bahn station, 'You come back when you're finished with your *friend*, I make you very happy.'

Alec smiled and lied, 'I may just do that, *danke.*'

'*Bis später.*' See you later, she said with a wink.

Alec crossed over to Nollendorfplatz station; the entrance was in what had the appearance of a bunker, a solid stone bricked construction with no windows, only an entrance, lit on either side by three-foot-high rectangular column lights. To the left of the entrance, the station platforms were raised and enclosed inside a glass-windowed structure, looking like two floors of an office block from the 1980s. The platform building was suspended over six lanes of road, which were broken up by supporting concrete columns. Above the station was a large, white powder coated, steel framed open dome, with a big 'U' in white text and blue background to indicate the purpose of the building.

The entrance was closed, it being a weekday, the U-bahn had shut for the night. Alec walked round to the right of the entrance; there was a poorly lit, paved area beside the station, where during the day commuters left their bikes. At night it became a place of drug dealers, and prostitutes. Fortunately for Alec on this cold December night, it looked as though the drug dealers had stayed at home, they usually weren't much trouble, just persistent. There were a few women there still hoping to pick up a last-minute customer or two.

Alec heard Brigette before he saw her, her strident voice booming out over the low-level conversation at the southern side of the station. Alec crossed under the train tracks overhead and headed towards her voice. He had always had a lot of time for Brigette when he was out in the field. She was very smart and knew how to obtain information, such as which diplomats had a predilection for streetwalkers in the Bülowstraße - Kurfürstenstraße area, who visited the strip clubs, brothels and sex cinemas in the area, even who were attracted to the young boys down Martin-Luther-Straße. Alec regularly gave her photos of foreign and British diplomats to study and would see her every few weeks for an update. Alec paid her well and had always enjoyed her company. Taking care not to cross the line into customer territory no matter how much

38

he had wanted to, they had enjoyed time together, saw the occasional German-language film in the *kinos*, and had dinner in the numerous restaurants in the area. She was easy to speak to, a charming, flirtatious manner. Alec didn't know if she ever wanted to take it further than that, he knew if he did it would be the end of his time in the service. An officer couldn't have a prostitute as a girlfriend or wife; he would have been sent back to England. Brigette was German and had walked the streets since she was nineteen; Alec first met her when she was in her mid-twenties. She had a voluptuous figure, usually over-spilling the tight clothes she wore on the job. When she was with Alec, she usually dressed more conservatively. She had a classic German face, full jawed, prominent nose, fair skin, dark hair, sometimes with multi-coloured highlights or lowlights. In her case, it all pooled into a breath-taking combination that was very good for business. Alec had always maintained she should have been in movies, but she didn't want to leave the life she knew so well.

He turned at the edge of the paved area and went towards the station's southern entrance; opposite was the imposing *Neues Schauspielhaus* building, now home to the Goya gay nightclub, with its dancing nude figurines on the facade. Alec had visited the place regularly back in the 90s when it was a concert venue. He saw Brigette standing by the entrance, amongst a group of four other women, all younger than her, her voice raised and a slight slur to her words. She appeared to be telling them about the good old days before the influx of Eastern European "whores", when the women could earn a decent wage without being undercut by the pimped-out crack addicts.

'Hallo, Brigette,' Alec called out as he closed the

distance.

Brigette looked around for the owner of the voice and finally saw Alec approach. Her eyes narrowed, and she unleashed a torrent of abuse at him, she pushed one of the women out of her way and marched over to Alec, her volume increasing as she got closer, and as she got within arm's reach, she started swinging. Alec was unprepared for the violence, and she got a couple of blows in before he could defend himself. He felt the impact of each one and painfully lifted his arms to block the strikes. He let Brigette expend her energy and calm the hell down so he could find out what her problem was. She stopped quicker than he thought she would and then heard a feminine voice behind him say: 'Brigette, you want me to stick him?'

Alec span round and saw a much younger girl, barely eighteen, holding a vicious looking knife in her right hand and looking mean enough to use it.

'What?' said Brigette, her eyes widening as she saw the blade, 'No Ingrid, don't. It's alright, I know him.'

'You sure? He looks like a creep; you always said, "Never give the creeps the chance to get near".'

'Brigette, call your girl off, you know I'm not a threat.' Alec said.

'It's ok Ingrid; he's just a guy I used to know.' Brigette said.

Ingrid put her knife back into the small handbag hanging from her shoulder.

'Watch yourself *Herr* Creep,' Ingrid said, 'you hurt our *Puffmutter* we'll hurt you.'

'Ingrid, enough,' Said Brigette. 'Customers are coming. I'll deal with him.'

Ingrid walked back to the other women, her posture changing as she walked from showing menace to offering a night of seduction and wickedness. Alec turned back to face Brigette; he could see the fury had left her eyes, he hoped it could stay away.

'She is sure feisty,' Alec said. '*Puffmutter*? You're now a madam?'

'That's what happens. You either marry Prince Charming or become a madam when the customers no longer fight for your affections.' Brigette said, the sadness evident in her voice. 'Why are you here Stefan? What do you want? Have you seen the error of your ways and are finally going to be my Prince Charming and whisk me away from all of this?' She opened her arms wide to indicate the grubby station entrance.

'I need your help, Brigette, I'm in trouble.' Alec said.

'You need my help?' Brigette said. 'You show up after all these years, looking for a favour? Where have you been? Why should I help you?'

'Brigette,' Alec said. 'I am in serious trouble, and I know I've been no friend to you for a long time. I am so sorry for that, I have no excuse, I would never have come here, but I have no one else I can go to.'

Alec truly did feel bad, looking at Brigette she had aged far more than ten years, her once carefree, beautiful face, now had hard lines around the eyes and mouth, Alec could see the nicotine staining of her teeth as she talked, the light in her eyes had dimmed as time and the streets had taken their toll.

'What is in it for me?'

'I am desperate; I'll give you whatever I can.' Alec took out his wallet and pulled out several Euros in high denominations.

Brigette looked at his wallet. 'I want that.' She said pointing at the black and white picture of a woman showing in the photo window of the black leather wallet.

Alec shook his head, 'That's all I have left of her. I cannot give that up.'

'Who is she? The photo looks old.'

'Her name was Stefanie. I got her killed many years ago.'

'Stefan and Stefanie? How *adorable*,' Brigette paused for a moment. 'Ok, in exchange for my help, I want twenty thousand Euros. I know you cannot get me them now, so I will hold the picture of Stefanie as collateral. How does that sound?'

Alec frowned, 'I'd rather not let it go… but I have no choice, I accept.' He pulled the picture out of the wallet and held it out for her.

'At least this way, you get to see me again; try not to leave it a decade though.' Brigette opened her handbag and pulled out a large purse. She put the picture in the purse, 'So what do you need me to do? Tell you what happened to the Russian ambassador last week?' She asked.

'Do you know where I can find Makary?'

'Makary? Is that all? You're willing to give me twenty thousand Euros for that?' Brigette sounded incredulous.

'It's important to me,' Alec said. 'When it's over I'll come back, get my picture and tell you all about it, maybe over a coffee?'

'I'd like that, I've missed you, you know,' she thought for a moment. 'Makary is usually found in the Golden Dolls on Potsdamer Straße.'

'Sounds like a strip club,' Alec said. 'I don't know that one.'

'Really?' She arched a tattooed eyebrow, 'I remember going to quite a few with you once upon a time.'

Alec coughed uncomfortably, 'I'm far too old

nowadays for that kind of thing, definitely a case of "*Herr Creep*",' he said.

'You're only as old as the women you feel,' Brigette said with a wicked smile. 'It is where the Hollywood Club used to be.'

'Used to be? When did that close down?'

'Oh, around seven years ago or so. Didn't I take you there once?' She asked.

'… Yes, once was more than enough, if ever a club was stuck in the 80s, it was that place.' He laughed at the memory, *more a school disco than a nightclub in a major city*. Cheesy Europop, the occasional female Serbian singer to attract the crowds, bad dancing, and cheap drinks.

'Stefan,' Brigette said, her voice suddenly serious, 'Why didn't you come back to see me?'

Alec thought for a while, unsure how to answer. *She deserves the truth.* 'I was promoted at work -'

'- Oh, poor you.'

'Let me finish… I was promoted at work, but the job was different. Made me different. I had to act a certain way, behave a certain way. I shouldn't have accepted it; I loved what I did before, the work wore me out, dragged me down. Then my b-brother and his wife died in a car accident. I shut myself away, couldn't face the world. I was like a zombie, hitting the bottle too hard and far too often. They should have fired me; it's only because my friend is my boss, that I'm still there.'

'Oh Stefan, I'm sorry,' she reached out and pulled him close, her hand rubbing his back in comfort, 'you could have come to me. I could have helped.'

'I'll remember that next time. *Danke.*' He bent his head down and kissed her forehead. '*Danke.*' He repeated.

43

Now it was Brigette's turn to be embarrassed, she disengaged from Alec, 'It's getting late, Makary won't stay there all night.'

'You're right, I'd better go.' Alec looked straight into her eyes, 'I will be back… I promise.'

'I hope so.'

Alec thought her eyes looked brighter, her posture straighter than it was before, *that might just be wishful thinking though,* he thought.

'*Bis bald.*' See you soon, Alec said

Brigette blew him a kiss; turned and walked back to the group of women, who all excitedly started talking. When she got there, she looked back at Alec, smiled and shooed him away with a wave of her hand. Alec got the hint and left the station entrance the way he came.

6

Alec turned onto Bülowstraße to avoid the Romanian prostitute from earlier, thinking of Brigette. He felt ashamed of the way he had treated her, *you treated her just like a whore, paying her for information and paying to leave with no strings attached or feelings involved. You can blame the people not liking the fact you had a prostitute as a friend all you like; you know its rubbish. Nothing would have happened if you'd continued seeing her. You were just scared of how close she was getting to you, how she was unlocking that dead heart of yours. You've been that way since Stefanie. You did the same to Claudia, luckily, she had the sense to get over you quickly and marry Roger. That was the best thing she ever could have done. You're damaged goods, old man, damaged goods. You're fifty-one now, you are going to be alone forever.* He turned on to Potsdamer Straße, past the Commerzbank buildings on the left. Retracing his route from earlier. *You are lucky she came around and gave you Makary's location, many others wouldn't have, and then you would have been screwed. What is Makary going to do? You dropped him, just like Brigette. All those times drinking together, the occasional helping him with his 'business dealings', he was your friend too. I wonder whether Arthur realises he is on borrowed time or not.* Alec promised himself that he would make things right with Brigette, *if I survive this of course.*

45

He walked past the LSD sex shop and instead of turning left on to Kurfürstenstraße as earlier, he continued straight on, past the Woolworth store, he continued walking for another five minutes or so, past shops long closed for the night until he reached the Golden Dolls strip club, he heard the music before he saw the club, muffled heavy bass lines. When he saw the club, he was pleasantly surprised at how tasteful it looked. The exterior was brightly lit in orange lights, which contrasted elegantly against the smoked glass windows. A narrow red runner carpet led to the doorway, framed by a red rope barrier connected to a pair of chrome poles. Only the Geldautomat ATM lit up in yellow, right next to the entrance spoiled the look. *That's what these places are all about*, he thought, *when the money flows so does the dream.* He checked his wallet before entering, satisfied he had enough money on him. It was something he had always done, carrying plenty of cash. *You never know when you need it and not everywhere takes credit cards, especially not in this business, or the one I'm about to enter either, in our world cash is king. I can always get more from the machine if necessary.* He nodded to the doorman, who checked him over, for in Berlin looking semi-casual or casual is the correct way to dress. *If anything, I'm probably a little overdressed, I am wearing a tie, and this isn't the Berlin Philharmonic.* The doorman unclipped the rope and stepped aside for Alec to enter. '*Danke,*' Alec said as he went into the club.

There was an abundance of red, and black, throughout the entrance to the club. Padded leather on the walls, and the front of the bar, with its array of bottles standing up, looking for attention from the clients. A partially curtained cloakroom to his left, with an assortment of jackets and coats on hangers designed to get a person more comfortable, less likely to leave quickly, *Probably have to wait around for a while, "have a drink while you're waiting", "they may be some time, would you like a private dance while you wait?" spoken by a beautiful young woman with an exotic accent, and little clothing, all the tricks of the trade designed to extract the most money in the least painful way from the client.* A hostess came over to Alec, she was slim, brunette and very pretty, wearing black lingerie, she asked if he wanted to leave his coat, her accent was Romanian, her words German. Alec refused politely but took it off and hung it over his arm, *I may have to leave quickly*, he thought. She led him to a small table slightly set back from the main stage, the stage was around twenty metres long, with a floor to ceiling pole at the end, it was surrounded on three sides by open booths, black padded leather upholstery, most of the booths were occupied, gold voile curtains hung down the back of the stage. Alec was surprised by the opulence of the club; it wasn't what he was expecting and a far cry from the gaudy Hollywood Club he had experienced all those years ago. He asked the hostess for a beer, and she went to get it. The music stopped, and a girl came on to the stage through the voile curtains. A spotlight shone on her, revealing an appealing, blonde woman, her hair down to her waist. She was wearing high platform heels, a sparkling silver bra and matching panties. She marched to the pole and indicated to the DJ to start the music, a heavy techno beat came thumping through the speakers around the club and she started to move. At this point, Alec's attention was drawn to the DJ behind his stand: *Makary Kalinowski.*

Alec watched his friend work. He was in his fifties but

looked a decade younger. His shaven head nodded in time to the beat, large headphones covering his ears, Alec knew the left one was torn up, the result of a fight twenty years ago. Makary kept his focus on the mixing desk in front of him. Alec was tempted to walk straight up to him but held back. When the hostess arrived back with his drink, he asked her to give a message to Makary, a fifty Euro note smoothed the transaction. He stayed in his chair and drank his beer and waited. The woman on the stage came to the end of her dance, rapidly spinning around the pole as the music's tempo increased and ended in the splits as the music stopped, leaving a pause soon filled by applause from around the room, Alec included. Alec could see the dance had left her breathless as her chest rapidly inhaled and exhaled, with a smile on her face, she stood up, bowed and left the stage. The generic dance music restarted. Alec saw the hostess move round to the DJ booth and speak to Makary. She pointed in his direction, and Makary looked over, his eyes widened, and his mouth opened. Alec raised his glass in salute. Makary glanced at his watch and held up his hands, fingers signalling against his palm, *twenty minutes*. Alec smiled and nodded his agreement. Makary shook his head in disbelief and dismissed the hostess. She came back round to Alec.

'Would you like some company while you wait?' She asked.

'No, *danke*, another beer would be nice though.' He replied.

'No problem.' She said and walked away, Alec watched her go, her hips swaying invitingly, in her lingerie. *Stop it, Herr Creep; she is far too young for you.* He drank the rest of his beer and thought about how to handle Makary.

He is bound to be angry at me. The last time I saw him,

he had just helped me out with a problem. I had to store an informant for a couple of days until a safe house vacated. I couldn't use any hotels, as they require ID for each guest. Makary sorted out an apartment in the Neukölln district, amongst the Polish community there. My informant was well looked after and has returned since to meet up with the people who cared for him. Makary is a part-time DJ and part-time black-market smuggler, specialising in arms, drugs and information. He has been a good friend to me in the past; I just hope he is not too angry with me. I'll have to come up with a reason for my absence. Alec looked up and saw Makary looking at him, Alec grinned, Makary returned the grin. *I can tell him I was posted to Britain or another European country for the past eight years; he knows I work out of an embassy, just not which one. I've dropped subtle hints over the years about Russian or as it was then, Soviet treatment of the Poles after the war, and made sure I carried those ghastly Russian cigarettes and always made a point of bumming a Western cigarette from him and savouring the taste. Yes, I'll blame the Russians, he should believe that, and it should let me off.*

With that settled in his mind, Alec finished off his beer just as the hostess brought over the new one.

'Thanks,' Alec said, giving her a ten Euro tip, 'Can you bring over a couple of whiskies when Makary finishes his set?'

'Of course.' She said, with a smile that didn't reach her eyes. *She mustn't have forgiven me for snubbing her company; it's worth money to her after all.*

Alec sat drinking his beer, foot tapping to the generic beat. His fingers danced in time, the familiar ache for a cigarette. *They are a great way of wasting time when you're waiting,* he thought.

'How you been you old fart?' Came a deep voice from in front of Alec.

Alec looked up, 'Makary!' and stood up.

Makary held out his arms and walked closer to Alec and squeezed him tightly in a rough embrace. Alec returned the hug, even though it hurt his back. There was a moment of manly back-slapping, and they parted.

'Come sit,' said Alec. 'It's great to see you.'

'You too, Stefan, you too,' said Makary, 'it's been too long. I thought you'd forgotten about your old friend.'

'Never, Makary, I've been away, on business, the *company* sent me to England if you can believe it. Miserable place, always raining, and the beer, God, it's good to be back in Germany.'

The hostess brought over the two whiskies Alec had ordered. He gave her another ten Euro. She smiled at Makary, not at Alec, and left.

'I'm glad you're back, we'll have to catch up properly when I'm not working.' Makary said, lifting his glass in acknowledgement to Alec.

'We will. Definitely,' Alec said, copying the gesture. 'I saw Brigette; she told me you were here.'

'I see her around occasionally; she's not doing too well.'

'Yeah, I could see that. That's one tough life for a person.'

'I would have thought you'd have taken her with you, you always were very close.'

'My bosses would have thrown a fit if I had. A Rus… An embassy official taking a prostitute to London? They would have sent me straight back home.' Alec laughed, mirthlessly. 'I feel bad for her, I didn't realise I'd be away as long as I was, I should have sorted something out for her, got her off the streets.'

'I usually slip her some cash when I see her,' Makary looked at his watch. 'I've got to head back for a bit. Are you going to stick around?'

'Actually, there's another reason I'm here, I need a favour from you.' Alec held up his hands, 'I know I shouldn't ask.'

'It's cool, we're like family, you know. Family looks after family.'

'That's a big relief, I'm in trouble, serious trouble.'

'What do you need?' Makary asked.

'A phone and, if possible, a gun.'

'What do I look like? Siemens Mobile?' Makary laughed, 'That shouldn't be a problem, do you need any *other* help?'

Alec knew that Makary was offering his specialised protection services, 'No, I should be ok with that. If I do need you for that are you still on the same number?' Alec rattled off a series of numbers from memory.

'How the hell do you do that?' Makary asked, impressed, 'Yeah, that's still my number.'

'Magic,' Alec said, making an arcane gesture with his hands. 'I'd tell you, but I'd get kicked out of the *Magischer Zirkel*.' The Magic Circle. Makary laughed.

'Alright, keep your secrets, Stefan. I'll find out one day.' Makary stood up, Alec followed suit. 'I've got to put on a song for the next dancer, then get your stuff. Stick around for a while, enjoy the club's hospitality, you look like you need it!' He punched Alec in the upper arm, deadening the nerve, 'Damn, it's good to see you.' He walked back to the DJ stand.

'You too, Makary, you too.' said Alec to his friend's back, as he sat back down, rubbing his arm. He signalled to the hostess and held up the half-full beer glass. She nodded and turned to the bar.

The music changed and 'Schools Out' by Alice Cooper blasted through the speakers, there was a loud cheer from one of the booths by the stage. Alec lifted his head and saw what the noise was about. On the stage a new dancer had come out, she had her dark hair in pigtails, she was wearing large rimmed glasses and dressed in a school girl uniform, well the stripper version anyway, high heels, hold-up stockings, tartan miniskirt, white blouse tied up at the bottom exposing a flat stomach. *Are those freckles drawn on her face? Really trying to sell the look,* and it was working. Alec could see the backs of the loud party in the booth, three of the men were standing up, trying to get as close as they could to the stage for a better look, the other four in the booth were cheering them on. Alec smiled and looked back down at his drink, picked it up and swallowed.

He heard a commotion coming from the stage and looked up. He could see the club's bouncer rushing towards the stage, where the dancer was screeching at a man, is *he wearing a dress?* Alec asked himself, *it can't be.* He stood up for a better view. The bouncer had arrived and pushed the man in drag back, the rest of his companions got to their feet and started shouting and gesticulating at the bouncer and the dancer. *Seven men, one's wearing a dress? That can't be the stag party from earlier, could it?* Alec stood up for a better look. *That's Peter and his mates. I better go and help them,* before *they bring the Police here.* Alec walked over to the booth.

7

'Come on mate, he was only having a laugh.' One of the group said.

'No need to get all Naz-' another started to say

'-That's enough of that.' Alec said, interrupting the comment that would have quickly caused a beating. 'Guys, sit down I'll handle this for you.'

'Stefan?' said Peter. 'What are you doing here?'

'Just sit down, all of you!' Alec said, his voice raised. 'Peter, sort these guys out, or they'll end up in a cell for the rest of the night.' He turned to the bouncer and the dancer.

'It's okay, tell me what happened.'

'Who the hell are you?' said the bouncer.

'I know these guys, this isn't their normal behaviour. What did they do?'

The dancer screeched in German, 'That one in the dress stuck his hand up my skirt while I was dancing,' and pointing at the group, 'you filthy pigs!'

The men started to argue again, Alec turned around and shouted at them to shut up.

'He can't do that. They'll have to go,' said the bouncer. 'They are the club rules, or I can call the Police.'

Oh crap. 'No, there's no need for that, I'm sorry about him, English drunkards, you know how they are. German beer is too strong for them; they're too used to drinking that piss water they call beer.' He smiled, as the bouncer nodded in agreement at the state of the English. 'I'll sort them out. Make them behave. It won't happen again, can they stay?' As he was speaking Alec pulled out his wallet and took out a number of bills. Both the bouncer's and the dancer's eyes were drawn to the money.

'I am really sorry, perhaps this could make up for the offence caused, 'Alec said, as he handed three hundred Euros to the dancer, 'and perhaps the club rules could be bent?' He handed the same amount to the bouncer. *One good perk of the promotion I got to Head of Section is that I have access to petty cash funds, I'll put this down to 'informant expenses' and claim it back. I'll definitely have to go to the ATM though.*

'Any more trouble from them, they and you will be out of here.' The bouncer said, putting the money in the inside pocket of his coat.

The dancer took the money, looked at the men sitting in the booth, spat at the floor in front of them, then turned on her heels and strutted to the back of the stage and went through the curtain.

'There won't be any more problems, I promise. I'm sorry, I'll deal with them.'

The bouncer took a long look at the group, shook his head, and said, 'If he waited until the end of the dance, he could have had a lot more than a grope up a skirt, a lot cheaper too.'

'Thanks.' Alec said. 'I appreciate it.'

The bouncer walked back to the doorway. Alec turned to the group.

'What the hell were you thinking?' He demanded.

'Sorry Stefan,' Peter said.

'Yeah, sorry mate.' The rest of the group said, apart from the groom to be who appeared to have fallen asleep on the sofa.

'Come and join us,' said Peter, 'we owe you a drink, at least. Come on guys, move up, and give Stefan some room.'

Alec shook his head at their behaviour and sat down with the group, between Peter and the now snoring groom.

'Stefan, what the hell are you doing here? We last saw you hours ago at the tube station.' Peter said.

'I came here to see an old friend,' Alec pointed to Makary at the DJ booth. 'I only knew I was coming here thirty minutes ago. I see you guys found the place ok.'

'It wasn't too hard, we got off at the stop you said and then asked a couple of passers-by for directions. I'm sure one of those we asked was a prostitute.'

'You did ask for directions to the *Reeperbahn*,' Alec laughed, 'not what you expected?'

'Not really, seems very seedy. Is it legal? In the UK you can get arrested for kerb-crawling.'

'Kerb-crawling?' Alec asked, playing dumb, not knowing English idioms. 'What's that?'

'You know, picking up prostitutes on the street.'

'Oh, I see, yes it's legal in Germany. I wouldn't recommend it though, from what I hear, it's not the most romantic, or even, sexiest experience.'

'What do you mean?' Peter asked.

'I heard that they take you to a nearby car park and you do the business there.'

'Really?'

Alec pulled a face of disgust and nodded.

'I'll let the guys know, doesn't seem like the nicest or safest way of getting your rocks off.' Peter changed the subject. 'Stefan, how much did you pay the dancer and bouncer? We'll have to pay you back.'

Alec thought for a second, *the money doesn't mean anything to me, it's not mine, and normally I'd tell them not to worry about it, but it might make them curious about how I can write off so much money for people I've just met.*

'A couple of hundred, or so, we can sort it out later. It's not a problem.'

The hostess came over with the beer Alec had ordered at the previous table, she approached nervously. Alec saw that she wasn't too keen on getting close to the group. He stood up and said to her in German 'It's okay, nothing like that will happen again. I'll make sure they give you a decent tip at the end of the night,' he smiled his most charming smile. 'Can you get beers for the rest of them and add it to his tab?' Alec pointed at the sleeping stag.

The hostess nodded and went back to the bar.

'So, Peter, how long are you and the guys here in Berlin?' Alec asked.

'We have another two nights; this is our first night here. We didn't plan to get so drunk so soon, to be honest. Hopefully, it won't spoil the rest of the trip.'

'What have you got planned? Sightseeing or just bar crawling?'

'None of us have been here before, so we planned to do the touristy bits during the day and then hit the bars and clubs at night. We want to see the Berlin Wall, Checkpoint Charlie, Hitler's Bunker, and there are a load of museums we want to see.'

'You'll have a problem with Hitler's bunker.'

'Really? How so?' asked Peter.

'We covered it over with a car park. There's a plaque there which is the only thing to signify it was ever there. It was important not to turn the place into a shrine. Turn it into a holy place for the wrong elements.'

'I suppose that's a fitting gesture. Is the wall still standing?'

'There are sections still there: The East Side Gallery is about a kilometre long covered in art, or what passes for art. A bit too modern for my tastes; there is some at the Topography of Terror Museum-'

'-that's on our list, the museum about the Nazi atrocities, isn't it?' Peter interjected, 'Oh I'm sorry Stefan, are you ok talking about this? I don't mean to be insensitive.'

'Don't worry about it. It's not like that British comedy... the one in the hotel... "Don't mention the war!" with the man from Monty Python...'

'Fawlty Towers?' Peter suggested.

'Yes, that's the one. Very funny, even for us Germans. We are open about what happened during that time, it's the best way to prevent it happening again. Older Germans, well, older than me at least, are more sensitive, they were closer to that time than us, so it was more their shame.' *I think I'm being authentic, that's how it was explained to me when I came over to Berlin back in the late Eighties. However, I never found Fawlty Towers that amusing; I think I was too young to get the humour and by the time I was old enough I just didn't find it that funny.*

'What is it you do Stefan?' Peter asked.

'I'm a *beamter*... a civil servant in the Federal Ministry for Family Affairs, Senior Citizens, Women and Youth.'

'The what?'

'Basically, it revolves around looking after families and different generations, children and their grandparents. We Germans, believe the family is very important and looking after it makes society better. What do you do, Peter, and the rest of the group?'

'I'm a corporate lawyer, so is Simon over there,' He pointed at one of the group, sitting sullenly, and waiting for the next dancer to come out. 'Mark is in wine; John, the groom is an actor, that's the reason for the dress...' He paused to see if Alec would want that explained, but Alec just nodded, *typical stag-do behaviour, Acting seen as less than a manly profession, hence the dress*, 'It was Simon's idea, anyway, where was I? Oh yes, John's an actor; Dave is an estate agent, Alan an accountant and Anthony, or Tony, as he prefers to be called, is a market trader.' As Peter mentioned the rest of the group, he indicated which man went with each name.

'That's quite a group, how do you know each other?' Alec asked.

'We all went to school together and kept in touch. Simon got me a job at his company after I left the army.'

'I thought you had a military air about you, either that or you play rugby.' Alec said, having noticed Peter's physique, broad shoulders and composed demeanour, 'Why did you leave? If you don't mind me asking, of course.'

'It's okay, it's not a secret. I joined the army when I left school; it was something I had always wanted to do. Back in 2006 I was stationed in Afghanistan and deployed to the Helmand Province, I'm sure you've heard of it.'

'Of course, that was where your Prince Harry was sent, wasn't it?'

'I heard he was there, I never saw him though. Anyway, we were in Sangin on patrol, five of us in a Land Rover, stuck in a traffic jam; I think a car had broken down ahead or a cart or something. We were all on our guard, in case this had been a planned ambush. I saw our CO,

Commanding Officer go as pale as a ghost and followed his gaze. I saw an Afghan boy approaching the vehicle with a basket from a side road; he must have been around six or seven years old, wearing dirty and ragged clothes, one of his sandals was broken and flapped with every stride.

'My CO ordered me to shoot the child. I raised my rifle, the boy was about fifty metres away from us, and I looked at him through the scope,' Peter mimed the action as he spoke, 'I couldn't see into the basket, but I saw his eyes. There was no malice there in those wide, dark eyes. No fear. I've seen suicide attacks, I know the difference. With the suiciders, there's either hatred in their eyes, or they're so nervous they look like they are going to pass out. This kid had none of these signs. I told my CO this, and he just told me to shoot anyway just to make sure. I refused; I wasn't going to murder an innocent child. He ordered me again and again I refused. He then ordered one of the other guys on the patrol, and they casually gunned the child down, no thought, no hesitation. The child cried out and fell; he dropped the basket he was holding.

'I saw the shock and confusion on his face and watched it turn from pain to nothing, his eyes glazed over, and he went still. I looked at the basket and saw the pomegranates, apricots and figs spread around the boy.' Peter wiped a tear from his eye.

'When we returned to base, I was court-martialled and dishonourably discharged for disobeying a direct order. I was lucky I could have been sentenced to a ten-year prison sentence. Simon pulled a few strings and got me a job at his firm. And here I am.' He took a deep breath and exhaled loudly.

'I'm sorry… I didn't mean to pry.' Alec said.

'It's okay. It's good to talk about it. As far as I'm concerned I didn't do anything wrong. I wish I could have saved the boy though, his face still haunts my dreams sometimes.' He shook his head, as if to clear out the thoughts, and drank some of his beer.

Alec stayed quiet for a moment.

'I'm sorry Stefan, that was a bit heavy for a strip club chat with a stranger.'

'Don't apologise.' Alec said. 'Thank you for sharing that with me. It's good to know there are still men like you... with a conscience... you don't see that very much these days. The newspapers and television are full of scandal and corruption. It seems that everywhere people are treating each other like animals.'

'Ain't that the truth. Another drink?'

As Peter spoke the music changed and another dancer came out on to the stage, dressed in a long sequined red dress, split at the thigh, she looked at the group with disgust.

'Keep to your seats, fellas,' Peter warned. 'Stefan, I think your mate wants you.'

Alec looked over, and Makary was waving at him. Alec stood up and walked behind the booth to the DJ stand keeping the row of booths between him and the stage to set the dancer's mind at ease. She inclined her head slightly at him in appreciation of the gesture and started her dance.

'Stefan, making friends I see,' Makary smiled.

'They're alright, just a young boisterous group of guys. We were like them once, I'm sure.'

'I don't remember you wearing a dress.' He laughed.

'Well, not exactly like them I admit.' Alec laughed too, *come on Makary have you got the stuff?* He thought impatiently.

'I got what you asked for,' Makary said. *Yes!* Makary handed over a small parcel. Alec tucked it into his waistband.

'That's great, Makary, thank you.'

'For you, not a problem. Here is the number for the phone.' He gave Alec a strip of paper. Alec looked at it and memorised the numbers. He was taught long ago a method for memorising telephone numbers based on assigning images to numbers based on their shape. Zero is an egg; two is a swan and so on. When he was sure he had the numbers in his memory, he went to screw up the paper but thought twice about it and decided to slip it inside his suit jacket pocket.

'I'm sure I've said this before,' Makary said, 'but one of these days you are going to have to show me how you do that.'

'I promise.' said Alec, 'thank you for this, how much do I owe you?'

Makary smiled, 'You can repay me with a drink together soon.'

'Are you sure?' Alec asked. 'It seems like I'm forever in your debt.'

'You're my friend, you've helped me out in the past, and I'm sure you'll help again if I need you.'

'Without question.' Alec said.

'So, we have a drink together, and we'll be all square. What is it the Russians say? *"Druz'ya poznayutsya v bede, a ne v radosti"*, Friends show their love in times of trouble, not in happiness,' Makary said with a wink.

Alec laughed, 'I'll have to take your word for it.' and returned the wink.

Makary clapped Alec's back in joy.

'How about we meet back here on Saturday, say around

ten o'clock?' Alec suggested, 'I should be sorted by then.'
And the Minister, whoever he is, could be dead... As he
thought it the nagging voice in his head started up.

'Are you ok?' Makary asked, looking at Alec carefully.

'What? Oh yes,' Alec replied, pausing the voice for the
moment, *I'll come back to that in a minute,* 'just thought
of something… work related. It'll keep for a while.'

'You looked like you had seen a ghost.'

Alec's eyes narrowed as he thought for a second, 'No,
I'm alright, Makary, something just flashed in my,' he
poked the side of his head with his forefinger a couple of
times, 'in here. It's ok, nothing to worry about. So,
Saturday then?' He asked changing the subject.

'Sure, that'll be great. We're not going to meet here
though are we? I do work here, you know. I'm not sure
they'd want to see me in the state we usually get into.'

'No, of course not. I know, as I've been out of the
country for so long, you can take me to any new spots that
have opened up that are worth going to. I'll even bring you
a dress to wear.' Alec laughed, this time clapping Makary
on the back.

'As long as you don't get horny for me as you drink,
you old lech, I know what you're like after a few drinks.'

'I don't think there's enough drink in the world to make
me hit on you, my ugly old friend.'

Makary lifted his fists in an old-fashioned boxing
pugilist style, 'You take that back.' He said laughing,
'God, I've missed you.' He changed his stance and opened
his arms, 'give me a hug for old times and get on your
way. I've got to get on with work.'

Alec hugged him, their hands slapped each other's back
in the way men do when they are showing emotion but
wish to maintain their masculinity.

'Thank you Makary, I will repay you, I promise.'

'See you Saturday, Stefan.'

'Bye, Makary.'

Alec returned to the booth with Peter and his friends, he adjusted the parcel in the small of his back before sitting down, *I don't want that falling out anytime soon.*

'You guys seem pretty friendly.' Peter said.

'Yeah, we've known each other for a long time, I haven't seen him for a while though.' Alec replied, looking at the beers on the table, 'which one is mine?'

Peter pointed out one, 'That one I think.'

'*Danke,*' Alec lifted the glass to his lips and drank about half of it, 'I'm going to have to make a move soon.' An idea came to him. He liked Peter and was starting to feel like his old gregarious self like he was before his promotion and the death of Mark and Sophie, *this mess should be sorted by then, I need to let loose a bit.* 'You guys are here for two more nights, you said?'

'That's right.' Peter confirmed.

'How about on Thursday night I take you and the guys out to the best bars in Berlin-' he stopped as he saw the doubt in Peter's eyes, 'It's ok, I'm not an old German pervert, I'm not trying to get my wicked way with you guys,' he laughed, 'my niece, Sara, is coming into town on Thursday, we normally go out drinking on her first night here. I thought you guys might like to join us, see some of the decent bars Berlin has to offer rather than the typical bar crawl bars tourists go to. We'll even go for a proper German kebab, I know a great place, not like the greasy, tasteless elephant legged monstrosities you get in England.'

'Ok, you've sold it. Sounds like a great idea. Why not

tomorrow?' Peter looked at his watch, 'Well, tonight, I mean?'

'Do you think John will be up to another drinking session that quickly?' Alec gestured towards John, now slumped forward, head on the table.

'I guess you're right.' Peter admitted.

'Give me your number, and I'll call you with directions on Thursday.'

Peter pulled out his wallet from his jacket, retrieved a business card and handed it to Alec. Alec looked at it and noted the number in his memory. He took out his own wallet and slipped the card in one of the card holder compartments. He reached into his suit jacket pocket and took out the piece of paper Makary gave him with the number for his phone.

'Sorry, I've just got a new phone, here's the number.'

'Thanks,' Peter took out his phone, pressed a few buttons on the screen and gave the paper back to Alec, 'I've added you to my contacts, so you can keep the paper.' He showed the screen to Alec. The entry read 'Stefan, Not an old pervert.'

Alec laughed, 'Well you got that right. I'm going to head off now,' He stood up, picking up his coat, he swayed slightly as all the drinks he'd had that night caught up with him, 'I'll call you on Thursday, enjoy the sights of Berlin, you can tell me all about it.'

The group waved at him, Peter said, 'See you on Thursday.'

Alec moved away from the booth and headed towards the exit. He saw the hostess that had served him and the group behind the bar and made a beeline towards her.

'Can you send the table another round from me? And what do I owe?'

She said she would and tapped a few buttons on the bar's electronic till and told him the amount. He removed his wallet and opened it. He saw that he didn't have enough cash in there.

'I'll just get some more from the machine. Hold on.' He told her.

He went to the ATM next to the bar and inserted his company card, the writing on the screen was blurred. Alec squinted to focus his eyes and entered the PIN when prompted. He mulled over the amount for a few seconds, the machine beeping at him incessantly, before selecting the maximum, one thousand Euros. The machine whirred, and the cash dropped into the tray below the keypad. Alec removed the card and collected the money. He returned to the bar and paid his bill. He added an extra fifty Euros as a tip for the hostess, 'For your charming hospitality.' He said with a straight face.

The hostess looked at him properly, for the first time since he snubbed her company, 'Just a trick of the trade, sir.' She smiled, 'Would you have been so generous if I had continued to hassle you all night?'

He thought for a moment. 'No, I suppose you're right, well done.' Alec admitted. 'I may come back another night and take you up on your offer of company.' He winked and pulled on his coat. 'Goodnight, my dear.' He said and walked out of the club into the cold night.

8

'Sir, we may have a hit on Foster,' Likhachyov Ilyich, Junior Lieutenant said, the excitement in his voice noticeable, as he looked up from his computer screen and turned towards the Captain.

'Where is he?' Captain Lukin Olegovich asked, sitting up in his chair, his attention focused on the junior officer. Olegovich looked older than his true age of thirty-two, which had aided his rapid promotion in the SVR. A narrow, but deep scar along his left cheek, a result of a childhood accident, was accentuated by piercing, cold blue eyes, that gave him a menacing appearance,

'In the Mitte District, Potsdamer Straße 8,' the officer replied reading the Cyrillic text on the screen. 'He used his MI6 account card at an ATM.'

'That's strange, he must know we'd be monitoring the accounts he uses.' Olegovich said to himself. *Is he mocking me? Taunting me with his arrogance? We should have picked the old man up hours ago; he shouldn't have been able to get that far from Polyakov without us finding him.*

'Sir?'

'Nothing,' Olegovich said. 'Ensure the collection party is ready and wake my driver. I'll go with them to pick him up.'

'Yes, sir.' He picked up the telephone receiver next to his computer screen and spoke instructions into it.

Olegovich stood up from his desk and collected his coat from the stand in the corner of the operations room. He was wearing a grey suit, tailored to hide the shoulder holster he always wore. He returned to his desk and opened the long, narrow drawer beneath it. He removed a gun and ammunition clip, checked there wasn't a round in the chamber and inserted the magazine. He put the gun in the holster and left the room.

***

'Andrei, How much longer?' Olegovich asked the driver of the black Mercedes, a hint of impatience showing through.

'We're about four minutes out, sir,' the driver replied politely. Olegovich only knew him as Andrei, he hadn't bothered trying to find out any more.

Olegovich, sitting in the back, looked at his watch, an ornate golden face on a plain brown leather band, a gift from his father for graduating fifth in his class and joining the SVR. Over the past eleven years, he had already eclipsed his father's rank. His father had to retire early, when he was four years old, due to an injury that occurred on duty, and although it was touch and go whether he would survive at first, he beat the odds and lasted another seventeen years, albeit with severe health problems. Olegovich was his father's main carer from the age of ten until the end as his mother had been killed in a road accident. His father survived until he was twenty-one, three months after he had graduated. Olegovich always felt as if his father carried on by sheer force of will, to see him join the SVR and let go once his task was done. He always tried to emulate his father's drive and determination, which was one of the reasons he was picked for this job.

His superior officers believed he was headed for great things, a two-week mourning period after his father's death the only blot on his copybook when he went off the rails, getting excessively drunk and violent, ranting about the British influence on Russia and Russia's interests. He soon cleared his head and resumed his search for perfection. He swore off alcohol and emerged from that period even more focused. He went from a man who was quick to smile and laugh, to someone much darker and more serious.

'Sir, we're two minutes out.' The driver advised.

Olegovich's mobile vibrated in his pocket, against his leg. He retrieved it and looked at the caller ID. It was from the office.

'Sir, I thought I should call you to let you know I have identified the address Foster was at,' Ilyich said. 'It is a place called the Golden Dolls. A strip club.'

'Thank you.' Replied Olegovich.

'You're welcome, sir.'

Olegovich terminated the call.

'Andrei, contact the other vehicle and tell them to pull up where they can, we need to go over the approach. There may be a complication.'

'Yes, sir.'

Olegovich saw Andrei pick up the hand-held two-way radio from the centre console of the car. He tuned the driver out, knowing his instructions would be carried out. *A strip club? The balls of the man! Kills someone he has known for twenty years, who mistakenly considered him, if not a friend, a worthy ally or adversary, then heads off to the nearest brothel to get his rocks off. I look forward to cutting those balls off.* Olegovich's face reddened, apart from the scar on his cheek that burned white in contrast.

He felt the car slow and then stop. He looked down to his lap and saw that his fists were clenched tight, the nails pressing deep into his palms. He forced them to open and waited for Andrei to open the door to the leader of the four-man team that made up the collection party for the SVR. The men were part of the SVR special operations arm, also known as the Zaslon.

Lieutenant Sivakov entered Olegovich's vehicle. He was out of uniform, wearing a loose-fitting charcoal coloured suit, that didn't hide his muscular physique.

'Lieutenant, I have been informed that the target is inside the Golden Dolls strip club,' Olegovich said.

'A strip club? The randy old goat.'

'There may be other patrons in the establishment,' Olegovich said, 'so it might be prudent to use discretion. We don't want the Berlin Police to be any more involved in this mess than they are already.'

'That's understandable, sir. We can ambush him outside when he leaves,' Sivakov offered, checking his watch, 'It's four-thirty now, these places close at five o'clock-'

Olegovich raised an eyebrow.

'-or so I've been told, anyway,' Sivakov continued. 'One man either side of the entrance, our SUV parked outside. The sick pervert leaves the club. We can have him in the vehicle in less than thirty seconds.'

'Your men know what he looks like?'

'Yes sir, each of us was issued his photograph before leaving the embassy.'

'I approve the plan,' Olegovich said.' Oh, by the way, Lieutenant, if he makes a fuss or resists feel free to inflict some retribution.'

'Of course, Sir, that goes without question. We all worked with Polyakov in the past, he was a great man.

We'll make sure this Englishman regrets his actions.'

'Good,' Olegovich said, looking at his watch as a dismissal.

Sivakov understood the gesture and exited the car and returned to his vehicle.

'Andrei, continue,' Olegovich said.

'Yes, sir.' He started the vehicle and pulled out.

***

'Sir, we're here, where do you want me to stop?' Andrei asked.

Olegovich looked out at the window, the contrast between the dark interior of the car and the blazing orange lights of the club dazzled him, and he blinked to clear the afterimage.

'Park just ahead of the entrance, so the others can be directly outside.'

'Yes sir,' Andrei said. He checked for traffic coming the other way, crossed the lane and parked where he was told. He saw in his rear-view mirror that the black SUV had followed behind him and three men exited the vehicle.

'Now we wait,' Olegovich said. He watched two men take up position either side of the entrance and the Lieutenant stand by the open door of the SUV. *I'll get you, you bastard.*

9

Alec crossed over the road opposite the club. There was a covered entrance to a car park, and he could shelter from the heavy rain that greeted him as he appeared from the closed-off sanctuary of the Golden Dolls. His coat collar was turned up to protect his ears and neck from cold. He stood in the relative dry thinking about his next step. *I'm going to have to sleep soon. Man, I'm going to crash so hard. All that alcohol and adrenaline I'm lucky it hasn't hit yet. Where can I sleep?*

He noticed a silver sedan car pull up outside the club, a black SUV with tinted windows pulled in behind it. Alec edged further into the car park entrance, deeper into the shadows, moving any further was prevented by a heavy gate blocking the entrance. He saw three men exit the SUV, the biggest one stayed with the vehicle watching the entrance. The other two went either side of the entrance and appeared to be watching for someone. Alec watched the rain splatter against the roofs of the vehicles, streak down the windows. His mind frantically searching for an exit, a plan of action, anything. *There's no way of escaping if they see me. They look like Spec Ops soldiers. They are younger, fitter, and stronger than me, better equipped and there are more of them. I'm toast.* He pulled out the package from his waistband. It was a large brown enveloped wrapped around itself and taped. Alec carefully opened it at one end and unwrapped it. He removed the phone. He put that in his coat pocket. He next took out the gun and magazine, he put those in the other pocket. Alec tipped the parcel up, and a small SIM card dropped into his palm, he put this in the pocket with the phone and slowly folded up the envelope and placed it into his back pocket. All the time he was watching the men across the road. He took the gun out of his pocket and slowly checked it was in working order. The sound of the rain hitting the pavement and the vehicles would hide any noise he made, however, he wanted to minimise any movement that could draw attention to him. He considered dropping to the floor like he did earlier, but they obviously didn't know he was there and his view would be obscured by the vehicles. Alec checked the magazine, depressing the top brass bullet to gauge the magazine's condition. The bullet sprang back up satisfactorily when he let go. Alec inserted the magazine into the gun and removed the safety. *That extra second may be all the advantage I have.*

He saw the men either side of the door tense up as Peter, and the group left the club, practically dragging John with them. They paid no attention to the men outside the club. *Probably think they are doormen.* They turned right and headed down Potsdamer Straße towards Kurfürstenstraße, he saw them turn onto Lützowstraße. *They must be getting a taxi from there to their hotel, lucky bastards. The Police would have given my description to all hotels and taxi companies by now.* The man by the SUV went to the other vehicle and spoke into the back window. Alec could see his close-cropped hair, *no grey there*, and his massive head squared like a weightlifter's on his bull-like neck. The man shook his head and then nodded. He left the car and walked purposely to the other men. They spoke for an instant, and one of the soldiers went into the entrance of the club. The strongman took station in the vacant space beside the doors and waited.

Alec slowly, bent his legs, so he was lower, a less distinct silhouette amongst the other shadows of the alcove. *I could phone the embassy to get help and try to escape in the confusion, but then they'd be able to track me through the phone, and I don't know who to trust there anymore. I'll hold tight, they don't know I'm here... yet.* One minute, then two, Alec waited crouched, his back and his legs were aching from the effort of holding the position. At the entrance, there was a commotion, and the soldier was pushed out of the club by the bouncer Alec had dealings with earlier. There was a lot of shouting. From the back of the silver car a man got out and strode over to the argument. Alec identified the commanding way he carried himself, the man quickly took control of the situation. The soldier looked like he was apologising and backed off. The officer took something out of his jacket and showed it to the bouncer. The bouncer looked at it and nodded. *Oh shit.* The bouncer pointed in the direction Peter and the guys had gone. The three soldiers and the officer turned their heads following the bouncer's gesture. Alec saw a scar on the face of the officer. *I'll recognise you again, that's for sure.* The officer and the bouncer shook hands, and the bouncer returned to the club. The big soldier told the other two to head down the street, they obeyed without question. He then turned to the officer. Although Alec couldn't discern what was being said due to the rain he could see the officer was angry at the turn of events, his chopping gestures were made clear when he prodded the larger subordinate in the chest a couple of times. Alec could see the muscular man's neck redden and then he abruptly walked back to the SUV and got in the back. Alec and the officer watched as the SUV started up and made a rapid u-turn in the street and headed in the direction of the other two soldiers. For barely a moment the vehicle's headlights swept over Alec's position in the shadows. Alec closed his eyes quickly to prevent being blinded by the glare. When he opened them, he could see the officer looking in his direction, peering intently into the gloom. The officer stayed like that for what felt to Alec to be a good minute or two, he didn't dare move. *Just get back in your car, goddamn it!* Alec's nose began to tickle. He willed his arms to remain by his side. The tickle grew stronger, more insistent, more demanding, like a creature had flown into his nostril and was burrowing around, looking for scraps. He remained still, he tried to slowly wrinkle his nose, ensuring his mouth remained closed to prevent the whiteness of his teeth showing, to relieve the pressure, but that did not work, just as it became too much for him and his hand started involuntarily moving, the officer snapped his gaze away and strode back to the car. He opened the back door and got in. Alec, remembering the headlights from the SUV, dropped to the ground. The hard, wet concrete floor shook his knees and back. He tried to splay out to disguise his body shape, become more like a homeless person sprawled on the ground or a pile of rubbish bags left out for the morning collection. As he was adjusting his position, the car's engine growled to life. Alec went motionless, the nasal tickle forgotten. The car's wheels shrieked as it turned and sped down the road, its headlights barely getting a chance to highlight anything, the driver in such a rush. Alec exhaled loudly. *Got to get off the streets, I've been lucky so far, that can't hold, with the Russians on my trail and those two goons earlier. Get off the streets and speak to Arthur.* Alec stood up with a wince and brushed down his jacket. He gripped his nose between his thumb and forefinger and rubbed them together hard. *That's enough of that, you traitor,* he admonished his betraying body. He put the safety back on the gun and put it in his jacket pocket.

Alec started walking up Potsdamer Straße, away from the strip club and the soldiers, towards the River Spree. He kept under the covered walkway and was relieved when the two lanes of the road split and became a dual carriageway separated by a grassed median strip with the occasional sparse tree. *Anything that might obscure someone's view of me is a blessing.* He checked his watch: *it won't be sunrise for another hour or so, where can I go?* As he was walking, he considered where he was and who he could trust. It didn't take him long. Newbury lives in Neustaaken in the Spandau district. *It's a bit of a trek, over an hour away,* he thought for a moment, *and the bus will take me back past the strip club. No, safety first. There must be someone else?* Alec started to despair; his self-imposed isolation for the past few years was really making its presence felt.

He used to be very popular among his peers and acquaintances, always being invited to weddings, dinner parties, nights down the pub, restaurants. He never noticed the invites disappearing, the calls drying up as he withdrew into himself. They used to go out as a gang, Stefan with Brigette and Makary, or Alec with Arthur and Julia, Roger and Claudia, and Simon and Judith. *When did it end?* Simon was posted back to Britain and Judith followed. Arthur and Julia broke up. Roger and Claudia, well, they had children and… *Roger and Claudia, where did they live again? It wasn't too far away, was it?* Alec thought back to the last time he remembered being at their apartment. *Roger had just died, hadn't he? So, it must have been eight years ago? God, that long ago? Julia was there, and Arthur.* He could see the looks they gave each other from across the room. Arthur's expression: one of hope and reconciliation. Julia's one: of betrayal and bitterness. *I told him to get rid of that secretary before it got too serious. Stupid Arthur. Twenty-five years of marriage brought down by that age-old cliché. The married man and the attention from a younger, attractive woman.* Alec shook his head at the futility of the situation. *Simon and Judith came over from England. I had stopped hanging out with Brigette and Makary by then. After the funeral, we had all gone back to the apartment, but it became too much for Claudia, too many happy memories in those walls. So, we all went to that godawful bar nearby that Roger loved, what was it called? It had a toilet seat on the front door... Klo Bar. My goodness, what a place. I don't think Roger ever grew out of his potty humour and that place sure was full of potty humour. Some of the seats were toilet bowls, and toilet brushes were hanging from the ceiling. Draught beer served in chambermaid pots and urine sample bottles. One table at the back of the bar was a glass-topped open coffin. We always had fun there though, mainly mocking Roger for his choice of bars. They didn't live far from there, and I haven't heard that Claudia has moved. The bar was on Leibnizstraße, and they lived around the corner from there, on Mommsenstraße. I can get the bus from outside the Neue Nationalgalerie. Should only take 20 minutes or so on the bus.*

Alec walked with purpose, the effects of the alcohol wearing off in the cold air, the rain had stopped, and a few snowflakes had taken its place. He came to the large intersection with Schöneberger Ufer which during the day was crammed with vehicles, but sparse at this time of the morning. Alec was grateful for the lack of traffic as it meant he could quickly cross the large wide roads without having to be exposed waiting at the kerb for the traffic lights to change. He crossed over the River Spree, glancing down at the dark water below him. He could see the New National Gallery in front of him. The unusual looking building with its sloped flat roof and large glass windows. He turned onto Reichpietschufer and saw the bus stop ahead of him. There was no one there, so Alec, when he reached it, sat on the bench and waited. *I'm exhausted. Cold, tired and hungry, I hope Claudia lets me sleep before telling Arthur where I am.*

The bus came quickly, and Alec joined the early workers on their daily journey. He stood near the middle doors, ready to press the emergency exit button if necessary. He stood to keep himself alert, knowing it was only a short bus journey. He didn't want to fall asleep like he did on the U-bahn. He watched out of the window for the sedan and the SUV, and also the silver Mercedes from earlier. He knew he was getting close to Claudia's when the bus turned on to Kurfürstendamm, Berlin's main shopping boulevard. Here were all the posh stores, Cartier, Rolls Royce, Hermes, Louis Vuitton, and others. Their store's windows lit up displaying their goods, along with small glass cabinets on the wide pavement allowing a closer look.

He stayed on the bus until it had passed the Leibnizstraße junction, then he alighted at the bus stop between Leibnizstraße and Lewishamstraße, which had always made him smile. *Such a strange street name to have in the middle of Berlin.* Alec doubled back to Leibnizstraße. He passed the Starbucks on the corner and continued up the road, he saw the Klo Bar ahead, closed for the night. A pang of regret hit Alec in his heart as he remembered Roger.

Roger was tall, well over six feet, slim and very handsome. He was only forty-four when he died of lung cancer; slightly older than Alec. When Alec found out Roger had cancer, he quit smoking the same day in solidarity with his friend's plight. He hadn't gone back to it since. Roger had worked in a different department at the embassy, he worked under the Ambassador, and there was office talk that he would be replacing the Ambassador within a year. Claudia, his wife, worked with Alec and had hidden Roger's condition until his cancer had reached stage four.

Alec remembered that Roger always had a ready supply of awful one-liners to fit any situation, from the clever to his favourite subject toilet humour. The Klo Bar really was his perfect place and probably why he and Claudia moved as close to it as they did. Alec pictured Roger's face at the Klo Bar the first night Arthur took Julia with them. He didn't tell her of the trick they play on you as you enter the bar: opening the door activates a small water hose that squirts people as they enter. Julia was, for a second, not amused as the jet of water struck her in the face, had soon joined in with Roger's infectious laughter. The owners told him once that it gets the customers in the right frame of mind for the bar and is a big success. Alec wasn't so sure, but Roger found it hilarious, and he always warned the group not to warn anyone new about it. Alec always wanted to take Brigette and Makary there, but they were from his other world. Stefan's world.

He turned right at Walter-Benhamin-Platz, a large concreted open square, surrounded by apartments and imposing columns, a fountain in the middle of the square reminded Alec that he had drunk a lot that night and had a pressing need. He crossed the square past the closed boutique shops and restaurants to Wielandstraße. It was only a minute from here. Alec turned right onto Mommsenstraße and saw the apartment. *It's so much nicer than the road my flat is on.* The road was a lot narrower than the typical Berlin thoroughfares and always reminded Alec of the leafy Mayfair streets in London. The apartment building was three storeys high and painted in a clean, grey colour. *How to ask her to let me in? Well, I do need the toilet I suppose, so I wouldn't be lying to her.* Alec took a deep breath and then pressed the intercom for Claudia's apartment, heard the harsh buzzer sound and waited for her to answer.

10

Alec waited a minute, but there was no response from the intercom. *Come on Claudia,* he willed. Another minute passed, he stabbed the intercom button hard with his finger, leaving the button depressed for a second or two longer than he should have. Nothing. He reached out his hand to do it a third time, but before he could press it, he heard a sleep-befuddled voice.

'Who is it?' Alec recognised Claudia's plummy German through the tinny speaker of the intercom.

'Claudia, its Alec.'

'Alec! What are you doing here? Do you know what time it is?'

'Can you let me in, I'm busting.'

'It's a quarter to six for goodness sake.'

'Come on Claudia,' He pleaded. 'I know it's early. Please.'

'Come on then.' The intercom clicked off, and the door buzzer sounded. *Thank you.* Alec grabbed the handle and opened the heavy wooden door.

Alec walked up the three flights of stairs, slowly, with heavy legs. The staircase was spotlessly clean, with a delightful floral scent coming from the vases of flowers on each landing. When he came to Claudia's front door, he took a deep breath and knocked gently.

'Who is it?' Claudia asked from behind the door. Alec

could see light changes through the wrong side of the peephole.

Alec laughed. 'Very funny, let me in, please.' Alec began to overdramatically hop from side to side to indicate the urgency of the situation.

The door was unlocked slowly, far slower than Alec wanted. His jostling around had accelerated the pressure, and the simulated urgency became very real very quickly.

'Claudia,' Alec said, elongating the syllables. 'I wasn't joking about being busting.'

'Oh sorry,' Claudia said, as she opened the door fully. She stood there in a nightgown and robe. 'You know where it is.'

Alec wiped his shoes on the mat outside the door, 'Do you want me to take them off?'

'Don't worry about it. Just go and do your business.' She looked at him, her blue eyes widened, 'You look like a state. Are you ok?'

'I'll tell you all about it in a sec.' Alec quickly went to the bathroom.

Alec looked in the mirror, while he washed his hands. His hair was sticking up in random clumps; there was a dirty streak down one cheek, a red burn mark on the other. *Was that the bullet in the club?* His hands began to shake, and his red-rimmed eyes had a wildness about them that he hadn't seen in a long time. His coat was filthy, drying mud down one sleeve and a tear next to the left elbow. He lowered the toilet lid and took out the gun, phone, SIM and wallet from the pockets. He removed the jacket and started cleaning it in the sink. When he finished, he laid it over the side of the bath and returned to the mirror. His coat had protected his suit jacket, but his shirt collar had tracks of

81

mud across it. *Probably from the dive over the hedge.* He placed the jacket with the coat on the bath and removed the shirt and cleaned the collar. He put the shirt on the growing clothes pile and looked at his body in the mirror. He twisted left and right to see his back. There was a patch of mottled, purple bruises down his left side, already beginning to yellow at the edges and a large fist-sized bruise in the centre of his back, *a present from the goon at Berliner Straße, I really hope they get in the shit for losing me.*

'Alec, are you alright in there?' Claudia asked through the door. Her voice was tinged with worry.

'I'll be fine, Claudia, I'm just cleaning up.' He altered his accent to full-on Cockney, knowing that it would help reassure her. 'You were right, love, I'm in a *proper two and eight.*'

'Ok, then Alec. I've put Roger's dressing gown by the door, so I can wash your clothes.'

'Thank you, that's great. I'll bring them out when I'm done. I shouldn't be long.'

'There's a hot cup of tea waiting for you too.'

'Thanks.'

Alec returned to the sink and washed his face and neck. He wet his hair and styled it as best as he could with his fingers. *A little more presentable now.* He looked down at his trousers, and the knees were caked in mud, his shoes were almost as bad. He kicked them off carefully, the soles were a lot cleaner thanks to the mat outside, and he wiped them down and placed them on the toilet. He then removed the trousers and washed off the main mess. He added the trousers to the pile. His knees were killing him, but there were no external signs of damage. Alec wrapped a large white towel around his waist, almost as high as his nipples, to hide the bruising down his side, opened the door and bent down to reach for the bathrobe. His back sung in protest, so he crouched down and scooped it up. He returned to the bathroom and put the robe on, it was a couple of sizes larger than he would normally wear. Roger being almost half a foot taller than Alec. The soft cotton felt luxurious on his skin. He cleaned around the sink, wiping any stray muddy marks and used some tissue to dry it. Alec replaced the gun, wallet and phone in the coat pockets and folded it over his arm. He then bundled up the clothes, shoes on top. He groped for the door handle and left the bathroom.

'Where do you want this lot?' He called.

'In the utility room please dear,' Claudia said from the kitchen.

Alec padded to the utility room opposite the kitchen in his socks, carrying the bundle like a small baby. He smiled at Claudia as he looked into the kitchen. She had a quizzical look on her face. In the small room, he placed his shoes on top of the washing machine and dropped the bundle of clothes on the floor. He laid his coat next to the shoes and crouched to open the machine door. He threw in the clothes and looked at the controls. *Yeah, that's not going to happen.*

'Claudia, how do you work this thing?'

'I took you to be a sophisticated man of the world,' Claudia said with a smile as she entered the room.

'Well, I'm having a break from that for a while. It gets a little tiring at times.'

Claudia laughed. She put some liquid in the machine and adjusted a few of the settings and paused before turning it on.

'Your socks? I can smell them from here.'

Alec trod on the toe of one and pulled his foot out and repeated the motion for the other. He picked them up between his toes and lifted his leg, so his hand could catch them. He waggled his eyebrows at Claudia, looking like he was waiting for gushing appreciation of his skills.

'You haven't changed one bit,' She said, stepping to the side. 'I'm not touching them though.'

Alec bent and opened the machine and threw the socks in. Claudia started the machine.

'Come on, your tea will be getting cold.'

Alec stood in the kitchen, his hands wrapped around the plain, white mug, sipping the steaming tea. Claudia had thoughtfully added a few sugars without asking. The kitchen hadn't changed since he was last there. It had the same white wooden cupboards, black granite worktop, small dining table along one wall. Claudia was sitting at the table staring at him with her large blue eyes, her expression one of amusement rather than anger. She was a few years younger than Alec, in her forties; however, time had been kind to her. When she had joined the embassy twenty-five years ago she had turned a lot of heads, Alec's included. She had always looked like she had come from a magazine shoot, wearing the latest fashions, not a single long blonde hair out of place, her minimal makeup applied perfectly. There was a slight, faded, narrow scar above her right eyebrow: the only imperfection. Alec and Claudia had dated, punching well above his league and it was looking serious, but Alec couldn't or wouldn't commit to the life she wanted. She worried every time he went on a mission, knowing that he had a reckless streak that could be his downfall. She wanted him to leave the fieldwork to others, start climbing the organisational ladder, start being home at a regular hour, and start staying safe for her and the children she desperately wanted. Alec refused to change, so they broke up. The split was amicable, and a year later Claudia and Roger were married.

'So, what brings you here at six o'clock in the morning? The clubs kicked you out finally? I must say when you came in I thought you'd had a heart attack or something,' she asked.

Alec thought for a moment. *I know I can trust her, but how much can I involve her in this mess? Should I have come here at all?*

'It's been a tough night,' He took a deep breath, *here I go.* 'Jaromir Polyakov was killed in a bar last night.'

Claudia gasped, and stood up, 'Oh my god! Are you okay? I know he was your friend, how did it happen?

'We were in a bar in East Berlin, when he was shot in front of me. Assassinated. I obviously got away and ended up here.'

'Do you know who did it?'

'Some Eastern European goon dressed as a waiter. They chased me for half the night,' He noticed Claudia's involuntary look towards the door. 'It's okay I lost them hours ago. There's no way they can know I'm here,' he said, reassuringly.

'How did they find you?'

'I'm a little rusty, they tracked my phone signal. I dumped it on a couple of drunken girls heading west when I realised.'

'That doesn't sound like you. You've always been more switched on than that.'

'I know. I'm out of practice I guess. I also used an ATM this morning, company card and twenty minutes later a posse of Russians turned up looking for me,' Claudia's mouth opened in surprise. 'It's okay. I hid from them, they never saw me.'

Claudia recovered quickly, 'That certainly sounds like an eventful night. Why didn't you go to the Embassy?

'I was headed that way, missed my stop on the U-bahn, found I was being followed by Tweedledee and Tweedledum, and decided that someone in the embassy must be behind it all, not many people would have the knowledge that I was meeting Jaromir or the resources to track my phone and put a couple of thugs on my trail.'

'That makes sense. Have you slept at all?' Alec shook his head. 'Ok, drink up and go and sleep in Chris's room. I'm supposed to be working today, but I'll call in sick.'

'I'm not sure that is best. Arthur will know if you don't come in and put two and two together. I can't risk it. The wrong person might find out.'

'You don't think Arthur is involved in this? That's absurd.'

'No, I think Arthur's clean. He has to be. It'll be someone else at the embassy. Jaromir told me, before he was shot, that someone was planning to assassinate a minister before the end of the week. I think the target is the Prime Minister.'

'Oh god! You have to tell someone.' She exclaimed.

'I will... I'll tell Arthur, but only when I've figured out who is planning it. Arthur will just call off the visit, or flood the area so our conspirator will just fade away, or worse, be part of the security and strike knowing where the weaknesses are.'

Claudia thought for a moment. 'You're sure about this?' Alec nodded. 'You're right then, I have to go into work. It'll be too suspicious otherwise.' She continued.

'Will you be okay?' Alec asked. 'You'll have to pretend

to know nothing about any of this.'

Her voice turned professional, 'Alec. You stay here and get some sleep. Don't worry I'll be fine. They won't find anything out from me, and I may be able to help you while I'm there.'

'Ok, I believe you. I've seen you keep a secret before. Even the Stasi wouldn't be able to extract anything from you.' Alec said, referring to her keeping Roger's cancer a secret.

'Good that's settled,' she looked at the clock on the wall. 'I better get ready. It takes me longer nowadays.'

Alec shook his head in disagreement, and said matter-of-factly, 'I've always said that you're always the most beautiful woman in any room. Makeup or not.'

'Shut up you idiot and go sleep.' She smiled at his compliment though. 'You look like you're going to collapse.'

Alec walked out of the kitchen, kissed the top of her head as he passed, 'Thank you for this. Claudia.'

'Sleep!' She ordered.

Alec went into Chris's room. Chris was twenty-two. Claudia and Roger's eldest. He had left the family home three years ago, abruptly leaving Berlin's Technical University mid-way through his first year to start up a tech company in Munich. Claudia and Roger's other child, Erika, had joined Chris there last year, going to Munich to study at the Bavarian Academy of Fine Arts. The room was sparse of Chris' belongings; *he must have taken them to Munich with him,* the last time Alec had seen the room, going on six years ago, Chris was showing Uncle Alec a program he had designed to catalogue the MP3 files on his computer. He had looked amazed when Alec asked him what an MP3 file was. Chris' shelves had been stacked with textbooks and computer magazines. His desk covered in computing hardware. *I'm not surprised he quit university so soon; he was far more advanced than they could teach him.* The posters of video games had been taken off the wall, leaving the occasional tell-tale putty adhesive grease-stain the only indicator they had been there.

Alec removed the dressing gown and laid it on the desk chair. He pulled back the covers and laid down on the soft mattress. He was asleep before he closed his eyes.

11

Alec was restless and fidgety in his sleep; he had kicked the covers off himself, his eyes moving rapidly under his closed eyelids. He groaned and shifted his position.

I walk down the steps at the Schlesisches Tor U-bahn station down to the street, there is a thick mist billowing around my feet. I cross the boiling River Spree via the bridge with the strange battlements and turrets which support the U-bahn train line. I have been this way many times, across many nights. I'm not worried I know what is coming. After the bridge, I turn left on Mühlenstraße, and I reach the East Side Gallery. I am the only one there this night, and every night come to think about it. I stop at the first mural and stand at the edge of the pavement to take the full image in. The mural is over three metres high. The subject of the mural is Jaromir, sat slumped in the booth, hole in his forehead. Dark red blood leaking out of the hole, dripping down his face to his bushy moustache, and further onto the pavement. His eyes look at me, I hear his voice. 'You failed me Alec.' Tears start to drop from his eyes. I close my eyes, try to breathe, there's tightness in my chest. I steel myself and reopen my eyes. The mural had changed.

This one I had seen before. Roger lying in his hospital bed, connected to machines and tubes. His, once strong once powerful body reduced to skeletal frailty. Claudia sits beside the bed holding his hand, gently. The machines breathe for him, the regular hiss of the ventilator expelling carbon dioxide. Roger's head slumps to one side, his jolly face with its ready smile now slack and grey, his eyes closed. The EKG machine beeps in time with the weak pulse in Roger's neck. The beeps slow and then stop. The mural doesn't change, but I can see Claudia standing up suddenly, leaning over Roger, and crying for assistance from a nurse. An alarm starts its panicked wail. Roger's eyes open and look at me. A sibilant hiss of a whisper assaults my ears. 'You failed her Alec.' I try to scream my denial. 'She always loved you more.' I shake my head. This is new. Roger has never spoken to me before. I normally just look and cry at the futility. I hear myself murmuring over and over 'No. Not me. Not me.' I cover my ears to block it out. My eyes can't take seeing him anymore. I screw them up tight. I want to hold my fists against the sockets to stop me seeing what I know is coming next. Tendrils of mist creep up, and I remove my hands from my ears. The sudden shock of the icy non-fingers on my flesh forces me to open my eyes.

It was the scene I knew so well. Mark and Sophie in their car, their faces were happy, smiling. Mark had probably just improvised an imitation of a waiter or a barman from wherever they had come. He was a natural mimic. They weren't looking at the car coming towards them from the side. That had shot the red light. I can see Sara there standing outside of the car and pointing at the threat heading her parent's way. She is much younger in the mural. I draw my gaze back to Mark. He has changed. He is younger too. My little brother. Too small to see over the steering wheel. His smiling mouth displaying the braces he used to wear. His small hand on the gear stick, Sophie's hand covering his. I always see him this age when

90

I picture him, wearing short trousers and our green prep school blazer. Pens sticking out of his shirt pocket. He looks at me. Looks into me. His pubescent voice wavers. 'Don't fail her Alec.' It increases in pitch, 'Don't fail her, don't fail her, don't fail her.' Repeating over and over, higher and higher. 'Stop!' I yell. I always do. It never works. I fall to my knees and hit the hard pavement, my hand lost in the mist. I beg 'Stop, please stop.' The mist forces my head up.

The painting has changed again. A red-walled room. Brigette lying on a bed, a silhouetted man over her, on top of her. I hear the sound of a slap, and then a punch. Blood and mucus pour from her nose. Her bruised eyes are wide with terror. The sound of another slap strikes my ears. Her scream shatters inside my head. The shadow turns and speaks with a menacing growl, 'You failed her, Alec.' I can't take any more. I push my face into the mist, fight against its pull, refusing to submit. I feel the vapour crawl into my mouth, my nose. Creep down past my throat into my lungs. I cough hard to force a breath and then harder still. I try to rid my body of the foreign spirit. I lift my head. The suffocating fog gradually retreating as my breathing becomes easier. The mural changes before my eyes. The old canvas brushed away, and a new one began.

A ball of fear hits my stomach. The dread of what I know is coming next. I try to turn away; my feet stuck in the concreted mist. Its creeping arms wrapping around my body. It hands holding my head facing the wall. Its fingers force my eyes open. I am unable to stop looking at the tableau forming in front of me. My Stefanie on the ground, café chairs flung around her, like mourners at a funeral. I look at her white skin with the fading blush on the cheeks, the line of blood steadily trickling down from the side of her mouth to her jaw. Her sharp silver eyes look at me. I look back, seeing the pupils enlarge and then contract. The tears from the sides of her eyes pulled by gravity down her cheeks to merge with the trail of blood to her jaw. I try to step forward. To touch her beautiful face one more time. I can't move. She coughs a mouthful of blood. I scream pre-emptively, 'I'm sorry! I failed you!' The mist won't let me turn away. She closes her eyes. I try to blink away the tears from mine. The mist holds them open. Through the watery blur, I see her face change to Claudia's, then to Brigette's, then to Sara's, then back to Stefanie's. Each one's eyes tear at my heart. They continue changing into each other. Each change occurring faster and faster while an ever-increasing tempo of voices shriek 'You failed us Alec.' The changes blur as my eyes can't keep up. The voices merge into a single word. 'Alec.' Repeated over and over. 'Alec.', 'Alec.', 'Alec.'

'Alec,' Claudia said. 'Come on wake up.'

'Alec!' She called out.

Alec grasped for her voice, reached out from the depths of sleep. He surfaced, gasping for air, his back soaked.

'Claudia?' He said weakly.

She held him in her arms. 'Yes, dear. I'm here.'

Alec shivered in her embrace, his breathing slowed, his pounding heart faded. Alec could smell the faint trace of this morning's perfume on her neck. He closed his eyes and sighed heavily. *Shit, that was a bad one. They're not normally so intense.*

'Was it a nightmare?' She asked.

'Yeah.'

'You still get them?'

Alec was momentarily confused, and then he

remembered that Claudia had seen him experiencing them many years before.

'Every night, some are worse than others. That was a bad one.'

'I'd say so,' Claudia said, as she broke the embrace.

Alec became very aware that he was only in his underpants and attempted to pull the cover onto him a bit. In doing so, he exposed the bruises down his side.

'Oh my god!' Claudia said, pointing, 'You didn't tell me about this.'

Alec followed her finger, the mottled bruising from the night before had turned into a bruise that took up almost half of his torso. 'It wasn't this bad last night. I swear. It was from when I jumped over a hedge.'

Claudia raised a perfect eyebrow. 'A hedge?'

I better not mention the clump to the back I took off the driver. I bet that looks much scarier. It feels like it does anyway.

'It's okay, it looks worse than it is. Getting old, less cushioning I guess.'

'You should have tried to land on your stomach or bum then.' Claudia teased.

Alec reached behind him for a pillow to throw and his back spasmed, he gasped in pain and fell back on to the bed.

'I'll get you some painkillers; I've got some co-codamol from the UK. That should help,' Claudia said. She left the room to get them.

Alec gritted his teeth and raised himself up. He reached out his arms and grabbed his feet. Tears welled in his eyes. He pulled and stretched his back. He felt something give, and the pain subsided, leaving a dull ache. Claudia came back into the room with a glass of water and a couple of tablets. She saw Alec's back and dropped the glass in shock.

'That didn't happen falling over a hedge.'

'That's where I was punched by Tweedledum. What does it look like? I can't see.'

'I can see the knuckle marks from his fist. They are black, the rest of the area is a dark purple. It looks horrific.' She walked over to him, and gently stroked his back. He flinched at the coolness of her touch.

'Sorry that was the hand I was holding the glass with. The marks are raised. Was he wearing brass knuckles?'

'I don't know I didn't see them. He was a big fella though.'

'You're lucky that's all he did. You let me know if you see blood when you pee. I'll get you to a hospital. Here are the tablets, I'll get you another water.'

'Don't worry about it.' Alec swallowed the tablets dry. He coughed a couple of times, wincing at the movement.

'Alec, you're not Superman, you know. You have to start looking after yourself better.'

'I know, Sara tells me that each time I see her-'

'-She's right. You should listen to her, she's very sensible for her age.'

'She really is. She's coming here tomorrow,' Alec paused for a moment, 'what time is it? '

'A little after seven.'

'Seven? Did I sleep all day? How did you get on at the office?'

'Fine. How about you get dressed, I'll make you a tea and something to eat, and I'll tell you all about it. Your clothes are on the chair over there,' Claudia said, pointing at Chris' desk.

'Sure, sounds like a great idea.'

'I'll see you in the kitchen, bacon sandwich ok?'

'Perfect, thanks, Claude.'

Claudia smiled at Alec's use of the old nickname he had for her and left the room, closing the door behind her. Alec struggled to his feet, stretched to work out kinks in his back. *She wasn't wrong; I'm no Superman, that's for sure. I don't think I've ever hurt so much.* His knees creaked, and each foot had a large blister on the heel. He gingerly walked over to the chair and slowly got dressed. The nightmare already fading in his mind.

12

Alec walked into the kitchen, the smell of the frying bacon making his mouth water. *Is there a greater smell?* He asked himself.

'Your tea is on the counter,' Claudia told him.

'Thanks, Claudia,' Alec took the tea to the table and sat down. His hands shook with a little tremor he put down to stress.

'So, how was work?' He asked.

'Well, according to the rumours you are either a double agent, a patsy, insane or an assassin, or all four at the same time. The whole embassy was talking about it, from the secretaries to the department heads. Lots of people came up to me asking about you.'

'Did you see Arthur?'

'Yes, he was waiting at my desk when I came in, said he wanted to tell me the news himself before I heard the gossip.'

'What did he say?'

'He told me that you met with Polyakov last night, Polyakov was shot and you escaped. He spoke to you on the phone just before eleven, and you said you were heading in. That was the last he heard from you. He did say there was a report that the Russians caught you at a strip club, but he didn't believe it. After all, why would you go to a strip club when you're wanted by the Russians, Berlin Police, the assassins and us?'

Alec coughed uncomfortably, 'There was a valid reason.'

'Oh Alec,' Claudia laughed shaking her head. 'You really haven't changed, still the same reckless man from twenty years ago. Come on then, what was the reason? Some drink and some fun before spending the rest of your life in a Russian prison?'

'I needed a phone and a gun, I found out a contact I used to use was working at the club, so I headed there. I may have had a drink to avoid suspicion. I'm far too old for strip club fun. That's if you could even call it fun anyway.'

'Methinks the lady doth protest too much. You forget Mr Foster, I know you too well.'

'Claudia,' Alec said, hurt evident in his voice. 'I don't frequent those types of places.' *Anymore.*

'That's a shame, your seediness is one of your more attractive features,' Claudia said. 'Here's your sandwich.'

Alec's head tilted in puzzlement at her remark, but before he could comment his stomach growled at him in anger at his neglect. 'Thank you,' He said, lifting the sandwich to his mouth. 'What else did Arthur say?'

Claudia sat down opposite him, a cup of tea between her hands. 'He asked if I had seen you or if you had contacted me last night. I told him I hadn't, and that since Roger died, I have barely spoken to you at all, just a passing nod in the office or uncomfortable small-talk in the lift... why do you do that? When I needed you the most you retreated and avoided me?'

Alec said a muffled apology, his mouth full. He indicated the reason for the delay in responding with his finger and thought how to answer. *The truth was that I had shut everyone away. The death of Roger and then Mark and Sophie so soon really affected me. I didn't want to get close to anyone again. I didn't stop to think how others needed me.*

'I'm sorry Claudia, after Roger and then Mark and Sophie I stopped talking with anyone. I couldn't bear to be close to someone and risk losing them. I guess… I guess I gave up. I surrendered and retreated to my own prison. It wasn't fair on you, Chris, Erika, even Sara.'

Claudia's eyes began to water; she wiped it away with the palm of her hand before it could spill into tears. 'We could have helped each other through it. That's what friends do, you know. They emotionally support each other in times of need. What am I saying? You've always had the emotional depth of a… used teabag. It's one of the reasons loving you was always so hard.'

'Claudia that was a long time ago.'

'Really, you haven't changed a bit. I'm kind of amazed you came to me for help. The all-powerful Alec Foster needing someone, I'm surprised the skies didn't crack.' She stood up abruptly, her cheeks and neck flushed; she clasped the back of the chair. She screamed and threw the chair to the floor and stormed out of the kitchen.

'Clau-' Alec started, but stopped his mouth wide open, blinking. *Give her some time to calm down or go to her? What should I do? I don't know. I can't sit here with a mouthful of bacon sandwich, like a robotic, what did she call me? A used teabag? A robotic used teabag? I don't want to be one of them. That doesn't sound good.* Alec stood up, took a sip of tea to wash down the now hard to swallow sandwich in his mouth. His guilt making his tongue swell. He followed her out of the kitchen.

Where did she go? It's not the biggest apartment in the

world, but I don't want to be knocking on her bedroom door or the bathroom while she's in the living room. He stopped for a second in the hallway to see if he could hear her. Muffled screams were coming from the bedroom. Claudia and Roger's. Alec had never been in there before. He imagined a room filled with pillows, frills and romance. He knocked on the door and waited a beat for a response. Nothing. With a deep breath, he twisted the handle and pushed the door open.

Claudia was lying on the bed, face into the pillow, her shoulders shaking violently. Alec took a step towards her; he noticed that the skirt she was wearing had risen and she was displaying a lot of stocking-clad leg. He looked away guiltily and moved closer to the pillow end of the bed.

'Claudia,' He said softly, reaching out a hand to her shoulder. To comfort and apologise.

She flinched at his touch, lifted her face and said, 'Go away, leave me alone, that's what you do best.' Her makeup had run, and there were streaks of mascara on the pillow.

'Claudia,' He repeated, his voice stronger this time, his touch firmer. Saying he wasn't going away, he was there for her.

She sat up straight on her knees and looked at him. She launched a slap, which struck with a clap. 'How dare you, I needed you. Chris and Erika needed you.'

She tried slapping him again, Alec stepped back, and she fell forward, overbalanced. Alec caught her and lifted her back onto the bed. Claudia struggled against him.

'I'm so sorry Claudia. I let you down. I failed you... and the children.'

Claudia didn't try to stop the tears that fell, darkening patches on the grey duvet cover, she launched herself at him again. Her strength surprised Alec and his legs gave way, and he fell backwards onto the carpeted floor. The cushioned blow to his back still hurt his already tender body, and he cried out. Claudia fell down on top of him and started beating his chest with the outsides of her clenched fists. Tears dropping onto his face. The punches weakened and then stopped, and she collapsed on top of him, shuddering. He could feel her breath on his ear, her fists caught between their bodies. He wrapped his arms around her and held her. Tears flowed from his own eyes. Tears for the pain he had caused, tears for the guilt he felt, tears for the pain in his back, getting ever stronger. He kept murmuring his apologies into her hair. How long they were like that Alec didn't know. Eventually, both of their crying ceased, Claudia's, and then Alec's. Claudia lifted her head and looked into his red-rimmed eyes. Her eyes narrowed, her face questioning.

'That's better,' Claudia said. 'I've wanted to do that to you for years. Let me up now.' Alec released his arms and Claudia sat up straddling his thighs. 'I can't believe it's taken you so long to let go. I'm glad you did though.' She tapped his forehead. 'Mr Roboto does have emotions.'

Alec felt battered, fragile and more than a little embarrassed. He sniffed a couple of times and coughed to clear the hoarse feeling in his throat. 'I'm sor-'

Claudia put her finger to his lips, silencing him. 'I know, and you're forgiven. Don't say it again. Now help a lady up.'

Alec bit his tongue at the obvious retort and held up his arms for Claudia to support herself on.

'Thank you, now let's go back into the kitchen and sort your problem out,' She said with a smile, straightening her clothes and flattening her hair. She left the room with Alec still flat on his back. His breathing ragged, his eyes wide and confused. He stayed there a minute to recover, then rolled onto his front and ungainly and with a lack of grace scrabbled to his feet. *What the hell was that? It worked whatever I did.* He shook his head in wonder and again followed her.

Alec entered the kitchen, and Claudia was making another tea.

'They went cold,' she said. 'Do you want another sandwich? That's gone cold too.'

'Nah, a cold bacon sandwich is still an enticing prospect,' Alec said. *Are we going to talk about what just happened? Hey Claudia, you remember the time you started beating me? The time we cried like babies? Do you want to talk about it?*

'Don't just stand there like a lemon. Go and sit down.'

Alec sat and absentmindedly started picking bits of bacon out of the sandwich and eating them. Claudia brought over the new cup of tea.

'One of these days, you'll finish one of these,' Her eyes were sparkling, and she had a great smile on her face, as though a lover had given her an expensive present for Christmas.

'Things keep getting in the way, I guess?' Alec said tentatively.

'Where were we before... oh, I remember I was telling you about Arthur and the office. Yeah, so Arthur was worried about you, he looked like he hadn't slept all night. To be honest, though, he didn't look as rough as you did when you came in this morning. That was frightening. I said that I hadn't seen or heard from you, but I'd keep him informed if you did contact me. He went around the whole office asking everyone.'

'I feel bad about not letting him know I'm ok.'

'He'll get over it. He may beat you around a bit, but he'll get over it. After he had left the whole office started talking. Rumours going round include: you killing Jaromir to start World War Three; Arthur and you in on a plot to kill Putin; you're holed up in a Berlin jail for being drunk and disorderly; Jaromir split your drink, so you killed him; a lot of them were drink related, a particularly nasty one started by Stephen on the EU desk – you finally fell into your bottle and drowned.'

'That's quite funny for him. He's just bitter because I refused him a transfer to my department. He saw it as a fast-track to Head of Section, as I won't be there forever. After last night he might be right. Anyway, there's a reason he's stuck on the EU section, nothing ever happens there, so there's nothing for him to mess up. Arthur will never accept him as a Head of Section. Anyone say anything else?'

'Richard in Counter-Terrorism was unusually silent; he normally has something to say about everything. He just stayed in his office with a concerned look on his face.'

'That's nice,' Alec said. He didn't get on with Richard, mostly due to his outspoken views on terrorism and the money being spent on it. Richard took that kind of stuff personally.

'I brought my laptop home with me; we can access the network from here and have a root around to see if we can find anything we can take to Arthur.'

'We?' Alec said, surprised.

'You come back into my life, well, come barging your way back into my life. With a tale of assassins, conspiracies and near-misses, and I got to see a side of you that I had never seen before. So, of course, I'm with you in this.' Her tone brooked no argument.

'I wasn't saying you couldn't be. You just surprised me that's all,' Alec said. *Don't make her angry, you won't like her when she's angry.* He smiled at his own joke.

'What are you smiling about?' Claudia asked.

'I'm glad we're going to be doing this together. At least you'll be able to use the laptop. I type like a ninety-year-old woman counting change in her hand.' He mimed a palm held out in front of him and with his other hand jabbed the forefinger into the palm slowly and firmly, looking for the correct change. Claudia laughed.

'Ok, I'll just wash these up,' indicating the sandwich plate and teacups. 'then I'll get the laptop and set up in the living room.'

'Oh, I better give Sara a call. She'll have texted my old phone her flight details. I usually pick her up from the train station.'

'Alright, I'll be in there when you've finished.' Claudia took the plate and the cups over to the sink. Alec stood up and went to Chris' room.

He took the phone out of the jacket pocket and rummaged for the tiny SIM Card. He sat on the bed and looked at the phone, *that looks like something from Star Trek.* He pretended to scan his body with the phone and in his best Bones McCoy voice he said, 'He's dead, Jim.' He laughed at his own joke. The phone was a lot more advanced looking than his usual medieval model. *Where are the buttons? How am I supposed to work this thing?* He turned it over in his hand and used a fingernail to pop the back off. He removed the battery and inserted the SIM card. *Thank god it has the little notch to tell me which way in it goes.* He replaced the battery and the back cover and then pressed the chrome buttons on the sides of the phone to start it. *One of them will do the trick.* The phone's screen came to life in a riot of colours and sounds. He waited for the exuberance to die down so he could call Sara. The display changed to a welcome screen with a dumpy robot and then asked him for his email address, a keyboard appeared on-screen. Alec slowly looked for the right letters and typed in his email address. He had trouble with the '@' symbol but eventually found it. The phone then asked if he wanted to connect to a Wi-Fi signal. *No, I just want to make a call, thank you.* He skipped that. An end-user agreement showed, and Alec scrolled through to the bottom and pressed the Accept button on the screen. *Come on now.* He was then asked to set the time-zone, date and time. He blew out his cheeks in frustration and slowly entered the information, looking at his watch for the correct time. *That's got to be it now, surely?* Finally, the home screen appeared with a whole host of different coloured icons. Alec chose the one that looked like a phone, *thankfully that is a pretty universal symbol.* The screen changed to a blank contact list. Alec looked at the different icons shown and chose the one that looked like a landline push-button keypad. *This is ridiculous. How is anyone supposed to do this in an emergency?* He jabbed at the numbers on the screen and pressed the green phone icon to place the call and held the phone to his ear. A series of electronic beeps sounded and then the ringing tone. A strange woman's posh voice said to him. 'You have reached the voicemail of...' then Sara's voice interjected, 'Sara!' and the posh lady's voice continued, 'Please leave a message at the tone, once you are done, please hang up or press the hash key for further options.' *Damn voicemail, I hate these things.*

'Hi Sara, it's Alec. I… um… lost my phone and have got a new one. My new number is.' Alec rattled off the numbers he memorised in front of Makary. 'Can you text me your arrival time and are we meeting at Alex as usual?' Alex being short for Alexanderplatz station. 'I'll try to reply back if I can figure out how to do it, but my new phone is one of those fancy smartphones you're always telling me to get. You know they're called smartphones because using them makes you realise just how un-smart you are. Ok, going to run out of message soon. See you tomorrow. Love you.' He took the phone away from his ear and pressed the red phone icon to hopefully end the call. Remembering the debacle from the night before he removed the back cover and took out the battery and SIM card and placed them separately back into the pocket. He stood up and went back over to the chair and put the phone in the jacket pocket. *Right, let's go and work out who's behind this then.*

13

Alec walked into the living room. Claudia was sitting on the large cream leather sofa, her feet curled underneath her. Her laptop, sitting on the arm of the sofa, projected a blue glow onto her face.

'Did you manage to get hold of Sara?' She asked.

'No, I left a voicemail though. She's probably out with her friends, it's the last night of freedom before her obliged visit to her boring uncle.'

'After last night, I'd say you're not *too* boring. How's she doing? I haven't seen her in years.'

'She's doing really well, as far as I know. She got a first in her degree in English Literature and is currently doing an MA at Brunel University. She'll be looking for a job in the summer, hopefully with one of the big publishing houses in London.'

'Wow, impressive,' Claudia said, a genuine smile on her face. 'How's her love life?'

'It's not something we really talk about, to be honest. I'm quite happy with that arrangement.' Alec grimaced. 'She isn't married yet, she would have invited me to the wedding. I don't know if she has a boyfriend, or a girlfriend for that matter.'

'You're not *that* great an intelligence officer, then are you?' Claudia said with a sly smile on her lips.

'Probably why they stuck me behind a desk. Just a washed-up old has-been put out to pasture, ready for the knacker's yard.' He brushed away an imaginary tear from his eye.

'Oh, poor you! You better go and sit in the armchair,' She pointed at the matching cream chair facing the sofa. She slipped into an accent more suitable for London's East End. 'It's gone six o'clock, you must be ever so tired. Here, put your feet up, and I'll make you some nice soup. Don't want you catching your death. I can put another bar on the fire. Warm you up a treat, Love, it will. Warm them tired old bones right up.'

Alec laughed with surprise. 'God, I don't think I've heard you speak like that in almost twenty years.' He plonked himself down on the sofa beside her.

Claudia gave Alec a smile, 'It's not an accent I use too often. Only for embassy parties to ward off lecherous ambassadors or-' She looked at him with a wrinkled nose of pretend disgust. 'over-familiar intelligence officers.'

'Ahem, Head of Section, remember?'

'Of course, you have the nameplate on your desk and the etched writing on your office door. "Alec Foster, Head of Something or Other." Well done.' She patted his head in praise.

Why does it always feel like she's a few steps ahead of me in these exchanges? Alec changed the subject. 'It's getting late, you've been up all day, and I woke you up early. You must be getting tired; shall we get started?'

'Spoilsport,' Claudia said, as she lifted the laptop from the arm onto her lap. She wiggled her finger on the trackpad, and the screen came to life. She entered her password to enter the system. 'It just needs a moment to connect to the Wi-Fi and then we can get started.'

'Have you got a notepad I can use, I work better with paper?'

'Yes, in the drawer next to the fireplace, over there,' she said pointing.

Alec lifted himself off the sofa with an effort, his legs and back still hurting from the night before and the fight earlier in the bedroom. He went over to the mahogany wall unit next to the marble effect fireplace. Photos of Roger and Claudia, with and without the children, smiled at him as he opened the drawer nearest the fireplace. He smiled back. In the drawer was an A5 reporters' spiral notebook with a pen inserted into the coils. He removed it and closed the drawer. He flipped through the pages of scrawled writing and doodles to a blank page.

'Did you know that your doodles can reveal aspects of your personality and how you are currently feeling?' Alec asked.

'Really? What does mine say? "I'm bored of being on hold, and no I won't press *eins* or *zwei* to go to this or that, please can I speak to someone human?"'

'I'd imagine so, there's a lot of heavy crossing outs and zigzags,' Alec said as he sat back down.

'I swear those systems were only put in place to make people hang up in frustration.'

'They probably make money from the number of calls they receive, so by getting you to hang up and call again it increases their profit.'

'Mr Foster, I think you may be right,' Claudia said. 'Right where shall we begin?'

'I was thinking about this last night, and there are a few ways they could have known about my meeting with Jaromir.' He ticked off from his fingers. 'One. They had Jaromir's phone tapped. Two. My office phone is tapped. Three. They followed Jaromir. Four. They followed me. Five. I logged my conversation with Jaromir on the

Contact Log, and they can access that somehow.'

'Ok, write them on your pad, we'll tackle them to see if anything shakes out.'

Alec followed her instruction. 'The first one, we can't tell if his phone was tapped, so I'll put a line through that.'

'How often is your office swept for bugs?'

'As far as I know every day, first thing in the morning, way before I get there.'

'When was the last time a bug was found in there?'

Alec blew out his cheeks. 'I don't know, maybe three... four years ago. A cleaner working for the French kindly left a pen on my desk. It was far nicer than the ones I use, so the security staff noticed it straight away. I think it was a Montblanc.'

'They really didn't know you at all. Tatty biro is more your kind of thing.' She reached over and slapped the pen as it edged closer to his mouth. 'You may eat your own pens, try to leave mine alone.'

'Sorry, it's habit when I'm thinking.'

'You've got an oral fixation.'

Alec waggled his eyebrows at her. 'That has been said before.'

'Oh my god you pig!' Claudia's cheeks reddened. 'You know what I meant.'

'Of course, I did. I couldn't resist the open goal though.'

She shook her head. 'At least you've quit smoking though.'

'Well, after Roger... well, you know. I wouldn't want to put anyone through what he went through. I thought you were so brave the way you handled it. God, I miss him.'

'He loved you, you know? He always said you were like the brother he never had. He was so proud you stood with him until the end.' Her eyes filled with tears, 'Others backed away in case it was catching. You were the only one who came to see him at the hospital. Do you know that?' She wiped her eyes.

'Really? Not even Arthur? I thought they were close, they'd known each other far longer than I had, and they went to school together for Christ sakes.' He stroked his chin, the rough day-old stubble rasping against his fingers.

'He… he kept putting it off. Kept making excuses, but Roger knew Arthur was lying. It really hurt him and was why he so looked forward to your visits. You kept his spirits up with your gossip and your jokes. I honestly think you being there for him gave Roger and the kids and I extra time together. Without you, I think he would have faded faster.'

Alec's cheeks reddened this time, 'No I think that was all your doing. He adored you.'

'We'll believe what we want to believe.' She gave her eyes a final wipe. 'So… number two, your office being bugged. Put a line through it?'

'Yeah, I think so. It would have been picked up. Unless of course our man… or woman had access to the office during the day and could place and remove the bug at will. It seems a bit unrealistic.'

'I agree.'

Alec drew a line through it. 'Okay, three: Jaromir was followed. I don't think so. I waited after he arrived, and no one entered after him until I did. The waiter was already there.'

'Ok, we can rule that one out.' Alec marked the pad.

'Four: you were followed. You're not as young as you used to be and you were never that good to begin with.' Alec looked up from the pad, his mouth open. 'I'm just teasing. You're so easy to get.'

'Well, ignoring those hurtful remarks.' He stuck out his tongue. *Childish I know, but sometimes there's nothing else you can do.* 'I don't think I was followed. I walked for three hours in the cold in the most roundabout way to the bar, and as with Jaromir, the waiter was already there. They probably tracked me by my phone; I'll hold my hands up to that. But physically followed? No, they knew where I was going and when I'd get there.'

'I agree. Also, the waiter couldn't just walk into the bar and say "Hi, I'm working tonight." Shoot you guys and then wait for his wages. If it was me and I found out where you were going to be, I would enter the bar as a customer and then when you got there pretend to be your waiter. You weren't in the main bar area, were you?'

'No, the non-smoking area to the back, it was just Jaromir and me there. The toilets are back there so he could have been sitting at the bar, his partner telling him from outside I was there, he opens the door – the front of the bar was very busy and hazy with cigarette and cigar smoke so the bar staff may not have noticed, hell, he could also have paid them off – leads me to the back, takes my order and returns to the bar to collect my drink or his drink if he ordered as himself, brings it too me, shoots us both and then leaves, staff non-the-wiser. Becketts Kopf doesn't have CCTV. I check for that each time I go.'

'It's plausible. Pretty convoluted, but plausible. So that's another item off the list. What does that leave?'

'Someone accessed the contact log after Jaromir called me.'

'Ok, let's check the contact log.'

Claudia picked up the laptop, woke the screen with her finger on the touchpad. She signed into the system and went to the contact log. The speed she went through the system made Alec whistle. 'I should hire you to do all my computer work.'

'I think technically you do, you are my boss after all.'

'A raise may be necessary.'

'I'm not going to argue with that. What time did Jaromir call you?'

'It was just after the department head meeting. I don't think Harper likes me.'

'What makes you say that? Richard has always been pretty friendly and civil to the Russian section when I've seen him.'

'I think he thinks I don't take his department seriously enough.'

'You don't though. You think terrorism is not a threat to national security and his department gets far too many resources.'

'Well, that's true. I don't want him to know that though. The most deaths caused by a single terrorist incident were the World Trade Centre, and Pentagon plane hijackings in 2001 - just under three thousand. Now, I'm not making light of the tragedy. It's a horrible loss of life. It's just if Russia or China or any of the other seven nuclear-armed countries kicked off there would be three hundred thousand deaths or more in the first minute if they went straight to the nuclear option, and it wouldn't stop until millions more died.'

'You may have mentioned this before a few times.'

'My opinion hasn't changed. If anything it has become more entrenched since Putin became President. He was in Germany when the wall came down. Did you know that?'

'I remember reading, that when the wall came down, and the people came to the KGB offices to demand their ejection, Putin was there burning files and trying to contact Moscow. I think it was in the *Time* magazine *Person of the Year* article. 2013 or 14, if I remember correctly.'

'2014. Exactly, he's a dyed-in-the-wool KGB officer, and to him, we are still the enemy.'

'That's why we are still where we are. To keep an eye on them, make sure things do not get that far. Terrorism to many, especially voters, is the more real threat. The Government is, of course, going to do what they can to reduce that threat.'

'It just frustrates me that's all.'

'Try to keep a poker face in meetings; your life will go smoother.'

'I suppose so. Where were we? Oh yeah, the meeting finished just before eleven, we'd been in there since eight. I went back to my office, and Jaromir called me almost immediately after. Spoke for a minute and I entered it on the log.'

'Okay, let's look at the log.' Her hands hit a few keys and brought up the message. 'You really should work on your spelling, this is almost illegible. What does this say?'

'I was in a hurry. A telephone call from Jaromir Polyakov at 11:05, requested an urgent meeting for nine p.m. Becketts Kopf bar. AF. That's my initials.'

'Thanks, I gathered that. Okay, let's see who has accessed that since.' She dragged her finger on the touchpad to an icon and a list of names, times and dates appeared. '11:15 same day, user AN1 – that'll be Arthur, 12:24 same day, user RH7. I don't know who that is. 22:45 same day, Arthur again. 08:09 this morning, Arthur. It looks like Arthur opened it four or five times this morning. Here's another entry for RH7. 13:34 today. That was the last one until me.'

'Who's RH7?'

'I'm looking. It should be quite easy to find out.' She fiddled with the touchpad and touched a few keys. Alec leaned closer looking at the screen. *I have literally no idea what I'm looking at.*

'Got it. RH7 is… what? Why the hell is he looking at this record?'

'Who is it?'

'Your friend, Richard-bloody-Harper.'

14

'Harper, what's he doing on there?' Alec asked, his pad and pen dropped off his lap to the carpeted floor without him noticing. *Richard Harper? Could it be him? Why would he want the PM and Polyakov dead? Me? Well, it's a bit of a reach, but I suppose I could see the attraction of me being out of the way, maybe get one of his protégés high up in the department. What would he have to gain by killing the Prime Minister though?*

'That's what I asked. I have no idea.' Claudia replied. Alec saw in her face that she was thinking the same as him.

'We'll have to look into it deeper, it could be innocent,' Alec said.

'Yeah, let's not jump the gun yet.'

'Ouch, that's poor phrasing.' Alec said with a smile. 'If we're going to take this to Arthur we need to have more than this.'

'Sorry I forgot what you had been through. I agree this will not be enough to convince anyone.'

'Where to start though?'

'I don't know. Pick up your pad and let's come up with some ideas.'

Alec looked down at his lap with surprise. *When did that happen?* He leaned forward and saw the pad below him the pages askew. Alec groaned as he got off the sofa, his joints seized up from sitting. On his knees, he picked up the pad and pen. He looked up at Claudia. He could see a smirk on her face.

'Don't you dare push me over,' he warned.

'I wouldn't dream of it. Really, Alec, you have such a poor opinion of me. I'm quite offended.'

He backed away from her on his knees, pad and pen in hand; his eyes narrowed watching her carefully. He stood up with a lack of grace. 'I'm sorry for doubting you,' He said. 'You had a look on your face that said you love to see me fall over and unable to get up.'

'How little you know me,' she looked away, her mouth twitching, shoulders shaking. Alec waited with an eyebrow raised.

'Oh my god! You'd be like an overturned turtle!' She shrieked.

Alec thought for a second and being one never to miss an opportunity to laugh at himself, threw the pad and pen onto the sofa next to Claudia, got back down to his knees, rolled over onto his back and started wiggling his limbs around. 'Help me! Help! I'm a turtle and can't get back up. Save me fair maiden.'

Tears were streaming down Claudia's face, 'You… really… are… insane.' She struggled to say.

Alec rolled over to his front and slowly stood up again, he made a little bow. 'Glad my audience is pleased.' He rubbed the small of his back, *the pain was worth it, I've missed that laughter in my life.*

'Oh yes, most definitely pleased. Back to work?'

'Unfortunately, yes.' He sat beside her again. 'So, Harper accessed the contact log, can we can see what other entries he's looked at? Also, have a look at his calendar for the past couple of months… see if we can make a timeline of his movements.'

'I could also see if I can get a copy of his emails.'

'You can do that?'

'Yeah, it's *company* policy and new recruits sign up for it when they join. Most don't read the contract, but it's in there. Every company issued mobile has a backdoor program installed so they can be monitored. I think it was put in place after the Cambridge spy ring fiasco. Although mobile phones and the internet weren't invented at the time, the language in the contract was broad enough to cover that.'

The infamous story of the Cambridge Five was drummed into me during training, they were a group of MI6 officers, Kim Philby, Guy Burgess, Donald Maclean, Anthony Blunt and John Cairncross, they were passing information to the Soviets during World War Two and afterwards. Their methods and exploits and how to counter them were taught to us.

'I didn't know it was there. What happens? Does GCHQ collect the information and we have to request it or can we, well you, access it?' Alec asked.

'I can't access it without authorisation; it needs a Head of Section to do that. Where can we find one of those?' Claudia's eyebrows lifted, 'How can you not know about this?'

Alec's cheeks reddened, a slow flush turned into flame. 'It just didn't come up-'

'-Or as soon as someone mentioned the word "technology" your brain turned off.' Claudia finished for him.

Alec coughed. 'That... is a believable hypothesis.'

'We should be alright. You do know your system password, don't you?'

'Of course, I do, I'm not that bad.'

Claudia gave Alec a long look, he held the gaze with a smile. 'Go on then, what is it?'

'I'm not supposed to share it with *anyone*. Security reasons, you know.'

'Alec,' she warned.

'Okay, you've tortured me enough. I submit to your questioning. I'll write it down for you.' He turned the page in the pad and quickly wrote a string of characters. He handed the pad to her.

'"Monday!23"?' She asked. 'That is stupid.'

'It's genius. No one will ever guess it. The exclamation mark instead of the one is inspired.' *Thankfully it was only changed on Monday, I forgot the previous password.*

'You are a walking, talking security risk. How the hell have you survived so long?'

'Oh, through a combination of luck, deceit, and dashing good looks and charm. Aren't all spies supposed to be like this? I've seen the movies.'

Claudia just shook her head and handed him back the pad. 'I don't think I'll need the pad to remember that one, *genius.*'

'Ok, so we'll go through his calendar and his email records. Anything else?' Alec wrote on the pad. 'Check his social media accounts? Sometimes pictures uploaded still have their location details on them.'

'What do *you* know about geotagging?'

'Not much more than I just told you. I heard of it from somewhere, and somehow it stuck.' Alec tapped his forehead with the side of the pen.

'I'm amazed, especially after the password. He might not have social media accounts; they are frowned upon in the service. Partly for the reason, you said. But he's quite new compared to us, barely into his thirties. He may have something, or his wife will.'

'He's married?'

'About ten years ago to Alison, his childhood sweetheart. Weren't you invited to the wedding? Roger and I went. It was a sweet occasion; they looked very much in love.'

'I may have been on a mission.' *Or in a bar somewhere with Makary and Brigette.*

'Ok, anything else?'

'What's in it for him? What's the motive?'

They both paused and thought for a minute. Alec spoke first:

'A terrorist attack on the PM. That would increase his purview exponentially, would put his department top of the pile, globally. Increased funding, being able to take the cream of the current officers and first dibs on the top recruits.'

'Don't they get that already? Counter-terrorism already gets tons of funding.'

'They do, however, in terms of status, Counter-Terrorism has an equal footing with the Middle-East and Africa department and the "friendly-countries" department. They're above War Crimes, Global Issues and the Technology departments, but below us, Asia, Nuclear Proliferation and Counter-Narcotics. A terrorist attack on the PM, especially if successful, would propel them to the forefront.'

'Is that motive enough?'

'The quest for power is a strong motivator for some. I don't know, I can't think of any other reason unless it's personal and the PM shagged his wife or something.'

'Our PM? Maybe, Berlusconi, that is far more likely. I can't picture our PM ever having sex, even if only with themself.'

Alec laughed, 'It was just a theory.'

'I can just see you going to Arthur with it. "Arthur, Richard Harper is going to assassinate the PM because the PM can't keep out of his wife's knickers."' She mimicked Alec's voice. 'He'd laugh you out of the building and hand you over to the Russians.'

'If I did that I'd probably walk out and give myself to them without Arthur's help.'

'Ok, we've got something to get working on, at least.'

'I think if we start by looking over the last two months on the calendar and see if there is anything there, to try to narrow down the search.' Alec said.

'Good idea. I'll bring up the Harper's calendar.' She opened Microsoft Outlook and went to the shared calendar's feature. She selected Harper and started scrolling through the dates. There were a lot of entries. Mostly internal meetings though.

'What's that one?' Alec pointed at a particular entry.

Claudia double-clicked on it to open it. 'Annual leave, started 21st November through to 28th November.' Alec wrote the dates on the pad.

'That was just over two weeks ago. Who starts their annual leave on a Tuesday?'

'It is unusual, most people, if they are having a week off will take the Monday to Friday off maximising the weekends. Here's another, two days, 13th and 14th November, not marked as annual leave, just blocked out.'

'Ok I've got that,' said Alec. 'Anymore?'

'Another week in October, at the beginning. The 3rd to the 10th. Tuesdays again, and a single day, Friday 22nd September, whole day blocked out.'

'Right, now let's bring up the emails to see if we can

see any explanation for these dates.'

Claudia returned to the laptop's desktop and double-clicked on an icon, labelled 'Tracker'. A dialogue box came up asking for Username and Password.

'This is where I put in your details. Username?'

'AF1, password-'

'-I've got it.' Claudia interjected, shaking her head. 'Okay, now I put in the user's name we want to look at and the date range.'

'Make the dates a couple of days before the ones I've got written down, he may have explained where he was going to be.'

'Good idea, shall we start with the earliest one?'

'Sure.' Alec read out the first date. Claudia entered the information. A list of email subject headings appeared in chronological order. Claudia started reading the headings out.

'Pay special attention to any replies he makes as he may tell the sender where he is going to be.'

'Yes, Boss.' Claudia smiled.

'I'm getting thirsty; shall I open a bottle of wine for us?' He didn't wait for a response. 'They still kept in the kitchen?'

'There's a white in the fridge, unopened, and some reds and whites in the utility room in one of the cupboards above the washing machine.'

'White still your preference?' Alec said, remembering.

'Yes.' Claudia had already gone back to concentrating at the screen.

Alec left her to it and went to the kitchen. He opened the fridge and took out a bottle of Barth Hallgartener Riesling Kabinett Trocken. *The Trocken on the label indicates that's a dry wine, are you supposed to have this with food?* Alec shrugged to himself; wines weren't really his drink of choice. *Should I put another in the fridge as a replacement?* Alec decided to do so and went into the utility room; he opened the first cupboard and was greeted by cleaning products. He tried the second, *towels?* He opened the third and final cupboard, and there were seven bottles, four red and three white. He took a white and closed the cupboard. He checked himself and opened the cupboard again and removed a red also. He returned to the kitchen and put the warm wine in the fridge and the red on the side. He went to the glass cupboard, *still in the same place I see,* and took out two wine glasses; they were a little dusty, so he looked around the kitchen for some kitchen paper. *Over there next to the kettle.* He tore off a couple of sheets and rubbed the inside of each glass, holding them up to the light to be sure they were cleaned enough. He threw the paper sheets in the waste bin and opened the screw-top on the bottle. The aroma of the wine caught in his throat as it was released. He coughed. *Must be good*, he smiled. He poured a generous amount into each glass and replaced the screw-cap.

'Alec, I've got something.' Claudia called from the living room, her voice sounded excited.

Alec put the bottle back on the counter and took the two glasses and returned to the living room.

'What have you found?' He asked.

'Come and sit down.'

He handed Claudia her glass and sat down beside her. She angled the laptop so he could see more clearly.

'There was nothing I could find about the dates we wrote down, so I went back another month. Harper took four days off in September, the 12th to the 15th. In this email from Arthur to him on the 5th, Arthur is giving him permission.'

'Permission to do what?' Alec asked.

'In an email earlier that day Harper sent Arthur a proposal to meet to with some ex-Bulgarian, Georgian and Uzbek KGB officers to discuss potential terrorists entering Europe and Russia through those countries from Turkey, Iran and Afghanistan.'

'We should have been consulted on that.'

'I know, Arthur does suggest it to Harper, but Harper dismisses the idea. He states "Foster will only get in the way, try to take over. You know what he's like when it comes to his turf."'

'And Arthur just lets him?' Alec didn't sound happy to be kept out of the loop.

'Yes. It appears so. I don't know if they had a face-to-face discussing it before permission was granted or not.'

Alec took a gulp of his wine and made a sour face, 'What was the result of the meeting with the ex-KGB?'

'There is no follow-up from Arthur or any emails from Harper to say what was discussed or any further proposals.'

'That's unusual, can you check the contact log to see if Harper had entered anything in there about the meeting?'

'I already have done. There's nothing around the dates he left.'

'It's not a smoking gun, but persuasive. I'm surprised Arthur didn't follow up. Wait, this was in September? That was when the PM visit was announced, Arthur was like a bull making sure of the details of the visit. He didn't want to be embarrassed on his patch. Did you know he is looking at leaving the service in the next year or so and taking on a cosy and well paid ambassadorial role in some friendly country?' Claudia shook her head. Alec continued

'That would partly explain why he was so frantic yesterday when he heard about Jaromir. Normally he'd trust me to do my job and return when it was safe. He's hoping Julia would come back to him once he's away from the stress of running the Berlin office.'

'I'm not sure she'll do that. She seems quite happy in her new life.'

'You see her still?'

'Of course, unlike someone, I didn't pick sides when they split. She's got a job in a florist making the most fabulous displays. She hinted at meeting someone new a couple of months ago but was very cagey about the details. I'm due to see her next week; hopefully, she'll tell me more.' She looked at Alec, her face set, 'You mustn't tell Arthur any of this.' Alec made the sign of the cross on his heart with his fingers and mimed zipping his mouth closed. 'You can trust me, I can keep secrets.'

'That's true enough I suppose.' She conceded. 'I've never known you to break a confidence. Anyway, do you think we have enough to take to Arthur?'

Alec took another gulp of wine, emptying the glass. 'We could look at his social media see if there's anything on there. I doubt it though.'

'Worth a try I suppose.' She brought up the internet browser on the laptop and typed in Facebook in the search bar. She clicked on the link and the page loaded.

'Do you have a log in?'

'No, it's frowned upon, do you? Of course not.'

'Never found the appeal to be honest. Sara is on somethings called Snapgram and Instachat all the time.'

'Snapchat and Instagram, you technophobe.'

'Whatever, can we still find him or... Alison? Without logins.'

'Possibly, we wouldn't be able to see what they had posted though.'

'Oh, that's a bust then. When we take it to Arthur, he'll be able to get Technology to look into it.' His stomach growled alarmingly.

Claudia looked at the clock on the mantelpiece. 'You must be starving; you've only had part of a bacon sandwich and probably not much yesterday if I know you. Shall I fix us something for dinner?'

Alec looked at his watch, just past eleven. 'We could always go out; Goldhorn's is just on the corner. I haven't been there since Roger took us that one time.'

'Aren't you wanted by the whole of Berlin?'

'Not the whole of Berlin, only by the Police, the Russians, and the service, of course. It's a calculated risk; the restaurant is literally one minute away. The windows are darkened so no one on the street can see in. If anyone were watching here, they would have been alerted by you looking at the log and come knocking. The food is lovely too.'

'I remember. Roger and I used to go there quite often. I haven't been since...' Claudia frowned.

'Oh, don't worry about it. It was a silly idea.'

'No... it'll be nice. Who knows it could be your final meal as a free man,' she said, her expression brightened.

'That's cheery, thanks.'

'You're welcome. You used to have to be a member to go there, Roger's membership ran out, but they did a day membership. I'll go on their site and see if they still do. While I'm there, I'll get their number so you can call them to book a table. You're paying by the way.'

'I wouldn't dream otherwise, it'll be just like the olden days,' he grinned.

Claudia punched his arm, 'I seem to remember you always taking me on dates and then paying me back on payday.' She typed in the restaurant name into the search engine and clicked on the relevant link, 'Yes, they still do the day membership.' She gave him the number of the restaurant and started looking at the menu.

'Are you drooling?' Alec asked as he looked at her.

She quickly wiped her chin, 'No, go on call them. The phone is over there.' She pointed to the bureau desk in the corner. Alec noticed her surreptitiously wipe her chin again as he turned his head to look in the direction she indicated. He smiled as he stood up and went to the bureau. He dialled the restaurant and spoke to them in German. He hung up and replaced the phone in its cradle.

'All sorted, made a booking for two in thirty minutes.' He said.

'I better get ready then,' she looked at him, 'you'll do I suppose, luckily Berlin is hot on shabby smart.'

'Why do you think I've lived here all this time? In London, I'd be lucky to get served in McDonalds.'

'That's for sure.' She placed the laptop on the sofa next to her, closing the screen. She stood up and said, 'I won't be too long. Put on the television or something while you wait. The remote is next to the phone.'

Alec stood up and picked up the remote and sat back on the sofa. He shifted the laptop onto Claudia's seat. He pressed the 'on' button and started flicking through the channels.

15

Alec saw his face on the television as he was flicking through. He went back to the channel to see what was being said.

'… you see this man, please contact the Police immediately, do not approach he is considered to be dangerous,' said the middle-aged news presenter on the ARD Tagesschau channel. She stood beside a grainy CCTV photo of Alec. Her aquamarine business jacket clashed with the blue studio backdrop. The presenter continued as the picture next to her changed to video footage of a film premiere at the Zoo Palast cinema. 'The stars were out in force at the premiere of Star Wars…' Alec tuned her out.

That's not a very clear picture of me; the Police mustn't have identified me yet. That's a bonus. I'll still have to be careful though, they may have clearer pictures they haven't shared with the media yet. It'll be twenty minutes or so before they repeat the headlines, I wonder if the other channels are running the story? He resumed his channel surfing, skipping past a number of phone-sex adverts. *Doesn't Claudia have satellite television? German television is awful.* He managed to circumnavigate the roster of channels on the television and returned to ARD, now showing highlights of the previous night's Bundesliga football games. *Hertha were playing at home last night? I hope that affected the journey of the goons following those two girls.* He laughed with a sense of *schadenfreude* as he pictured the waiter and the driver standing at a U-bahn station platform packed with the blue and white stripes of the Herta Berlin supporters.

'What are you laughing about?' Claudia asked as she came into the room, behind him.

'Oh nothing,' Alec said, 'something amusing from last night just came to mind.'

'I'm glad you can find humour in being chased across Berlin on a winter's night by hired assassins and Russian Special Forces.'

Alec turned and looked at her, and his mouth dropped open. She was wearing a black sequined evening dress, low cut at the front and with a long slash in the skirt displaying one of Claudia's perfectly toned and tanned legs.

'That's exactly the reaction I was hoping for,' she said.

'Claude, wow, I mean… wow.'

'Come on we'll be late for the booking.'

Alec stood up and walked over to her, unable to take his eyes off her. He said, 'You look beautiful.'

'Thanks, Casanova, go and get your jacket and shoes on. I'll be at the door.' She smacked him on the arm as he went past. 'Hurry! I'm starving.'

Alec went into Chris's room and put on his suit jacket and shoes. The shoes looked scuffed, and the polish was dulled on them. He breathed on them and with the inside sleeve of his jacket buffed them up. *That's a little better.* He put them on and did up the laces. He looked at the blue outer jacket on the chair and took his wallet from the pocket; he thought for a moment and decided to wear the outer jacket also. *Better to have the gun and the phone with me than to regret it like I did last night.* He left the room and went to the door where Claudia was tapping the jewel-encrusted watch on her wrist. She had put on a glittering black shawl to protect her from the cold.

'Finally, he emerges. Is Your Highness ready? Are you wearing the 'going-out' tiara?' She mocked.

'Ha ha, come on then let's go,' he said, the laughter spoken rather than expelled.

Claudia opened the door for him and bowed deeply as he passed. His laughter this time was genuine. He left the flat and started down the stairs. He paused and turned to admire her figure as Claudia locked the door above him. She turned, caught him looking and smiled.

'One foot after the other, Alec, it's called walking. If we miss the booking I won't make you anything.'

Alec started down the stairs, Claudia followed.

'You could have got an apartment with a lift,' Alec grumbled. 'This is killing my blisters.'

'Shut up. Just be thankful I'm not making you run down them.'

They reached the bottom; Alec opened the main door of the block and held it open for Claudia. 'After you dear lady.'

'Thank you, kind sir.' She stepped out. Her head slowly turned from left to right, looking for Police cars, or suspicious people loitering in the area. When she was satisfied, she turned back to Alec and whispered, 'it's all clear.'

'Why are you whispering?' Alec whispered back as he exited the building.

'I thought it was fitting, especially as you were skulking back in there.'

'Skulking?'

'Very shady behaviour. Like a criminal. I'm not sure I

should associate with the likes of you, what would the ladies at the bridge club say?' Her eyelids fluttered innocently at him.

'I'm not going to comment.' He held up his arm for her to take.

'Wise decision.' She wrapped her arm round his and snuggled close to his body. *Is that because of the cold or something else, something better?* They started walking to the restaurant. Light snowflakes fell, reflecting the streetlights. The ground was wet, but the snow wasn't settling. They avoided the larger puddles.

They crossed the road arm in arm and headed up Mommsenstraße, they crossed the junction with Wielandstraße. There was very little traffic on the roads, so Alec relaxed a little. *I'll be able to see any police cars or Russian SUVs.* Within a minute they were there. The restaurant's black awning with gold longhorn cattle head logo looked classy, as did the illuminated bushes in pots along the length of the pavement, their glow reflected in the darkened windows with "Der Private Businessclub" etched on them. Alec released Claudia's arm and went up to the door and held it for her. She went in, and Alec followed in behind her. The smell from the open kitchen was the first thing that Alec noticed, the charred smell of beef caused his nostrils to expand, and he savoured the aroma, his taste buds ached. The second thing was the large black carpet with the massive cattle logo woven into it. He approached the hostess at her lectern. Without staring, he noted the tight-fitting black sweater she wore accentuating her curves. *Come on Alec, what's got into you? You're like a horny teenager.*

'Guten abend,' Good evening, Alec said, 'I have a booking for two, under the name Duquesne.'

The hostess looked in her bookings diary, '*Ja*, I can see you need to register for the day membership.' She handed him a small form and a pen.

'*Danke*,' he said. He rested the form on the lectern and started to complete it. The hostess walked over to the kitchen window. Claudia came over and looked over his shoulder, her hand on the small of his back.

'Duquesne? The German spy?' She tutted and shook her head.

Alec turned and smiled, 'I'll tell you why when we sit down.'

'Ok, Frederick, or should I call you Fritz?'

'Shhh,' Alec said, putting his finger to his lips. 'Loose lips sink ships, remember?'

Claudia stuck her tongue out at him, 'Spoilsport.' She stepped back and haughtily turned her face away from him, she couldn't hide the smile on her lips though.

Alec completed the form and waited for the hostess to return. He went to put the pen into his jacket and stopped himself when he realised what he was doing, he put the pen down on the lectern. The hostess returned and asked, 'Have you been here before?'

Alec replied that he had, knowing that the hostess would give them a tour of the restaurant and the smoking lounge if he had said otherwise. *Better to keep a low profile.*

'Could you follow me, *bitte.*'

He turned to Claudia and held out his hand, 'My dear?'

She took his hand, and they followed the hostess past the five refrigerator cabinets displaying the available cuts of meat. Kept at the optimum temperature the sight of such an array made Claudia squeeze Alec's hand tight. Alec decided to keep his comment about her loving meat to

131

himself. The restaurant was reasonably busy with most tables taken by diners. It was well-lit with a large chandelier in the centre of the dining room, the bar was to their left, with mirrored walls, bottles of spirits and glasses lined up with parade-ground precision, that reflected the light back into the room. The hostess took them to a table in the middle of the restaurant next to the bar.

'Excuse me, could we have a table next to the windows? Bitte, more private.' Alec requested, having spied a free one away from the main area.

'Certainly sir.' She looked around for a moment and guided them to the table Alec wanted. It was back towards the entrance in the corner; however, three sides were enclosed by the blackened glass, meaning Alec could see anyone enter the restaurant and they'd have to walk past his table into the main area and turn around to see him and Claudia.

Alec pulled out the chair for Claudia, it faced the entrance window, the black surface mirrored the restaurant behind her. Alec took the seat in the corner facing outwards.

'*Danke*, this is perfect,' he said to the hostess.

'*Bitteschön*,' you're welcome. 'Your waiter will bring your menus.'

'*Danke*,' Claudia said to her. The hostess departed. Claudia placed her elbows on the table and rested her chin between her fingers, looked at Alec intently. 'So, you were going to explain why you use the surname of one of Germany's greatest spies as a cover name.'

'Well there are a couple of reasons. First, it's easy for me to remember. Second, in English it's pronounced Doo Cain, in German and Russian, it's Doo Quesner, which makes it hard for someone not familiar with the name to write down. Third, I just like it.' He poked out his tongue, copying her earlier expression.

'It's just another sign of how reckless you are.'

'I've been using it for almost thirty years, and apart from Arthur, you're the only one to have picked up on it,' he protested.

'That you know about.'

'Well... I suppose that's true,' he frowned, conceding the point. 'I'm still here though.'

'Your luck and charm have got you through this far despite your stupid name choice.'

'You think I'm charming?' Alec smiled.

'Are you fishing for compliments? That's very unattractive.' She returned his smile.

The waiter brought their menus over and asked them if they wanted to order a drink.

'Sparkling water,' Claudia said. Alec raised an eyebrow at her choice, 'and a glass of your house white, thank you.'

'I'll have the same.'

The waiter left them, allowing them to peruse the contents of the menu. Alec asked Claudia, 'Are you having a starter and main or just a main?'

'Just a main for me, as nice as the starters are, they are too much as well as a main. A girl has to watch her figure, you know.'

'How about I watch it for you?'

'I've seen you watching me since I entered the living room. You didn't even gawp at the pretty hostess with the big boobs like I expected you to.'

'She had big boobs? Where is she? I must see,' Alec said. He lifted himself off the chair, motioning to stand up and look all around for the hostess. He sat back down. 'I didn't notice. I must be captivated by your presence.'

'It's been a long time since you have been. It's been a long time since I've felt this way too.'

What is going on? Where has that come from? We have always been flirty together, even when she was with Roger, never like this though, with this intensity. This is like we were when we were together… what? Twenty-three, twenty-four years ago. What about Roger? He was one of my best friends. Alec shivered as he remembered his dream. The words from Roger rattled around his head: "You failed her," "She always loved you more." Alec closed his eyes to try to calm his whirling mind.

She reached out and took Alec's hand in hers. He opened his eyes in surprise. The touch of her hand was cool and gentle against his rough skin. She started tracing lazy circles on his palm with his finger, while looking into his eyes. 'I'm not wrong, am I? You are feeling it too?' Her voice wavered with uncharacteristic nervousness.

Alec didn't give himself a pause to think. 'To be honest, I don't think I could describe how I'm feeling right now. A part of me is worried about what Roger would say seeing us here. However, another part of me just wants to sweep you into my arms and hold you close until the end of time.'

A tear came to her eye. 'Wow.'

16

The waiter returned with the drinks. Claudia released Alec's hand and coughed to compose herself. The waiter placed the drinks on the table and asked if they were ready to order food. Alec looked at Claudia, her cheeks were flushed and eyes sparkling.

'Can we have a little longer? I'll call you over when we're ready.'

'Certainly sir,' he said, retreating.

'We'd better have a look at these. I know I want one of their steaks, that's all I've been thinking about since the living room. Well, that's not true, I've been thinking about-'

'- steak sounds good,' she interrupted quickly. She opened the menu and flipped the plastic-covered pages. 'I'll have the fillet,' she flipped a couple more, 'with the truffle potato puree.'

'I remember that being lovely.' Alec picked up his own menu. 'I'll have the prime rib Australian wagyu with grilled vegetables.'

Claudia turned to the steak page, and her eyes widened, 'The prime rib is one hundred and sixty-five euros!'

'Like you said earlier this could be my last meal, I'm going to treat myself. Besides, the company is paying.'

Claudia laughed, 'Really? In that case, I'll have some green beans too and a better wine than the house wine.'

Alec smiled, he sipped his wine and said, 'It's not bad, but everyone knows its red wine with steak. I'll get the waiter to choose a decent one for us.'

'Good, if it were schnapps I'd trust your opinion, but a good wine, you're okay, I'll go with the expert.'

'I wouldn't trust my schnapps judgement either to be fair. I normally go for the cheapest, although I keep meaning to go to Austria and do a few of the tasting tours. Maybe you'd like to join me?' He offered. While he was talking, he motioned to the waiter, who came and took their order. When the waiter left Claudia continued the conversation.

'Now you're thinking of taking a holiday? When was the last time you went away? Not just the odd day to recover from the night before.'

'It's been too long. I can't even remember. Possibly Mark and Sophie's funeral, I was away for that for almost a month, sorting out their stuff and making sure Sara was well.'

'That's not a holiday, also why didn't Sara come and live with you?'

'I spoke to Sophie's parents, and they were more than happy to look after her. They lived nearby so Sara wouldn't have to change schools and leave her friends. I thought that would be best for her…'

'… even though she was your only family left.' Alec's mother and father were both dead. His mother died when he was twenty, she had had a massive stroke at work and died on the way to the hospital, and his father two years later. Alec liked to say he died of a broken heart, but the truth was that he drank himself to death. Like father, like son.

'It was the right thing to do. I'm hardly father material, am I? I drink too much, I'm far too absorbed in my work, look at me I'm a wreck.'

'Weren't you worried it would affect your relationship with her?'

'Of course, however, I felt that uprooting her from her life at that time would make an already tough situation worse. She'd either resent me or hate me. At least this way I can still be a part of her life. We speak on the phone all the time. She's trying to get me to get a laptop so she can Skip me.'

'Do you mean Skype?'

'Yeah, something like that. She comes here four or five times a year for a few days, we go out to museums, bars, and exhibitions. I sometimes go to the UK to see her. I think she likes her cool Uncle Alec in Berlin far more than she would if she had to live with me.'

'You think you're cool?'

'Well, it's a relative concept. I'm no Justin Beaver, but compared to Sophie's parents and even Mark and Sophie themselves, to Sara, I'm like the Fonz.'

'I'm not going to comment on that, except to say you're more like Potsie.'

Alec put a hurt look on his face. 'I'm the clumsy, bumbling one?'

The waiter brought their dishes and laid them on the table. *Wow, that looks and smells amazing.* Alec's prime rib was charred to perfection, the fatty edge rendered golden, the juices spread out to the grilled peppers, mushrooms, courgette slices. Alec looked at Claudia's plate, her two-inch-high round fillet begged for attention. He could smell the truffle coming from the mashed potatoes.

'Yours looks amazing,' he said to Claudia.

'Thanks,' she picked up a knife and fork and sliced into the steak. The jagged knife slid through the meat like butter, the reddish-brown juices ran to the potatoes and soaked into the base. Alec could see the bright pink of the inside, a picture-perfect medium-rare. 'It's cooked just right too.'

Alec picked up his cutlery and cut into his wagyu steak, it too was cooked flawlessly, rivulets of rendered fat from the marbling oozed through the pink meat onto the plate and joined the pool surrounding the beef. He placed a sliver into his mouth savouring the taste. *Ah, that is heaven. A fitting final meal.* Alec caught Claudia looking at him often, each time with a shy smile to her lips, or a flush to her cheeks. *I probably look the same. I haven't felt this way since we first got together all those years ago.* At one stage he was looking at her face rather than concentrating on what he was doing and missed his mouth with his fork. The sharp tines of the stainless steel stabbed his top lip.

'I told you that you were Potsie.' Claudia smirked.

Alec scowled at her, his cheeks burning with embarrassment. 'I wasn't going to point out the meat juice in your cleavage,' he said, pointing with the traitorous utensil.

Claudia reached for her napkin and looked down at her chest. 'Where? Where?'

Alec laughed. 'Got ya.' He then had to dodge as the napkin arched through the air towards his face.

'You're such a dick, sometimes.'

The rest of the meal was uneventful. When the dishes were removed, Alec sat back in his chair, his appetite sated. 'That was delicious.'

Claudia smiled, 'A fitting meal for the condemned man and his glamorous assistant.'

'Thanks, Claude,' Alec said. 'Hopefully, it won't come

to that. Arthur will be furious with me though. It will take a lot of fast talking to keep my job.'

'What will you do if you can't talk fast enough? Will you stay in Berlin or return to the UK?'

'I've been here for over half my life, I barely know London anymore and know even less of the rest of the UK. I've got savings and my pension so I should be ok for money. Sara will probably stay in London, so I'll probably just stay here and drink myself into oblivion, unless...' He trailed off, unwilling to put his hope into words. *Unless there is going to be a future for us.*

Claudia stayed silent. Alec could see she was thinking. 'We better get back; we'll have to be up early to see Arthur.' he said. He gestured to the waiter and asked for the bill. He removed his wallet from his jacket pocket hung up on the back of his chair. He opened it and removed five hundred Euros, more than enough for the meal and a decent tip. He laid it on the table tucked under his glass.

He stood up and put on his jacket. Claudia also stood; she pulled on the shawl and smiled. 'Come on then,' she said, holding out her arm for Alec to take. They left the restaurant and headed back to Claudia's.

They arrived at the apartment without incident. Alec was breathing heavily from the stairs. *She really needs to get a lift.* Claudia opened the door and went in. Alec followed. He wiped his shoes on the coarse mat and removed them when he stepped inside. He closed the door behind him. He hung his jacket on the coat hook in the hallway. He could hear Claudia in the kitchen, glasses clinking as she took them from a cupboard. He joined her in the kitchen as she crouched down to get a bottle of wine from the refrigerator. He silently admired the shape of her figure, as her black dress clung to her in interesting places, the sequins glittering in the artificial light.

'I thought we might have a nightcap,' she said, standing up.

'That is a great idea.'

She poured the wine, dark claret, and passed him a glass. He held the glass up and toasted, 'To my glamorous assistant, without whom I would have been lying frozen on the street, or worse.'

Claudia clinked her glass against his and took a sip. 'You're lucky I have a soft heart.'

'I'm forever in your debt.'

'I'll hold you to that.'

Alec drained his glass. 'I'd better check to see if Sara has replied. Back in a sec.'

'Do you want another?' She said, indicating the bottle.

'Nah, better keep my head relatively clear for tomorrow.'

'Wow, that's a first.'

Alec stuck out his tongue and went to the hallway. He reached into the jacket pocket, took out the phone, battery and SIM and assembled the phone. He powered it on. Once it had started up and connected to the network, it dinged to announce a new message. "Hi Uncle Alec, flight arrives at 1:30. I should be at Alex for 2:30. I'll meet you at the usual spot." Alec was pleased she had replied. *Two-thirty, I should be finished with Arthur by then. Maybe I'll take Claudia with me if she'll go. Sara always liked her. Called me a fool when she found out we used to be together. She had a point.* He disassembled the phone and put it back into the jacket. He returned to the kitchen, Claudia was washing up the glasses.

140

'All sorted. I'm meeting her at two-thirty at Alexanderplatz Station. We should be finished with Arthur by then. Do you want to come?'

Claudia thought for a moment, 'Yes, that would be lovely.' She looked at the clock on the wall and said 'Right, we better get some sleep.' She dried her hands on the tea towel next to the sink.

Alec walked over to her and held her hands; he looked into her eyes, smiled and said. 'Thank you for everything, I would have been lost without you.' He kissed her cheek, the touch of his lips on her skin and intoxicating smell of her perfume made his knees shake. He let go of her hands before she could notice the tremor of excitement that flowed through him.

'Good night, Claude.'

'Night Alec,' Claudia replied, with a strange smile on her face. 'I'll use the bathroom first.'

'Of course, it's your home after all.'

As Claudia walked past Alec to leave the kitchen, her hand brushed against his, sending more tremors through him. *Really Alec? At your age? You shouldn't be having these feelings. I thought you dried up past a certain age.* He gripped the counter to support himself.

'It's all yours,' Claudia said from the hallway. Alec heard her open her bedroom door.

'Thanks,' he said as the door closed behind her.

He left the kitchen and walked down the hallway to the bathroom. Inside he washed his face and hands. He used a bit of her toothpaste on his finger to brush his teeth. *It wouldn't be right to use her toothbrush.* With his business done he opened the door and with a longing look at Claudia's bedroom door. He went to Chris's and opened it. He was about to go inside when he heard Claudia's door

141

open.

'Don't you think it would be more comfortable in here?' She asked.

Alec turned and saw her standing in the doorway, partially obscured by the bedroom door. She was wearing a thin satin crimson robe. The way her nipple was making the fabric protrude he was fairly certain she wasn't wearing anything underneath.

'Are you sure?' He asked, praying for the positive response.

'Of course, Darling,' she smiled, 'When have you known me to be unsure. If I remember correctly in the restaurant, you were saying something about sweeping me off my feet. I'd like that.'

'Well, in that case.' He closed Chris's door behind him and walked purposely to her, they embraced, mouths meeting, hands caressing. They walked into the bedroom still interlocked; Alec kicked the door closed behind him with his heel, the bed springs squeaked through the door, as their weight fell upon it.

17

Alec woke to daylight streaming through the open curtains, he squinted at the brightness. He heard breathing beside him and all the memories from the night before come flooding back to him. The way she tasted, the touch of her skin, her touch on him, her intoxicating perfume, her eyes gleaming in victory as he gave his all to her. Then repeated more slowly, less frantic, her moans as he pleasured her and the way her body shook and shivered as she submitted to him.

He looked over at her; she was facing away, her hair wild from behind, his gaze moved down taking in the body he had been admiring the night before. There were a few wrinkles here and there, areas where the skin wasn't as taut as it had been so many years ago. But compared to him she had hardly aged, especially considering she had had two children. He reached out and stroked her back gently. She shivered at his touch and pushed back against his hand. Her right hand came back and started rubbing his hip. He shuffled forward, lifting the duvet cover as he moved. His legs wrapped around hers, his chest against her back. He could feel her heartbeat, *or is it mine?* He reached around with his free arm and found her breast, he stroked the nipple and heard her gasp, she pushed harder against him, they were both breathing harder now. She turned towards him, her eyes a deeper blue than he had seen in a long time, they kissed passionately, tongues finding each other. Alec lifted himself up, and Claudia scooted under him, he lowered himself down, careful not to put his weight on her. She opened her legs wider, and he entered her, she exhaled with pleasure, he moaned with delight. *A third time? It's like I've become twenty again.* Her nails ran down his back, his hands on her hips pulling her towards him. He shuddered and a few thrusts later she did too. He collapsed beside her unable to support his weight any longer. For a while, all he could hear over the blood rushing around his head was heavy panting, *hers or mine? I don't care.* She turned and laid her arm over him, claiming him as hers. He willingly acquiesced, he turned his head to the side to look at her. She had a wide smile on her face, her cheeks were flushed, and there was a sheen to her forehead. He took in the crow's foot wrinkles round her eyes, the laughter lines around her mouth. *She has never looked so beautiful.* He told her so, and her smile widened into a grin, and she kissed him with passion.

'You're not too bad for an old man,' she said.

'I didn't have a stroke or heart attack, so that's a bonus. Although at times it felt like I would.'

'I'm glad.' She pulled herself on top of him. 'I'd hate to lose you now I've got you back.'

'I'm not going anywhere. My darling. I promise.'

She looked into his eyes, 'Well we have to soon, it's almost eight.' She slid off him to the floor and walked towards the door. He watched her move, her body graceful as though on a catwalk. Her long blonde hair, without a trace of the grey that dominated his own. *You're a fool for letting her go all those years ago. You are so lucky you've been given a second chance.* He laid there for a few minutes, his breathing and pulse returning to normal. He then sat up and rubbed his face. *I don't think I want to leave, this is perfect.* The image of the PM's head splattered by a bullet came to his mind. He begrudgingly got up and started picking up his clothes. Claudia re-entered the room, 'I've left the shower on for you.' She threw a towel at him.

'Thanks.' He wrapped it around himself and gave her a kiss as he passed her to go to the bathroom. She squeezed his bum through the towel.

***

After the shower, Alec went back to the bedroom, Claudia was not there. 'I'm in the kitchen, do you want tea or coffee?' She called.

'Tea,' he replied. He finished drying himself off and put on his clothes. He looked at the dishevelled bed and smiled. He half-heartedly straightened the cover and fluffed the pillows. He then went into the kitchen.

'Here you go,' Claudia said, handing him the mug. Hers was beside her on the counter. 'So, what's the plan Boss?'

'We drink this and stay here forever, only leaving to have dinner.'

'Sounds perfect.' A wistful look crossed her face. 'What's really the plan?'

'We'll get the S-Bahn to Friedrichstraße station, and walk to the embassy.'

'Wow, that's easy.'

'I know, there's no other way really, there is only the main entrance and the road is sealed at both ends to traffic, those terrorists making our life hard again. I think we should stay together. Hopefully, if they are watching, they'll be looking for an old man by himself. Not a horny teenager who can't keep his hands off the sexy woman next to him.'

'I like that, and if they do notice you?'

'We better hope they don't. The Russians the other night looked very serious.'

'Well, we only have to get to the embassy. If we come up the Unter den Linden and turn on to Wilhelmstraße, it's a shorter distance to the embassy than from the other direction. Less for us to run.'

'That's a good idea. I'd expect them to be stationed around Mohrenstraße station as that's the closest one and the one I was aiming for the other night. We also have to watch out for the two goons and also Harper.'

'We'll have to see what we can do to disguise you.'

***

Claudia opened the main door of the apartment block and stepped out. Alec could see her shadow in the bright sunlight. He waited, and she came back in. 'It's clear.' She said.

'Let's go then,' Alec said. He pulled her close and gave her a deep kiss. 'Just in case.'

They broke their embrace and Claudia took Alec's hand. 'I'm with you, you'll be fine.'

'I feel strange wearing Roger's clothes.'

'You look good. Much better than the scruffy old suit you normally wear. Maybe that'll be enough to hide from them. The Police would have been advised to look out for a tramp.'

'They're not that bad.' He laughed.

'They're not that good either. When this is over, I'm going to have to take you clothes shopping. I can't be seen with a vagrant. It's not good for my image.'

They stepped out of the building still holding hands. Although the sun was shining there was a bitter chill to the air. They turned left and huddled together as they walked. After a short while, they turned onto Bleibtreustraße, and it wasn't long before they could see the beige arches of Savignyplatz station. There were two Police officers outside the station, but they took no notice of the couple as they entered. Alec breathed a sigh of relief when they were passed. He listened for the crackle of their radio as they turned the corner to go up the stairs to the platform. *Nothing.*

'I think we're clear,' he said as they reached the top of the stairs.

'They would have been told to look out for a grey-haired old man, not a thinning brown haired old man.'

He playfully dug his elbow into her side, 'I'm not that old!'

Claudia squealed causing a few heads to turn in their direction. 'Stop that! I'm very ticklish there. We'll never keep a low profile if you keep doing that.'

He turned and kissed her cheek; his hand caressed her back. 'Anyway, I don't feel old.'

'Didn't you get enough earlier? Did you slip some Viagra into your tea when I wasn't looking?'

'Nope, it's just the effect you are having on me.'

'Well that's good but try to keep it in your pants. Low profile, remember.' She smiled at him.

'I'll try, but I can't promise anything.'

The train entered the station and people around them started shuffling towards the edge of the platform. Alec turned his head to look. Claudia grabbed both sides of his face and pulled him in for a hard kiss that caught his breath.

'Come on,' she said as the train's doors opened.

Alec stumbled on his weakened legs, and Claudia caught him from falling.

'Good to see I haven't lost my effect on men.'

They entered the carriage; there were no seats, as the train was packed with commuters. They stood near the door, close together. The train set off with a jerk and Alec, and Claudia banged into each other. They stayed that way, Claudia's arm wrapped around Alec holding him close. He could feel her breathing on his cheek. He knew if he looked at her he would be lost forever and would really cause a scene. She pushed herself closer against him, her breathing grew heavier, more rapid. *That's not helping.*

The train entered the next station, Zoologischer Garten, and some people got off, a few entered. Alec and Claudia stayed where they were, entwined against the side of the door. Alec risked a glance at her. Her eyes were half-closed, her cheeks glowing. She opened her eyes; the pupils were large and dilated. Alec bent forward and whispered in her ear. 'You're so sexy... I love you.' *Where the hell did that come from?*

She gasped, her eyes widened, and she hugged him tighter. The train started again. She couldn't stop smiling at him. They carried on the journey in silence, the noise from the tracks made it impossible to hear each other. By the time the train reached the penultimate stop, Berlin Hauptbahnhof, or Berlin Central Station, Claudia's head was resting on Alec's chest, her arms were no longer crushing him. *No doubt listening to the rapid beat of my heart, why did I tell her I loved her? I mean, I do, I always have, even when she was with Roger. We had different plans for life and decided it was best to split up, the way I* felt about her didn't change and still hasn't, but I didn't want to tell her so soon. If I've messed this up again, I'll never let myself forget it. Alec kissed the top of her head, inhaling the scent of her. Her subtle perfume and traces of shampoo merging to make an intoxicating concoction which made him feel light-headed.

To attempt to take his mind off Claudia's close proximity, Alec decided to run through the journey to the embassy in his head, think of routes to take and alternatives if they were spotted. *At Friedrichstraße station we'll take the exit onto Dorothea-Schlegel-Platz, it's not the main entrance so should be less busy, fewer people to notice me. Thankfully the Germans haven't installed facial-recognition in their stations.* Alec recalled a newspaper article he saw back in the summer about testing being done on a system and a trial being held at Südkreuz station. There was a lot of dissent amongst a population still wary after the monitoring of private citizens done by the Nazi Gestapo and the East-German Stasi. *I don't want to follow the route I took the other day heading towards Becketts Kopf bar – Reichstagufer and then Wilhelmstraße, they were probably tracking me then, so we'll go the other way, Georgenstraße onto Friedrichstraße, then down to Unter den Linden and across to Wilhelmstraße. It's a little convoluted but allows us plenty of scope to veer off and re-join the route later if we are discovered.*

Many passengers disembarked at Berlin Hauptbahnhof station, Alec expected this to happen. Berlin Central Station was the largest train station in Europe, with domestic trains to most German major cities including Munich, Hamburg or Cologne and international trains to Warsaw, Prague, Vienna amongst others. He turned to look at the remaining occupants. The carriage was about half full, most seats were taken, and few people were standing. He had been so lost in his and Claudia's world that he hadn't noticed the passengers surrounding them either disembark or sit down, they were the only ones standing at their end of the carriage. There was a lot of space around them, their obvious reluctance to separate had been noted by their fellow travellers, as Alec found out. The passengers he saw looking at them had knowing smiles and occasional smirks. He also noticed that several commuters were reading newspapers, with *Bild.de* being the most popular, and displaying the largest, clearest photo of him on their cover. He took a deep breath and tried to remain calm. He almost told Claudia, but he didn't want to panic her. No one had stood up and pointed at him shouting "J'accuse", perhaps they hadn't made the connection, maybe the hair dye had worked.

Claudia raised her head, 'Alec, what's wrong?'

She must have felt my breathing change. 'Nothing, darling, we're coming up to the station, just psyching myself up.'

'I'm sure we can handle it, it's not too far to the embassy.'

Alec felt the train slow, he looked out of the window he could see the double arched Friedrichstraße station approaching as the track curved, with the Fernsehturm, Berlin's famous television tower, high above it in the background. The train pulled into the station and came to a stop. The doors opened, and Alec and Claudia exited. The station was on Claudia's normal commute, and she led Alec to the nearest platform exit, the S-bahn line being on the upper level. They held hands, Alec savoured the touch of her skin against his fingers. *Concentrate, you old fool.*

They headed down the steps to the ground level, their pace matching the fellow travellers, not too fast, or too slow. They reached the ground floor, and Claudia directed Alec to the Dorothea-Schlegel-Platz exit. They went through the open doors to the triangular plaza outside. Alec saw the square had been taken over by the annual Christmas market, closed this early in the day. Alpine huts and stalls, their openings shuttered, protecting their wares overnight. Alec remembered taking Sara here two years ago, they sampled the different cheeses, meats, and *lebkuchen* or ginger-bread, and mulled wine. It wasn't the biggest or the oldest in Berlin, but they had enjoyed it nevertheless. Sara didn't come to Berlin last Christmas, she was touring Canada during her winter break with fellow students instead. Alec was loathe to go to the market alone, so decided to stay at home instead. However, after the lorry attack at the Christmas Market at Breitscheidplatz. Alec went to Berliner Weihnachtszeit at Alexanderplatz when they reopened a few days later, along with what felt like at the time, the rest of Berlin, in a show of solidarity with the city. Alec's reminisces were cut short when he saw two Polizei officers come from the right-hand side of one of the Christmas market huts at the side of the plaza, stopped and looked directly at Alec and Claudia. They were forty metres away.

'Claudia, I think we'd better get out of here.'

They headed left from the station entrance and crossed over the road past the taxi rank. They walked down Georgenstraße, maintaining a steady pace. Alec resisted the urge to look behind him, he had heard no shouts of "Halt" from behind him. They reached the junction with Friedrichstraße, and as they turned right to head south towards Unter den Linden Alec risked a glance behind him and saw the two Policemen were following them, now thirty metres behind.

18

Alec's heart started to race. *Shit, they're too close. I was hoping for more of a lead. They'll outrun us for sure.* He looked ahead and saw the yellow tram pull up to the Friedrichstraße tram stop.

'Quick Claudia, the tram.'

They ran, still holding hands, to reach the doors before they closed, and the tram would move on. Only ten metres, but several people were getting off blocking the doors. Alec pushed his way on to the tram, past startled tourists with their backpacks, he dragged Claudia with him. His usual deference on public transport long forgotten. The doors closed behind them as they sat in one of the vacant pairs of seats on the far side of the tram. The tram silently moved off, Alec looked to his right and saw the Police officers on the pavement run past the tram stop looking further down Friedrichstraße for their quarry. The tram turned left onto Dorotheenstraße and Alec, and Claudia breathed deeply. Alec kissed Claudia on the lips.

'That was exciting,' he said.

His relief was short-lived when he saw on the electronic journey map that there was only one stop before the tram would loop back and reverse its journey and return to Friedrichstraße. He pressed the bell for the tram to stop at Universitätsstraße.

'We have to clear this area quick it'll be flooded by police soon, and no doubt the Russians will be listening to the police channels too,' Alec said. 'Okay, if we turn on to Universitätsstraße and then cross Unter den Linden to Behrenstraße that'll take us to the south side of the embassy. If we need to we can keep heading south and make our way around, Französische Straße has plenty of places we can hide, like that shopping mall there.' 'Galeries Lafayette? You could buy me a ring!' Claudia laughed.

'Not a hope in hell, my love.' Alec said gently. He added a wink when he saw her face drop. 'Let's get to the embassy safe before you start making wedding plans and choosing colour schemes.'

The tram stopped just before the junction with Universitätsstraße, and they got off. Holding hands, they turned right on to Universitätsstraße, they walked along the Department of Social Sciences building on the right-hand side down to Unter den Linden. Alec thought he could hear the faint sound of police sirens coming from where they had been. Within a minute Alec and Claudia came to the wide thoroughfare of Unter den Linden, the Humboldt University of Berlin behind them to the left. They crossed the road quickly, stopping in the central reservation alongside the tall bronze statue of Frederick the Great of Prussia on horseback and waited for a break in the traffic. To their left, they could see the tourist hotspots of the Berliner Dom and the Fernsehturm in the skyline. When the traffic was clear they crossed to the other side and instead of heading west towards the Wilhelmstraße and the embassy, they turned east, and then south when they reached Bebelplatz, the large square infamous for being the site of one of the Nazi book burning ceremonies in 1933. Around twenty thousand books were burnt there for being "un-German", including works by Karl Marx,

Albert Einstein and many others. To the couple's left was the State Opera house, to their right was Humboldt University Faculty of Law and ahead of them was St. Hedwig's Cathedral.

Alec and Claudia crossed the pebbled square, passing the memorial to the book burning, a glass plate set into the floor, giving an underground view of many empty bookshelves. There were a few tourists taking advantage of the early morning to capture some clear photos. Alec and Claudia were walking slightly faster than normal walking pace and when they reached Behrenstraße Alec asked for a moment to catch his breath.

'I'm not as young as you, you know.' He said breathing heavily, 'I've also got those blisters from the other day.'

'Excuses, excuses. Come on darling, we have to move.' Claudia cajoled.

'It's only another ten minutes of pain, I suppose.'

'That's the spirit, then, of course, we have to hope security lets us through.'

'We have our passes, they should do.'

Alec took her hand and started moving. Behrenstraße was reasonably quiet, they were held up a few times by students pushing bicycles and talking in twos and threes. They didn't see any sign of the police. *Hopefully, they are searching north of Unter den Linden.* They passed restaurants getting set up for the day's trading. Just before they reached the junction with Friedrichstraße, they stopped and approached the intersection with caution. They looked to their right up Friedrichstraße, they could see the Unter den Linden and far beyond that the arches of Friedrichstraße station, the occasional flash of blue police lights in the distance.

'I think it's clear.' Claudia said.

'I agree, let's try to be casual.'

They crossed the junction. When they reached the kerb on the other side of the road Alec's heart jumped in his chest as a police car turned its siren and lights on behind them as it sped up Friedrichstraße towards the station.

'We should have checked the other way too.' Claudia laughed with relief.

'I think I'm going to need a change of pants.' He said waiting for the drumming in his ribs to subside. 'Come on let's get over there and have a breather.'

The 'there' that Alec was referring to was the covered walkway leading to the Westin Grand hotel. Wide pillars held up the hotel floors above the walkway. The pillars also provided cover for pedestrians from the gaze of anyone driving along Behrenstraße.

'I can't believe we didn't notice the police car.' Alec said, *I need this rest.*

'I know, talk about a rookie mistake.'

'We can't do that again, Claude. Oh my god. I almost had a heart attack.'

'I can't be having that. Not now.' Her face was serious. 'We're getting very close now, how about we take it a little slower and a lot more carefully?'

'That's a good idea.' Alec's heart had slowed to normal levels, his breathing calmer.

Claudia reached up and held his face between her hands and said, 'I told you earlier. I don't want to lose you. If you feel like you're going to drop dead, you tell me, and we'll stop, police arrest or Russian Special Forces be damned. We have the printouts showing Harper's involvement, and you're innocent. It may mean Harper gets away or the Prime Minister's schedule gets changed, but so be it. That's a much better option for me than not having you in my life again.' She patted his cheeks and smiled. 'We can do this, only a few more minutes and we'll be at the embassy, or...' Her smile turned devious, 'the Galeries Lafayette is thirty seconds away from here, if you look past this pillar you'll be able to see it, there's also a jewellers shop just across the way there too.'

'That's ok, I believe you,' he said. He put on an exuberant voice and exclaimed, 'To the embassy!' *When this is over, I may surprise her though.*

'You can have a minute or two to get sorted though. We're quite sheltered here.'

Once Alec had recovered they set off again. Just past the Westin Grand was the Komische Opera house, a modern boxy-looking building out of place with the other older buildings around on Behrenstraße. They soon passed it and crossed over Glinkastraße.

'Next turning,' Alec said.

Claudia squeezed his hand in acknowledgement. Alec noticed that she was breathing heavier now. He decided not to mention it.

They walked steadily towards Wilhelmstraße, unconsciously hugging the building side of the wide pavement as though using as a shield to hide them from their unseen pursuers. Alec could see the sign for Wilhelmstraße ahead and the line of car bomb barrier bollards indicating the start of the embassy. He knew from working there that there were two German guards armed with submachine guns and semi-automatic pistols permanently stationed on guard within the closed-off area. The entrance to the embassy further guarded by embassy security. He saw a black SUV turn off from Wilhelmstraße onto Behrenstraße and head towards them, *tinted windows, where have I seen that before?* The SUV passed them then Alec heard the screech of brakes, he looked around and saw the SUV doors opening. It was forty metres away from him. *The Russians! They must have heard of the police sighting and have been looking for me.*

'Run!' He shouted, dragging Claudia after him. They turned on to Wilhelmstraße at speed, Alec could see the embassy gate thirty metres ahead of them. He groped in his jacket pocket for his security pass as he ran. They splashed through the puddles left from overnight rain. He held the security pass in front of him as he ran. Claudia had recovered from his sudden acceleration and had kept pace with him. From the corner of his eye, he saw she had her pass out as well. He heard heavy splashes coming from behind them, gaining. He also heard shouts from the German guards, 'Halt!' He could picture them raising their guns and aiming at the pair of them. He hoped the passes and the chasing Russians would make them hold off firing. *We're going to make it.* He felt a strong hand on his trailing forearm, the strength in the grip made his body turn toward his assailant, his legs still carried him forward. The movement made him lose his balance, and he stumbled. He heard Claudia cry out 'Alec!' as he fell.

19

Alec felt the hand that had grabbed his arm loosen as he went down. He rolled into the fall like a paratrooper landing from a jump and inelegantly tumbled through the embassy gate. He still had hold of his pass, and he started saying in a loud, firm voice to the guards he knew would have their guns out and pointed at him, 'My name is Alec Foster. I work here. I'm British. I need to see Arthur Newbury.' He stayed on the floor and glanced behind him at the Russian who had almost got him. It was the big soldier from outside the Golden Dolls strip club, he was standing outside the gate. He had a look of hate on his face, he held up his hand and lifted his chin, he slowly dragged his thumb across his neck and turned away in disgust. Alec resisted the urge to give him the middle finger. He repeated his litany hoping it would get through to the guards.

He heard Claudia's voice, clear and commanding, 'Don't shoot. We work here. Call Newbury he'll vouch for us.'

One of the guards told him to stand up and not make any sudden moves. Alec slowly got to his feet. He found he couldn't quite stand up straight, he was slightly slumped over. *I must click my back into place. That fall was not what I needed after the other night.* He looked up and saw Claudia in front of him, she was facing him. She was still holding her pass up with her left hand. The other hand was in the air above her head. He looked around him and saw three security guards holding semi-automatic pistols in the weaver stance: both hands on the gun, and the feet in a boxing stance, one foot further forward than the other. Behind the guards Alec could see men and women looking at them with fear on their faces, frozen in place. He repeated his name and asked again for Newbury.

From a side room door, came more guards, these ones more heavily armed with submachine guns like the German guards outside on the street. They took station between the other guards, their guns up and aimed at Claudia and Alec. There was silence in the entrance hall. Alec could hear his breathing. He thought about saying his name again but decided against it. *Wait it out, let the tension dissipate. Reduce the chance of any accidents.* He saw Claudia come to the same decision as she half-smiled at him. He fought the urge to wink at her. After what felt like a couple of minutes there was a commotion from behind Claudia, Alec could see Newbury striding towards them coming from the lift area, his head a foot taller than most, pushing gawkers out of his way. He had a look of thunder on his face; he was staring at Alec as he came closer, his eyes boiling in anger.

Alec looked back at Claudia and jerked his head towards Newbury, she half-turned her head and looked behind her, Alec could see her body relax, her arms dropped an inch, and she looked up at the ceiling in relief.

'I see you finally decided to show up Mr Foster,' Newbury said, his gravelly voice carrying around the entrance hall. He looked at Claudia, 'Mrs Hampton? Why are you with the most wanted man in Berlin?'

Alec saw people behind Newbury whispering to each other, recognising his name from the television and newspapers.

'Arthur, maybe we should take this upstairs?' Alec suggested.

Newbury looked around, seeing the people in the entrance for the first time. 'You may be right.' He turned to the guards, who were still pointing their weapons at Claudia and Alec, although not as intensely. 'It's ok; I'll deal with these two.'

Alec breathed out. He stretched out his back hearing the click as it straightened.

***

They came out of the lift into the busy office. All chatter ceased at the sight of them. Alec smiled at the few faces that looked at him with welcoming expressions. He made his smile even wider to the ones that didn't. Newbury took them straight into his office; he slammed the heavy door behind them and went behind his desk. Alec removed his jacket and hung it on the back of the functional wooden chair in front of the desk. Claudia sat closely next to him. There was silence as each person waited for the other to start speaking. Newbury's eyes bored into Alec's. Claudia's hand found Alec's. Her touch gave him the strength to start.

'Arthur, I know you're angry at me. There's a good reason-'

'-There better bloody-well better be. You've been missing for two days,' Newbury said cutting Alec off. 'Berlin police and the Russians have been looking for you, thinking you murdered Polyakov. The ambassador is going out of his mind trying to deal with the fallout. I've had our people out looking for you too. And you just stroll in here like it's a beautiful summer's day after a bit of sunbathing in the *Tiergarten*. Tell me why I shouldn't sack you here and now and send you back to the UK?'

Alec paused and gathered his thoughts.

'Arthur,' he began. 'I didn't shoot Jaromir; my gun is still in my drawer in my office. He was shot by someone pretending to be a waiter at the bar. A short man with a long nose, brown hair and wearing a hair band. He had an Eastern European accent. I was sitting there talking with Jaromir. The waiter brought over my drink and shot Jaromir in the forehead with a silenced gun.' Alec brought his free hand up and indicated where Jaromir was shot.

'And he let you go?'

'No, he shot at me, a bullet grazed my cheek.' Alec's hand dropped from his forehead to the mark on his cheek. 'I threw my drink at him, blinding him, kicked him in the leg and then the head and got the hell out of there. I decided to take the long way to a U-bahn station, rather than getting caught up by the Police. The waiter and his companion, a brute of a man, found me, but I got away from them and onto the train.'

'That's when I spoke to you, and you said you were heading in, "be there soon." were your words.'

'Well, I missed the stop,' Alec omitted falling asleep on the train. 'Then when I headed back I saw the two goons waiting for me at the station. They were tracking me by my phone signal. I gave them the slip, dumped my phone and got the hell out of there. I wandered around the city for a while.'

'You went to a strip club. What were you thinking? We saw the transaction on your company card account. A strip club? Come on Alec that is taking the piss, even for you.'

'I thought it was too dangerous by then to return to the

embassy, the police and the Russians would be staking the place out.'

'You were right there, there were meat wagons either end and a number of Russia's finest outside.'

'I needed a phone, so I tracked down where my old friend Makary was. He works at the club. The Russians turned up just after I left the club. I saw that Captain you told me about, nasty looking guy with a scar on his face. Olego-something.'

'Olegovich,' Newbury supplied.

'Anyway, I hid from them, and they went away looking for me. It was about five, six o'clock and I was dead on my feet, so I thought about where I could hole up and get some rest. I thought about going to yours, but it was quite a trek at that time of the night, and I would have had to go in the same direction as Olegovich. I thought that was too risky so I went to Claudia's.'

'I wondered where you came into it,' Newbury said to Claudia.

'He turned up looking like he'd been dragged through a hedge,' she said. 'He told me what had happened and I let him get sorted and sleep at mine.'

'But you came into work yesterday and didn't say anything. I even asked you if you had seen him.'

'There was a good reason-'

'-Another one? You two are as thick as thieves. Don't think I haven't noticed you holding hands there either. Are you together again?'

Alec looked at Claudia and then at Newbury. 'Yes Arthur, we're together.' He stared at Newbury as if daring him to say something. When he didn't Alec continued. 'Claudia didn't tell you where I was because I told her not too, because of what Jaromir told me in the bar before he

163

was killed.'

'So, what did Jaromir say to you that was so important?' His eyes narrowed, and he leant forward, his arms resting on the desk.

'You may find this hard to believe, I didn't at first. He told me that a government minister was going to be killed, here in Berlin, before the end of the week.' Alec stopped to let Newbury take that in.

Newbury was silent for a few moments. Alec could see him processing the information. Alec then decided to up the ante. 'Arthur, I believe it was the PM he was talking about.'

'What? That's impossible! Their security is water-tight. I've dealt with it myself.'

'It's an inside job. That's why I didn't come in yesterday; Claudia and I were figuring it out. If we had come to you with that yesterday we would have had nothing to prove this, and you would have had to cancel the visit or even worse, tightened the security bringing the person closer into the fold.'

'It's being organised by someone in this building? Everyone has been thoroughly vetted. There is no way.'

'I'm telling you, Arthur, it is. We can even tell you who it is: Richard Harper.'

Newbury started laughing, 'Harper? I hope you are joking. I know you, and he don't get on. Accusing him is ridiculous. He's a Head of Section for Christ's sake!'

'We couldn't believe it ourselves. We have some proof, but it'll need further work to make it ironclad.'

Claudia took the printouts from her bag, unfolded the pages and laid them on Newbury's desk. 'This is Harper's leave schedule for the past three months and an email trail between him and you, Arthur. I have also printed off his

164

contact logs since September also.' She said.

Newbury took the pages and spread them out over his desk. 'What am I looking at here?'

Claudia and Alec walked him through the pages, they explained their suspicions, mentioning the contact log – both Harper checking on Alec's and also the lack of entries on Harpers. They told Newbury about Harper and his wife's social media profiles and their inability to access them.

'Ok, I think you're right it is not enough, but it is promising. Is there anything else? Have you thought of a motive? What's he getting out of this?'

Alec said, 'I think it's about power, a terrorist attack on the PM, especially if successful will propel Counter-Terror to the top of the food chain, ahead of Russia and China, and when you retire next year he'll be going for your job, once there he can go anywhere. Ambassadorships, government positions, UN envoy, you name it.'

'It seems a high price for not much gain. If he wants my job that badly he only has to ask, it hasn't brought me much power, and a lot of heartache. He's welcome to it,' Newbury said with a resigned tone to his voice.

'You're still the "Guvnor" here, Guv,' said Claudia.

'Thanks, Claudia, did you know I'm leaving at the end of next year?'

'I had heard rumours, to be honest, I think it's a mistake, the service needs people like you… and Alec. But, it's your decision, where do you think you'll go?'

'Somewhere peaceful and warm in winter, these old bones cannot take the Berlin winter's anymore.'

'You're Rogers's age, aren't you? He used to moan about the winters too, usually when I had chores for him to do.'

'Yeah, when you get to our age the cold seeps into the joints, it's not fun. Do you think Roger would be ok with you two? Together again, I mean.'

'I think he'd be fine with it. He'd rather I was happy than mope away my life, he said as much in the hospital. It's been eight years, and I've decided not to mope anymore. Besides Alec and I have unfinished business.'

Alec looked at her and smiled. *Was she just having a dig at Arthur pining after Julia then? I wonder if Arthur realised.* 'Yes, it feels like we have a new chance and I'm going to take full advantage of that, this time.' He reached over for her hand.

'It's good to see you both happy, I suppose,' Newbury said. 'It's been long enough.' He picked up the papers on his desk. He looked at Alec, 'What's with the hair colour, you're not turning vain on us, now are you?'

Alec laughed, 'I'm incognito.'

'It's taken about ten years off you. Anyway, you two lovebirds wait here; I'll go and put things in motion regarding Harper.'

Newbury stood up and walked to the door; half opened it and turned back, 'No canoodling on my desk.' He winked, 'there's a ton of cameras in here.'

Claudia and Alec laughed. 'We promise we'll keep it PG rated for you.' Alec replied.

Newbury held up his finger as though to make a point, then thought better of it and left. Alec left out a huge sigh of relief. 'I'm glad that's over. Hopefully, he'll forget about firing us, he didn't mention it.'

'I suppose it depends on what he can find out about Harper.'

'I thought I was a goner when the Russian grabbed my arm.'

'He grabbed your arm? I thought you just fell over due to your age. Are you ok?'

'My back hurts where I fell on it.'

'I'll kiss it better later.'

'I'll hold you to that.'

Claudia blew him a kiss, 'I nearly pissed myself when those guards pointed their guns at us.'

'It seems that all I've been getting over the past few days is people pointing guns at me. It's not getting any easier.'

'Well, that should be the end of it now. Arthur will inform the Berlin Police and the Russians of your innocence, Harper will be arrested and hopefully give up those two "goons", as you put it. What will you do then?'

'Well I want to stay in bed for the next month or so-'

'-interesting, need company?'

'Oh, without a doubt I will.' Alec paused and thought for a moment, his eyes opened wide, and he said, 'Shit.' He looked at his watch.

'What's wrong?'

'I've just remembered Sara is coming in today. It's already midday; I don't know how long we'll be stuck here. We won't be able to meet her at the station.'

'Wouldn't she just go on to your apartment?'

'Yes, but the Russians are watching that, and if they don't get the word about Harper out quickly enough, they could pick her up. Shit!'

'They wouldn't harm her.'

'I don't know, they seemed pretty angry at me the other night. Jaromir was one of their most decorated officers; he had his own cult of personality over there, I'm sure more people wear that hideous moustache of his in his office than they do in the whole of Russia.'

'So, what can we do? I can ask Arthur to go.'

'After our entrance this morning I don't think he'll let you go anywhere. Also Harper could have seen you with me and put two and two together. It's not a risk I'm willing to take. There must be someone.'

Who else do I know? Brigette? Makary? I don't really want Sara to be that exposed to Stefan's world. Also, they'd figure out pretty quick that I wasn't who I've said I was all these years. Sara knew about Alec's alter-ego, Stefan, because when she turned eighteen she came over to stay with Alec and they went out to celebrate her birthday. During the night one of Stefan's contacts attached themselves to them, and Alec had to quickly explain his double-life to Sara. He hadn't gone into too much detail that night, enough to keep her from blurting something out which would have backfired. However, over the next six years, he found himself telling her more and more about what he did and for whom. It was cathartic to finally tell someone, there had been no one else that had been close enough to him since he and Claudia split up to tell. He thought Sara got a kick about having a spy for an uncle. *Who can I ask? Wait, what day is it? How about Peter from the stag party. He seems pretty switched on and his story about Sangin certainly revealed him to be a caring fellow, and I'm supposed to be meeting them later anyway to show them the city. I'll give him a call.*

Claudia had remained silent watching him work it out in his mind. She finally asked, 'You have someone you can contact?'

'Yes, there's this guy Peter I met the other night, he's ex-military and a pretty sound guy. He's over here on a stag do, and I'm supposed to show him and the guys the best bars in the city tonight. I completely forgot until now, it must have been the excitement. I'll give him a call see if he can meet her.'

'You were making friends? That's very unusual for you nowadays.'

'I know, when I was walking the city, I had plenty of time to think how I've been acting since Roger, Mark, and Sophie, and I decided I needed to change. I've shut people out for so long, to protect myself, that there were very few people I could turn to for help, and even then, there was a chance I'd be told to get lost.'

'I'd never say that to you.'

'Thank you, I wouldn't have blamed you if you had. I've been a dick to you. But, that is going to stop now. I'm going to try to be better.'

'So, a dinosaur can change its spots, I see.'

'I hope so, and that's enough of the dinosaur talk, missy.'

'Missy?' Claudia's voice raised a touch.

Alec blew her a kiss. 'I'd better call Peter.' He stood up and reached into his jacket pocket and took out the phone, battery and SIM. He reassembled the device and turned it on. He caught Claudia giving him an amused look.

'What?'

'I didn't expect you to have a top of the range smartphone. You always used to carry that brick around.'

'I got it the other night after I dumped my "brick". It's why I was in the strip club, remember?'

The phone started up with its now familiar welcome screen and accompanying jingle.

'I'm going to have to figure out how to turn that off, it's so annoying.' He said.

20

Alec opened his wallet and took out Peter's business card. With aching slowness, he tapped the number into his phone and pressed the connect button. The phone rang, and Peter answered.

'Hi, "Stefan, Not An Old Pervert" how's it going?'

Alec laughed, remembering the entry on Peter's contact list, he put on his German accent and said, 'I'm doing well, you guys enjoying the touristy parts of Berlin?' He could hear a lot of voices in the background.

'Yeah, we're in the DDR Museum at the moment. Have you been?'

'*Ja*, sorry, I mean yes.' Alec ignored the look from Claudia. 'I took my niece Sara there a couple of years ago. It was very interesting.'

'The nude centrefold in the locker was a surprise, as was the nude beach panorama.'

'We Germans have a different attitude to nudity than you British. If you really want to open your eyes go to a spa or even to the *Tiergarten* Park in summer.'

'Sounds like the voice of experience; maybe I should change the contact on my phone.' Peter laughed.

'Well,' Alec coughed, avoiding Claudia's eyes. 'I may have gone when I was younger. It doesn't hold the appeal anymore now I'm older.'

'I can believe that. So why are you calling?'

'I was checking to see if you and your friends still

wanted to do the pub crawl and kebab tonight.'

'Yeah, definitely, we even took it easy last night in anticipation. A few sedate drinks in the hotel bar was all. John has finally recovered. Yesterday he was a mess.'

'I can imagine, he's not wearing a dress tonight, is he?' Claudia's eyebrows raised quizzically as she listened to Alec's side of the conversation.

'No, we had to throw that rag out, after the cab journey from hell. I'll tell you all about it tonight, you'll laugh.'

'I look forward to it… There was another reason for my calling. My niece, Sara is coming into Berlin this afternoon, I think I told you about her, and I'm going to be caught up in work so I won't be able to collect her. Would you be able to get her, and I'll get to you as soon as I can?'

There was a pause, and then Peter said, 'Sure, mate, that shouldn't be a problem. She isn't a little girl, though is she?'

'No, of course not. She's twenty-four. She'll be getting in at Alexanderplatz station at half-past two. That's just down the road from you at the museum.'

'Oh, I know that one, that's where we came in from the airport. Are we that close? I've completely lost my bearings.'

'Yes, it's about a ten-minute walk, well, ten for me, five for you, it's on the same road as the museum you're at. You go up the steps next to the museum, and you're at the road, turn left, and it's down there. You can't get lost.'

'Ok cool, I'll head over there when we're done. How will I recognise her?'

'Of course, she'll be on Platform two; you don't need a ticket to get onto the platform, unlike the UK. She will be alone, quite young looking for her age and will have a large blue rucksack with her. She's dark-haired – brown rather than black - usually has it in a pony-tail when she's travelling and has blue eyes.'

'So, I'm to approach dark haired young-looking females travelling alone? Are you trying to get me arrested?' Peter asked with a laugh.

'No, no, of course not, she'll be looking out for you too. What colour clothes are you wearing?'

'Um, I'm wearing dark blue jeans, a red or burgundy Superdry sweatshirt and a heavy, long black overcoat.'

'Excellent, I'll let her know. I'll let you get back to the museum now, don't let John try on the virtual dresses in the bedroom, or you'll never get him out.'

'I'll keep an eye on him. Two-thirty, Platform Two. I'll be there.'

'Thanks, Peter, I really appreciate it. I'll get the first round in later.'

'No worries, I owe you from the other night anyway, see you later.'

Alec hung up the phone and looked over at Claudia.

'What?' He asked when he saw the smirk on her face.

'This new social you is quite the eye-opener. Consorting with men in drag, going to the *Tiergarten* to let it all hang out.'

'It's not as bad as it sounds. They were on a stag do, and the groom-to-be was wearing a dress, they needed directions and then later I met up with them by accident.'

'And the *Tiergarten*?'

'That was with a contact, years ago. They wanted to check I wasn't wearing a wire, but subtly.' *Well, that's not exactly lying. It was what Brigette said, although I think she had an ulterior motive.* He tried not to picture her laid out on the blanket in the park in all her glory. *It was an interesting afternoon for sure.*

'Don't think I don't notice your gender-neutral pronoun use. Or that little smile on your face.'

'Claudia! What are you suggesting?'

'Don't act all innocent. Mr Foster. We both know what I'm talking about.'

'Have you ever been?' Alec said changing the focus of the conversation.

'No, are you offering?'

'God no, I wouldn't want to subject anyone to the sight of this in the cold light of day,' Alec indicated with both hands his body.

'That's a shame. I liked what I saw last night and this morning. How about a spa instead? That will help sort out all your aches and pains from the past few days, including your combat fall, sorry, roll, this morning.'

'We'll see.'

'Have you heard of Liquidrom? It's a spa which has a salt pool that plays music and lights underwater as you float.'

'No, but it sounds interesting. Have you been?'

'I've haven't had anyone to go with, until now. Don't worry you have to wear a bathing suit in the pool.'

'Ok, you've sold it to me. I'll go with you. I'd better give Sara a call to tell her about Peter.'

He woke his phone from its sleep mode and dialled Sara's number. 'Voicemail.'

'She's probably in the air about now,' Claudia said.

'Hi Sara, something's come up at work so I won't be able to meet you at Alex. You can't go to the flat at the moment. I'll tell you why when I see you. I've arranged for a mate of mine, Peter, to meet you at the station. It's their last night in Berlin, so we're going out with him and his mates tonight to show them the cool bars in town, I hope it's okay…'

'Tell her what he looks like,' Claudia said. 'You don't want her going off with just anyone.'

'Oh, Peter's pretty tall, six-two or three, in his late twenties or early thirties. He'll be wearing dark blue jeans, a red Superdry sweatshirt and a long black coat, his hair is cropped quite short. You can get started on showing him, and his mates, a decent bar and Claudia and I will meet up with you guys. Text me when you meet up with him, so I know you're ok. Oh, by the way, he knows me as Stefan, so make sure you use that instead of Alec.' He hung the phone up and put it away in his jacket.

'Were you planning on inviting me?'

'You're coming aren't you? Sara would love to see you and…'

'And you can't bear to be away from me for a second. God, you're so clingy.'

'Well, in that case…'

'Of course, I'll come, stupid. I haven't seen Sara in years, and I'm just as clingy as you.'

Alec walked over to her and leant down and kissed her deeply. At that point, Newbury came back into the room.

'I thought I said no canoodling.' He smiled.

'I don't think we agreed to that. Aren't you happy for us Arthur?' Claudia said.

'Yes, I'm very happy for you both. However, there is another thing going on, which although it is not as important as your blossoming relationship, it does need thinking about.'

Alec sat down, with a lingering brush of his hand along Claudia's arm.

'I've got the Tech guys looking into what you gave me. Harper's actually been in the contact log a couple of times this morning too.' He told them about the other actions the Technology department were doing to narrow down Harper's movements and actions.

'Hopefully, Harper has made a mistake, and we can take him in bang to rights rather than with circumstantial evidence. I have requested a team from the Warsaw office to keep tabs on him; he may recognise anyone from here trailing him. They should be here in a few hours.' He concluded.

While Newbury was talking Alec's nagging internal voice was speaking to him. 'Arthur, it's just come to my mind something possibly even more serious has happened, not just about the PM.'

'Go on.'

'Well at the strip club I took money out of an ATM, and within twenty minutes the Russians were waiting outside for me. Luckily I had already left and was on the other side of the road thinking about what to do next.'

'So, you should have been aware they may be watching your accounts.'

'That's the thing Arthur, it wasn't my account. It was my company account.'

'Your company account?' He paused for a minute and then exclaimed, 'Bloody hell. I see what you mean. That could be far more serious.'

'Wait what's going on?' Claudia asked. '...Oh shit, I get it.'

'Yeah, if the Russians tracked that account it may mean they have the details of all our company accounts and can see where any of us take out money from an ATM or use the card in shops or restaurants. It'll make surveilling us around the city a piece of cake, they'll also be able to monitor our spending and identify patterns.'

'It may not just be ours here in Berlin; they could have compromised the whole company. They could track any of our officers around the world. They'd have the cover names too as they would be on the card.' Claudia added having taken the thought further than Alec had.

'How the hell could they have got that information?' Newbury asked.

'Probably from a source at the card issuing bank or within the company giving them details of every card issued. Tracking the leak down will be a nightmare,' Alec said.

'I better go and make a couple of calls,' Newbury said. He stood up and left the room. Alec and Claudia sat in silence for a few minutes.

'He didn't say we couldn't canoodle this time,' Alec said to Claudia to break the tension.

She smiled at him, 'Sorry Darling, I'm not in the mood at the moment.'

'No, me neither I guess.'

'There was something I wanted to ask you.'

'What's that?'

'Rumours are going around the office that you are going to retire when Arthur does. Is that true?'

'I was thinking about it. I don't know, Arthur's always had my back, practically carried me for the past five years. I just didn't enjoy being stuffed up in the office. With all that's happened in the past few days, I must admit I quite like the adrenaline. I missed it.'

'But you're not a young man anymore.'

'I know, and that has made itself extremely clear over the past few days as well. There have been times when I have really felt my age, and that will only get worse. There is also you and us for me to consider. Before we were together, the first time, I let someone down who loved me, because of that I couldn't commit fully to you. I felt I didn't deserve happiness and especially didn't deserve someone else to love me. So, I let you go.'

'You never said any of this at the time; you just kept volunteering for more and more missions. I rarely saw you and when I did you were always planning the next mission. Who was she?'

'Her name was Stefanie. I met her in the East, when it was still the East, wall and everything. She worked for the Stasi, and I was using her as a contact, one thing I hadn't planned was to fall in love with her. She loved me and wanted to come to the West, for us to get married and live in England. I pushed her for more documents and information. She was too high placed a source to bring her out, no matter how much I wanted to.'

'What happened to her?'

'Well, it was late summer in 1989, ironically only four to five months before the wall came down and she would have been free. We met in a café to transfer some documents. Truth be told, I just wanted to see her. Someone in the café recognised her and saw that she was meeting with a westerner, or maybe they had been following me all the time, I don't know, it could have been someone with a crush on her. I never found out. They pulled out a gun and shot at us. They missed me, and I returned fire hitting the man, I don't know what happened to him or care to be honest. Stefanie died in my arms on the café floor amongst the broken crockery and glass. I covered her with my jacket and fled back to the West.'

'Oh Alec, that's terrible. Why didn't you tell me years ago?' Claudia stood up and went over to him, wrapped her arms around him, her eyes filled with tears.

'I don't know. It felt too personal, the wound was too fresh.' Alec stood up and accepted the comfort from her. *It feels good to finally get that out, I've wanted to so many times.* 'It felt like I was letting her down being happy with you, loving you.'

'You should have told me. I would have helped you work through it.'

'I know that now. I went back to the café a couple of years ago. It's still there – Café Sybille on Karl-Marx-Allee. They've replaced the bullet holes in the ceiling and the tables. I sat in the same place and cried until I was empty. I then went for a walk along the Spree. It was only the thought of Sara that kept me from jumping in, what it would do to her.'

'You stupid, stupid man,' she said, as she kissed his forehead, his cheeks, his nose.

'I know.'

'And now? How do you feel?'

'It feels as though I have a second chance at life. I don't know what is going to happen with work, and quite honestly, I don't really care. I want to be better for you, Sara, and the friends I abandoned when Roger, Mark and Sophie passed away. My life has been on pause for so long, I want to make up for the lost time. Maybe it could start with a visit to that jewellery shop you mentioned earlier.'

Claudia hugged him tighter. 'I was only joking you know, there's no need to rush anything. We can just enjoy each other for a while if you want.'

'We'll see,' Alec said with a wink and then kissed her with passion.

'Arthur has been a long time, hasn't he?' Claudia said. She was back in her chair with a contented smile on her face.

Alec looked at his watch, 'It's gone three o'clock. I should have had a call from Sara by now.'

He took his phone from his jacket and turned it on, 'There a text from Sara. "Hi Uncle Alec, got your message. Since when did you have friends? Smiley face. Is he good looking? I guess I'll see at the station. I'll take them to Madame Claudes via the East Side Gallery. Tourists love that stuff. See you later. Bye." Madame Claudes? That's the ex-brothel with all the upside-down furniture on the ceiling.'

'That's an interesting choice. A brothel, Sara knows you well.'

'"Ex-brothel" I said. Wait, there's a ton of missed calls from Peter. I better call him.'

Alec pressed the button to call Peter back, it connected, 'Hi Peter, what's u-' Alec stopped and listened. 'What do you mean she's been taken?'

21

Alec felt like his world had been turned upside down and back to front, his hands shook, his mouth felt dry. 'What happened? Who took her?'

Peter's panicked voice over the line wavered, 'There was a short ratty looking guy and a massive fella, all weights and steroids. I saw her come off the train. I was at the other end of the platform. I called out her name, and she looked my way. Then the big guy grabbed her and dragged her to the exit. I chased after them, but the little one turned and shot at me with a silenced pistol. I followed them at a distance, but they got into a silver Mercedes parked outside the station and drove off. I'm sorry Stefan, I tried to get the licence, but they had covered the plates. I tried calling you a number of times, but it kept going to voicemail. Shit!'

'That's ok, Peter, you did all you could. Where are you now? I'll come to you.'

'The north side of the station, Karl-Libenicht Street. By the underpass.'

'I know where you are. Karl-Liebknecht Straße. Stay there. I'll be about ten minutes or so.' He hung up the phone, stood up and put on his jacket.

'Alec, what happened?' Claudia asked, alarm in her face.

'Sara was taken at the station by the two goons, they shot at Peter. I'm heading there now.'

'Alec, wait. We don't know if Arthur has got the word out to the Police or the Russians. You could get arrested or worse. Then you'll be in no position to help Sara. I can go instead. They aren't looking for me.'

'But-' Alec stopped, his heart pounding. The blood rushing around his head made it hard to think. He tried to calm himself down. He took a deep breath. 'You're right. That won't help Sara. You sure you can get her back?'

'I can try; don't forget you trained me, so I'm not an amateur. If the two goons were hired by Harper then they wouldn't have their own resources, they would be here to do the job and be out again. They would be either staying in a hotel or Harper would have set them up in the city, possibly at one of our safe houses. They couldn't take her to a hotel. I'll pick up Peter and try the safe houses first.'

'Ok. You be careful, they're quite vicious. They killed Jaromir and shot at me and Peter without any compunction. I don't want to lose you.'

'I'll be fine. It'll be alright. I'll get her.'

'I love you.' *It had to be said, just in case.*

'I love you too. Call me, so I have your number so I can keep you updated.' She left the room in a rush.

Alec slammed his fist down on Newbury's desk. He bellowed a stream of curses. He started pacing, his body a bundle of nervous energy. He kicked at his chair, which crashed over. *That arsehole Harper, I'll kill him when I see him. If anything's happened to Sara, I'll do worse than kill him, I'll blind him, and I'll rip his goddamn face off. I'll destroy him, make him scream and make him bleed.* He kicked over Claudia's chair and then started stamping on the legs and the backrest. The brittle wood splintered and then cracked. With a final thrust of his foot, the structure broke, and the chair collapsed. He kicked the pieces over to the corner of the room, where they settled like a drunk on a bench. Alec reached for his phone and went to throw it at the wall. *Come on Alec, get a grip. This will not help her, you need to think, and help Claudia and Peter get her back.* He reluctantly put the phone in his pocket. He could feel the gun next to it and stroked the cool metal surface. *You're an intelligence officer, it's time you started showing some.* He took a deep breath and righted his chair. He took his phone out of his pocket and dialled Claudia. He hung up once he heard the ringing tone. While he had the phone in his hand he looked along the side for a volume button, there were two next to other. He pressed one, and a message showed the volume lower. He pressed it until there were no bars and the phone vibrated in his hand. He replaced the phone in the jacket. He pulled the chair closer to the desk and sat down. With a shaking hand and a dull ache in his temple, he reached for a pen and a piece of paper. *Let's see if I can narrow down the search for them.*

So, their target is the PM, and it will happen tomorrow. The PM is only in town for the day. What's on their schedule? Alec tried to think back to the meetings he attended and the emails he received. *The PM will fly into Tegel airport at eight-something and head to the Schloss Bellevue to meet with the German President. After that they'll be going to the Berliner Dom,* Berlin Cathedral, *to attend the Christmas Advent Concert, if I remember correctly, the concert is Bach's Christmas Oratorio. The PM is a keen classical music enthusiast. Finally, they are going to the Reichstag Building to speak to the German Parliament before heading back to Tegel and fly back to the UK.* Alec wrote the headings on the paper – Tegel, Bellevue, Berliner Dom, Reichstag. He stood up and walked around the desk, moved Newbury's chair to one side and opened the bottom drawer. He pulled out a heavy crystal brandy glass that sparkled in the office lights and a bottle of Remy Martin XO Cognac, with its spear-bearing centaur logo silhouetted on the gold label. *Only the good stuff I see for Arthur.* Alec pulled the cork stopper from the cut glass decanter shaped bottle and inhaled the vanilla and grape aroma. *That is just what I need.* He poured a generous measure and returned to his own chair. He looked at the headings as he absent-mindedly swirled the amber coloured drink in the glass. He took a sip and savoured the taste; the rich smoothness of the liquid warmed his tongue and throat. He took another and started to think about how the assassination would happen.

Terrorists kill crudely, car bombs, IEDs and trucks. The killing indiscriminate and random. IEDs being improvised explosive devices, delivered in roadside, suicide and even animal attacks. *An attack on the PM would need to be highly organised to get past the security, but to be blamed on terrorists it would need to be carried off inexpertly.* Alec felt a shiver of excitement down his spine that had been absent since he became Head of Section, the events of the past few days notwithstanding. He felt a challenge to his expertise that brought a smile to his lips until he thought about the stakes. *The PM being assassinated, bad as it would be, would not compare to the loss of Sara. If the Prime Minister is killed another will take their place in a blink of an eye. Sara is irreplaceable.* He pushed the glass away from him, resolving to abstain until he had solved this conundrum.

Ok, Alec, you're a terrorist how would you do it? Start from the airport. Alec considered the different approaches a terrorist would try. *Tegel airport would be impossible for an unsophisticated attack such as a car bomb or vehicle attack. Too much security and no access to the runway for unauthorised vehicles. A sniper could lay up in the wide flat grounds waiting for a shot at the PM. Scaling the perimeter fence wouldn't be hard for a professional, the eight-foot-high razor-wire topped fence the only barrier and that could be defeated quite easily by a determined attack. However, apart from the D.C. Sniper attacks in the early '00s, which was a killing spree designed to hide the murder of an ex-wife of John Allen Muhammad rather than a wave of terror in the strictest sense of the phrase, a sniper attack isn't a typical terrorist method. Harper surely wouldn't go for that option.* Alec sat at the desk, tapping the pen against his lips as he thought some more. *A rocket launched as the plane came into land could be effective. It would depend on the Prime Minister's plane,* an RAF 'Voyager' Airbus A330, *and the counter-measures installed against rocket and missile attacks.* Alec recalled the rocket attack on the MI6 building at Vauxhall Cross in London. *Something similar could easily be done to a plane. I suppose. There was that attempt on an airliner in 2015. Sharm el-Sheikh, I think. The rocket missed in that attempt though.* He wrote under the Tegel heading on the paper, "rocket attack?"

Next, the Schloss Bellevue. The Bellevue Palace: The official residence of the President of Germany. *The Schloss is situated with the Spree running from the north-east side of the palace, down to the east. Tiergarten Park covers the remaining sides. There is a road running along the southern edge of the palace, crossing over the Spree. An attack could be made from there. A rocket attack, like Tegel airport, is a possibility. However, the assassins would need to know exactly which room the PM was in. There's quite a lot to choose from. A vehicle attack would require busting through the reinforced fence after leaving the main road, Spreeweg, I think it's called, and going along one of the two narrow paths to the Schloss gates. The whole centre section of the palace is protected from a vehicular attack by a concrete ha-ha.* A ha-ha is a landscape feature which was installed to prevent livestock wandering onto the manicured gardens of the palace. It consists of a ditch with a sunken vertical brick or concrete wall, its top is level with the garden, so it is invisible from the house or, in this case, the palace. *A vehicle attack would be a suicide attack for the assassins and a rocket attack ineffectual. I think this isn't a possible target.* Alec wrote a large "X" under the "Bellevue" entry on the paper.

Ok, now for the Berliner Dom. The church on *Museumsinsel*, or Museum Island. It's large green dome an iconic Berlin landmark. *The Spree backs onto the church to the North. The PM would enter the church from the Lustgarten side, arriving there by car. The assassins could strike by car bomb, operated remotely. The German police and the British security services will be checking any parked cars along the route, so there is a remote possibility of success. A sniper could work. There are a number of perches they could use that would give them line of sight to the entrance. However, as with Tegel, a sniper doesn't scream terrorist attack. A truck attack is a possibility, however, building up speed on the Schloßplatz,* the main road that leads past the church, *is difficult due to the traffic and there is street furniture in place to prevent these types of attacks. A truck attack is also very much a suicide attack, the drivers rarely survive.* Alec wrote "unlikely" on the paper. He then thought about it some more. *A rocket attack would work, especially a mortar attack, like the IRA attack on Downing Street in '91. The mortar attack was launched on a time delay or using a remote-control mechanism from a vehicle parked in a side street. I'd have to find out the range of a mortar, but that is a definite possibility, especially as they would know the PMs schedule and have a man on the inside giving them a running itinerary.* He put a line through "unlikely" and wrote "mortar" under it.

Finally, the Reichstag, possibly the most secure and defended building in the city, there are bollards in place to prevent a vehicle attack from Dorotheenstraße, armed guards on duty round the clock. The least you'd expect for the building containing Germany's parliament. A mortar attack from the Tiergarten park to the west of the building is possible. However, any mortar shells coming down would have to pass the Reichstag itself to catch the PM out in the open, which requires a precision I'm not sure the weapon possesses. They could bomb the building itself, but it would be touch and go whether they could identify which room the PM was in. Mind you, an attack on the Reichstag with the PM in attendance could be enough to increase Harper's purview, whether the PM was killed or not. Alec wrote "mortar" under the "Reichstag" heading and underlined it a few times.

I think the Reichstag is going to be the place for the attack, irrespective of whether the PM is assassinated. Any terrorist attack on the building would be worldwide news. Alec reached for the glass of cognac as a reward. He brought it to his lips but thought twice and placed it back on the desk. *Not yet. Need to find Sara.* He turned the paper over and drew a rough sketch of Berlin marking Alexanderplatz and the Reichstag on there. *The goons will have taken her to a safe house, but it will need to be within easy reach of the station and also the Reichstag. They wouldn't risk a long drive with Sara held captive. A routine traffic stop could end their plans. They also need to be relatively close to the Reichstag in order to set up for the attack, again wary of traffic stops; they won't want to be driving their vehicle carrying the mortar too far. I think they're probably based in Charlottenburg. After the traffic circle at Ernst-Reuter-Platz, it's a straight line into the Tiergarten on the B2 highway. Also, the other way from Alexanderplatz, again following the B2 it's a twenty-minute journey to Charlottenburg.* Alec circled a rough area on the map he'd drawn and marked it Charlottenburg. He drew in the B2 route. He then marked the approximate locations of the MI6 safe houses in the area. *Thrasoltstraße? That safe house consists of a whole six-story apartment block on the junction with Richard-Wagner-Straße, it hasn't been used for over a year, something about asbestos in a couple of the apartments, I think. It has a private car park which would be ideal for storing the mortar vehicle and the assassin's Mercedes. It also is about a two or three-minute drive to the B2. One of the reasons why we chose it. There are a couple more safe-houses in the area, none as ideally located or isolated as that one though.*

Alec circled the location on the map and put the pen down. He reached for the glass and held it to his lips, enjoying the alcohol fumes tickling his nostrils. *I'd better text Claudia so she can check it out.* He reached with his free hand to his jacket pocket. The door opened behind him. Alec stood up and turned. *Arthur.*

'Arthur, I've figured it out. It's the Reich-' He stopped abruptly as he saw the man who had followed Newbury into the office. He recognised the weasel-like face of the waiter, his nose covered in a bandage, wearing an awful smirk on his face. Alec's gaze looked down and saw the silenced gun from the bar pointing at him.

22

'Captain,' Ilyich said, his voice breaking Olegovich's thoughts.

'What?' He said, curtly, his mood dark. *How can one old man be so lucky? Foster is making a fool out of me. He's been on the run since killing Polyakov and just leisurely strolls back into the British Embassy, like a man after a liquid lunch. He's probably in there laughing at us. Having a whale of a time with his partner in crime Arthur Newbury. Sivakov had him in his grasp, and he still got away.* He rubbed the scar on his cheek. He always did in times of stress.

'Your idea of staking out the English safe-houses for Foster has dredged up an old friend. One of our teams has picked up Todor Kochanov.'

Todor Kochanov? Olegovich thought as he searched his memory for the name. 'The Bulgarian assassin? Built like a weight-lifter, ex-KGB?'

'That's the one, Sir. Well remembered. I had to look him up.'

Thanks for the brown-nosing. You'll go far. 'Where was he?'

'He was picked up heading towards the MI6 safe-house on Thrasoltstraße. He had a bag of groceries and was limping. One of the team recognised him, and they approached him to see why he was there. He took down two of them, delivering a broken nose and a broken arm, before the third managed to taser him into submission. They managed to manhandle him into their van, and they are on their way here now.'

'Did he say why he was in Berlin?'

'No, he attacked them as soon as they approached. He didn't give them any warning.'

'That's interesting. I wonder what he's doing here. Have him brought into the interrogation room when they get here.'

'Yes, sir. Oh, by the way, they tell me he already had a bullet wound in his thigh. I don't know if they are saying that just to cover themselves.'

I wonder what this is about. Olegovich turned on the computer on his desk, and after waiting for it to start up, he searched the records for Kochanov.

***

Olegovich pushed open the interrogation room door with force. It slammed into the wall leaving a dent. The two officers in the room jumped at the sound. Olegovich noticed that Kochanov, sitting in handcuffs chained to the wide table and legs chained to the floor, didn't. *A tough cookie, as the Americans say. We'll see.*

'Out,' he ordered.

The two officers left the room, and Olegovich sat down opposite Kochanov, his hands in his lap. He didn't say anything, just looked at the man. *He certainly paid for harming the two team members.* Kochanov's wide, ugly face was already beginning to swell. The lips, the right eye, forehead knotting up. *Hmmm, he has a scar on the left side too.* Olegovich resisted the urge to rub his. They sat in silence looking at each other. Five... Ten minutes. Waiting for the other to blink first. *KGB trained: he'll know all the tricks. Time to mix it up a little, try to put him off balance.* Under the table, Olegovich took the extendable metal baton from his pocket, and in one fluid motion he brought his hand up and whipped it towards Kochanov. The baton extended at the apex of the strike and came down with a hard slap across Kochanov's left cheek. Olegovich followed the blow instantly with another to the right cheek. He motioned another strike to the left cheek and noted with satisfaction that Kochanov flinched at the expected blow. Olegovich stopped the motion before it hit the cheek and quickly reversed his action striking the right cheek harder. Kochanov rocked in his chair and struggled to raise his chained hands. Deep, narrow welts showed on both cheeks, blood was showing through parts of the right cheek. Olegovich retracted the baton, and placed it on the desk, his hand beside it.

'Why did you attack my men?'

Silence.

'I want an answer.' He placed his hand on the baton.

'I thought they were after me.' *Yes!* Kochanov's eyes didn't leave the baton.

'Why would they be after you?'

Silence.

Olegovich swung the baton, this time coming down on the man's hands. He heard the crunch as a knuckle broke. Kochanov screamed in pain. Blood started dripping on the tabletop.

'Why would they be after you?' Again silence.

Kochanov's breathing had become heavy and ragged. Olegovich leant across the table and, with his thumb, pressed down firmly on the broken knuckle like he was putting out a cigarette. Kochanov's body shook rigid as though he was being tasered. He tried head-butting Olegovich, but the chains restricted him, stopped him getting close. Olegovich paused.

'Why would they be after you?'

Deep gulping breaths, then, 'Polyakov.' *What?*

'Polyakov?'

'I killed him in a bar.'

Impossible, it was Foster. I know what that man is capable of. 'Tell me what happened and why. Do not lie to me. It'll be worse if you do.'

***

Olegovich left the room, after a final look at the unconscious Kochanov slumped in the chair. His hands mangled, his right tree trunk of an arm bent inwards at an impossible angle, his face a bloody mush. Olegovich closed the door behind him and ordered the white-faced guard outside the room to call a doctor for the prisoner.

He returned to his office and sat in the chair and placed his hands on the desktop. They were still and calm like his heart. Ilyich turned to him and asked, 'How did it-' he stopped his mouth opened wide, his jaw slack. 'Sir, can I suggest you visit the bathroom to clean up?'

'Huh?'

'Sir, your face… it needs cleaning.'

Olegovich looked down at his hands, they were covered in gore.

'Thank you, Likhachyov.' His voice emotionless. He stood up.

***

The running water from the tap faded the dark red blood into a light pink as it swirled down the plughole. Steam rose covering the mirror with a fog of tiny droplets. Olegovich was glad. It meant he couldn't see his eyes. He rubbed his hands with a thin bar of soap oblivious to the heat of the water. He scrubbed them until they were raw and then cupped them together and splashed water onto his lowered face. Again, and again. He then started with the soap rubbing it deep into his skin, relishing the sting as it penetrated his closed eyes. Streams of pink water cascaded down his bare muscular back to the floor and to the waistband of his trousers, darkening the material.

Foster didn't kill Polyakov.

23

Alec reacted without thought; he threw the heavy cognac glass at the waiter and followed it up with a hard punch to the man's face and then a second, and a third. The waiter fell backwards to the floor, the door closing behind him. Alec fell on him and heard the gun cough and a second later heard a thud as it hit the wooden panelling behind him. He sat astride the waiter, pinning him to the floor. One punch, another, and then another. The waiter's bandage had come off, and blood was flowing steadily from his nostrils, his eyes glazed.

'Where is she? You bastard. Where is she?'

'That's enough of that,' Newbury said and lifted Alec to his feet from behind. He held him in a full nelson hold. Newbury grabbed Alec's left hand and twisted it tightly behind him and pressed down on his neck with his free arm. The waiter struggled to his feet, spat blood on to the carpet and punched Alec in the gut. Alec felt the air go from his lungs. He struggled for breath. The waiter followed up the punch with another to the face. Alec felt his cheek shudder, and his head snapped back, the neck held in place by Newbury's forearm.

'I said that was enough!' Newbury threw Alec to the floor and stood in front of the waiter, his hands on the smaller man's chest. 'Stop.'

The waiter spat again. Newbury winced, 'Do you have to do that? It's impossible to get blood out of the fibres.'

'It's just a carpet.' The waiter looked down and picked up the bandage. He straightened it up and reapplied it to his face.

'Put him in the chair, Mihael.'

Alec was slowly getting to his feet, breathing deeply. He launched himself at Mihael, the waiter, with a roar, knocking his chair out of the way. His fist landed on the man's chin sending him reeling. Alec fell to his knees and felt Newbury lift him up and then slammed him on to Claudia's chair. *What the hell?*

'You stay there Alec.' Newbury commanded.

'Like hell I will.' Alec countered, lifting himself back up.

Newbury swung a heavy fist into Alec's temple. Alec's world went black and then dimmed.

Alec felt the world swimming into focus, the side of his face was screaming at him. He could hear murmuring voices in the distance, slowly getting closer. He opened his eyes slowly and saw Newbury sitting at his desk.

'Arthur? What's going on?'

'Good, you're awake. I was going to have Mihael slap you in a minute or two to wake you up.'

At the mention of the waiter's name, Alec's body jerked up. He found his lower body was secured to a chair. A voice to the right of Newbury said, 'I don't think he likes me.'

Alec turned and saw the man next to Newbury, his face was a mess, the bandage across his nose was askew, and blood had seeped through. His eyes were bloodshot and starting to show bruising. There was a hard lump on his forehead. *That must have been from the glass.* Alec felt the warmth of satisfaction.

'Where is she?'

'She's safe,' Newbury said. 'I wouldn't hurt her... unless it was completely necessary.'

'Why are you doing this? You've known her since she was a little girl.'

'Well, that's your fault, I'm afraid. If you had just died at the bar like you were supposed to she wouldn't be in this situation.'

'Like I was supposed to?' Alec's head felt foggy. *Must be because of the punch. God, he hits hard.*

'I thought you were smarter than this. Maybe you're concussed. As soon as Polyakov requested the meeting and told you to take precautions I knew he knew about the plot. You should have listened to him. If you hadn't told me about the call, he'd be alive, and Sara would be safe. You failed them, Alec.'

Alec looked around the room and saw that his chair had been righted next to him, his jacket hung from the back of it. He realised his throat was dry, he was having trouble swallowing. 'May I have a drink?'

'Certainly. Mihael, get a plastic cup from the cupboard over there.' Mihael stood up. Newbury resumed talking to Alec, 'You seem to enjoy throwing glasses at my friend, so a little precaution is in order.'

'Why are you doing this?' Alec repeated the question.

Mihael returned to the desk with a clear plastic cup. Newbury opened his drawer and removed the Remy Martin. 'I can't believe you wasted this by throwing it. That's very disrespectful of you, Alec.' He poured Alec a generous measure, stood and placed the cup in front of Alec. Newbury sat back down.

Alec lifted the cup with his free hand and took a gulp of the drink. He paused and then threw the remainder at

Newbury. The amber liquid splashed his face and suit. The plastic cup bounced off his shoulder and onto the floor.

'I should have expected that I suppose. You always were so uncouth,' Newbury said calmly. 'Roger and I used to joke about how common you were.' He removed a napkin from his pocket and dabbed at his face. He picked up the piece of paper Alec had been writing on and looked at the map, 'You figured this out? I'm impressed. I thought you had left your brains in a bottle years ago.' He turned the paper over, 'That is really good work, you know. I agree if a terrorist was to kill the Prime Minister that would be the best way to proceed. Unfortunately, it's not about terrorism.' He turned on the shredder next to his desk and placed the piece of paper in it. The machine caught it and chewed it into multiple tiny pieces.

'So, what's it about then, arsehole?'

'I suppose there's no harm in telling you, seeing as you are going to be part of it.'

'What's that supposed to mean?'

'We'll get to that, later,' Newbury paused, framing his argument. 'We've had this discussion many times. I know you agree with me. It's to do with Russia.'

With those words, Alec knew what Newbury meant, what the purpose of this was. Newbury was proposing a return to the days of the Cold War, the clash of capitalism versus communism, fighting proxy wars against each other through third party countries around the globe, the days of open suspicion between the West and East. A return to the war that Russia never quit, they just changed their methods.

'And assassinating the Prime Minister? That's not a return to the Cold War, that's the opening salvo of world war.'

'It won't get that far. No one wants that. The Americans and Chinese will step in and stop that from happening.'

'You're wrong. The Americans are politically at their weakest since Watergate, and the Chinese, who knows, you can never tell what they are going to do. They could always side with Russia. You're gambling with the world. You're going all-in with a pair of eights.'

'It's better than watching Russia tear the West apart, turning us against each other: Brexit, the far-right against the far-left, their puppet in the White House. I'm not wrong, you just don't have the vision to see our political masters are so weak, so focused on the short-term, the current election cycle, the next week's headlines, that they don't look to the bigger picture, see what is happening around them.'

'They just need to see-'

'- And how will they do that? Who will they listen to? We cannot influence them enough for them to act. We're not one of their party donors. We work for them and have to follow their misguided and ill-informed decisions.'

Alec shook his head, 'It'll never work, you'll start a war.'

'I'm protecting our way of life.'

'No, Arthur, you can't do this.'

Arthur smiled, and Alec felt a chill down his spine. 'I won't be doing it, Alec, you will.'

'Like hell I will.'

'Oh, you will. Mihael's friend, the one you shot in the leg, was going to take the shot, but, he's been taken by the Russians. Luckily, I hadn't got round to telling him where and when. Information compartmentalised until necessary. You're taking his place.'

'There's no way, Arthur. I won't do it.'

'Think of Sara, Alec. You do this we'll release her unharmed. Refuse, and she won't see daylight again. We may pay a visit to the lovely Mrs Hampton as well.'

Alec's blood went cold, then flash-boiled. He struggled against the bindings that held him. The cords in his neck stood out, his face red from the exertion. He couldn't free himself. He collapsed, exhausted.

'Calm down, you'll have a heart attack.'

'You hurt them, I'll tear you apart. I'll destroy you.'

'You'll do as I want. That's what you'll do. Your life and the PM's for theirs. That is the deal.'

'How do I know you'll release her?'

'You'll have to trust me. You have done all these years; I'm not doing this on a whim. It is for the good of the country.'

'Trust you? I wouldn't trust you ever again.' *What choice do I have? She'll die if I don't. I can't live with that. I have to give Claudia time to find her. See if I can find a moment to tell her.* Alec stayed silent for the better part of a minute. 'Ok, I'll do it.'

'Good I'm glad you can see sense. I would hate to harm her.'

'Whatever. What do you need me to do?'

'Mihael's friend was going to be the marksman. I know you have had sniper training and excelled at it, so you're taking his place.'

'That was a long time ago Arthur.'

'Well, you better reacquaint yourself quickly.'

'Where is it going to be? Wait, it's the cathedral, isn't it. Building works are going on next to it. That is where I'll be shooting from.'

'I'm impressed you've figured it out so fast. It's good to see you almost back to your best. Yes, Mihael will be with you to make sure you go ahead.'

'And the gun? Where am I getting that from? I can't really walk around Berlin with a rifle under my arm.'

'You and Mihael will go and get it from a locker at Zoo station. It's broken down in a briefcase, so you'll be fine. It's a Russian model, of course.'

'I have to go with him? Won't the Russians be after him now they've got his mate?'

'I don't particularly want to be your babysitter either,' Mihael said.

'You'll do as you're told, Alec. Your handy work with the glasses has helped disguise him, so the Russians won't recognise him.'

'What about me? Aren't they looking for me still?'

'I've already put out the word that Mihael's friend was responsible for Polyakov so you should be fine. If you head to the building site after getting the rifle and hold up there for the night, you won't be around for them to pick you up.'

'Wait, you want us to sit on a building site all night and wait for the PM in the morning. You do realise its December, we'll freeze.'

'Dress up warm. I only care that you have enough movement to pull the trigger when its time.'

'This is shit. You always were a poor mission planner Arthur.'

'Ok, Alec, what do you suggest?'

'How about we check into a nice warm hotel and head out at daybreak?'

'What a hotel where you have to provide I.D.? The most-wanted man in Berlin, so the Police can pick you up, and you can tell them everything. Nice effort. You'll do as I say. Mihael undo him. Alec, you better not try anything, remember you're responsible for Sara's wellbeing.'

'I won't do anything. Cross my heart.' Alec made the sign of the cross on his chest with his middle finger. *He might have me by the balls, but I'm not going to be all sweetness and light.*

Mihael undid Alec's bindings. Alec stood up and stretched. 'Thanks,' he said. His voice like sandpaper. 'So, Arthur, when did you come up with this genius plan? Why now?'

'I'm retiring next year. I had planned to try and get back with Julia, take her somewhere warm. She's found someone else, so I decided to leave with a bang.'

'So, this is all because you can't stop pining for a woman that you didn't respect enough to keep your hands to yourself.'

'You're one to talk about pining. You've been pining over that German woman and Claudia for, what? Twenty years now.'

'Something like that,' Alec said. His voice deadly calm, his hands flexed.

'At least you got a second chance with Claudia, even if has only been a couple of extra days.'

'You're pathetic, Arthur. Just pathetic. I hope Julia's happy with her new man, she can't do any worse. I hope you die picturing them together, naked, and writhing. I hope the last thing you hear is their moans of pleasure reverberating through your skull.'

Arthur stood up, 'You get out of here now, before I end you.' He removed a piece of paper from his pocket and key and gave it to Mihael. 'This is the locker number and key. I'll see you tomorrow at the safe house to give you the rest of the money. Don't worry you'll get Todor's share too.'

Mihael pocketed the paper and turned to Alec and said,

'Come on Foster.'

Alec picked up his jacket and put it on; he was comforted by the weight of the pockets. He turned to Arthur. 'I'll see you again.'

'No, you won't. You do your job, and they'll be safe. Just remember that.'

24

The train slowed as Alec and Mihael stood up to alight at Bahnhof Berlin Zoologischer Garten. They had ridden seated next to each other, the silence only broken twice when Mihael had answered his mobile phone. Alec got the gist that Newbury was checking on them, and figured it was going to be a regular thing. *It's so frustrating. I could beat the crap of him here and now and be free to get Sara, but Arthur has his buddy on a tight leash. I can't risk him hurting her. I need to find a way of telling Claudia where she is. I'll bide my time, this Mihael doesn't seem like the smartest, so maybe he'll make a mistake, leave an opening.*

The train stopped, and they stepped off on to the platform.

'The lockers are this way,' Alec said. 'Come on.' He walked off knowing Mihael would follow. They walked down the stairs to the ground level, and Alec headed towards the lockers.

'Which locker is it?'

Mihael fumbled in his pockets for the piece of paper, '0217.'

'And the key?' Alec moved to that locker and held his hand out. Mihael was clearly subordinate in the two relationships Alec had observed him in: with the driver, and with Arthur, *maintaining an authoritative stance could help me later.* Mihael passed Alec the key. He placed it in the slot and turned, the locker popped open, and Alec opened the door wider. Alec reached in and took out the silver briefcase; it had a nice weight to it. He held it out for Mihael to carry. *That's one hand less for defending yourself.* Mihael took it without comment.

'Right, we need to get some gear. I know a place not far away,' Alec said.

'We're supposed to go the cathedral,' Mihael protested.

'You can go to the cathedral, sit out all night up on scaffolding in the middle of December if you want. Me, I'm already cold, and it's going to get worse during the night. If you don't want us to freeze to death, we'd better get some equipment and some supplies. You didn't do mountain exposure training in the KGB?' Alec said.

'No, I was based in Turkey,' Mihael admitted, with a flush to his cheeks.

'I went on a course with the SAS, one week up a mountain with the toughest guys you could ever imagine. Trust me I know what I'm doing.' *That's right, building relationships and compromising people's trust is what I do best.*

'Ok, we go get supplies. Don't try anything though.'

'Don't worry, Arthur has my niece, I'll carry out the job.' *Only if there are no other options.* 'Come on, let's go.'

They left the station through the main entrance on to Hardenbergplatz. Alec could see McDonalds and Dunkin Donuts opposite. They crossed over onto Joachimsthaler and headed south.

'Is it far?' Mihael asked.

'Just down here a little bit, not far.'

They walked past a florist and some restaurants until they came to the junction with Kantstraße, there was a large sporting goods store on the corner over the road, and opposite that on the other side was a skiing store.

'You were right, these weren't far at all,' Mihael said.

'Oh, those aren't where we're going; they don't have the right equipment. They're like Sports Depot in Bulgaria; we need something like Camping Rocks. These are more sports fashion than practical,' Alec said. *The amount of information in my head about the ex-Soviet bloc countries surprises even me sometimes.*

'I see. Yes. You're right. How much longer?'

'You'll be surprised,' Alec said.

They crossed over Kantstraße, walked past the Karstadt sports store and continued walking for two minutes until they reached the junction with Kurfürstendamm. Alec turned right onto "Ku'damm" and stopped as Mihael's phone rang. *Arthur again?* Mihael spoke into the phone, he didn't tell Newbury where they were going. *That's a good sign.* After the call ended Mihael asked, 'how long until we're there? You better not be trying anything.'

Alec put on a broad smile and pointed to the entrance of the Kranzler Eck Berlin shopping mall beside them. 'Here we are, I was about say before your call. We need to go to Jack Wolfskin, they'll have what we need.' Alec noted that Mihael was breathing a little harder. *Not used to walking? Maybe the broken nose isn't helping.* He smiled.

'That wasn't far. You were right.' Mihael smiled back.

They entered the shopping mall and looked at the store directory for Jack Wolfskin. Alec let Mihael find it on the plan. He already knew where it was located.

'Well done, Mihael, you'll be part of the SAS in no time.'

Mihael beamed at the praise.

In the store, Alec headed straight for the sleeping bags and chose the most expensive one.

'That's almost 300 euros, I'm not paying that,' Mihael protested.

'I'm paying, it was my idea.' *The company are paying. It is business related; I'll be able to justify the expense to the penny-pinching bean counters.* Alec smiled to himself. *If I live that long, of course.* The smile evaporated. 'We'll need the best if we're to survive the night. It's going to be cold.'

Alec bought two of everything: sleeping bags, rain covers, thermos flasks, self-inflating mats for the sleeping bags, and backpacks. They moved over to the clothing section, and Alec picked out a large parka for Mihael, a couple of jumpers for them, thermal undershirts, thick gloves and hats.

'You're going to need layers to stay warm,' Alec said. Mihael was wearing a beat-up, black leather jacket and jeans. *The bulkier you are, the more restrictive your movements will be.*

'Aren't you going to get a coat?'

'No, this is fine,' Alec said. He pulled the lapels of his jacket. 'It's windproof and has a fleecy layer. I'll be fine.' *I'd prefer to keep this, thank you.*

When they were at the till Alec added a penknife to the pile of items. Alec paid for the goods, and the sales assistant put them in the backpacks to make them easier to carry. Alec and Mihael left the store with the packs on their backs.

'Now for supplies,' He said. 'There's a Lidl round the corner.'

Outside the shopping mall, it had turned dark. They

walked the two minutes to the Lidl supermarket and stocked up on drinking water, cold meats, bread and cheese. *Not much of a last supper. We can't be having an open flame on a scaffold, now can we?* They returned to the Zoologischer Garten station area. There they stopped off at McDonalds and bought some coffees and a meal each. At the seating area, Alec took the thermos flasks from the backpacks and filled them with the coffee.

'Ideally, we should wash these out before using them. I suppose it doesn't matter too much,' Alec said.

'Why's that?'

'Dust from the factory they are made at gets inside and can affect the drink. We're more concerned with having hot liquid to keep warm than whether it tastes great.'

Once they had finished their meal, they stopped off at Dunkin' Donuts and bought a selection of doughnuts and bagels. Alec decided they had enough supplies to last them the night. They went into the station and boarded the S3 train to Hackescher Markt station.

***

They exited the station and came out onto Henriette-Herz-Platz, there were a number of restaurants under the red-brick arches supporting the tracks overhead.

'How come we didn't eat in there?' Mihael asked as they passed the BBQ Kitchen restaurant, 'it smells delicious.'

'It does, you're right. The food tastes pretty good there too. But we look like the world's oldest gap year students. That's not the sort of place where we'd go; we would stand out too much. Somewhere like McDonalds is great for maintaining anonymity. You get everyone there from businessman to families to backpackers. We're getting close now; you should be able to see the cathedral soon.'

They turned onto Burgstraße and followed the path of the Spree, as predicted the cathedral was in the near distance across the river. They crossed on to Vera-Brittain-Ufer, the waterfront promenade that runs parallel to the rear of the cathedral. They passed the nude bronzed statues of Berliners sitting on the wall enjoying the view, and went down the steps to the lower promenade, right alongside the river and below the terrace restaurants with their empty tables in the chilly air. The walkway was separated from the river by a grey ornate iron fence. *Too high for me to push him over, even if I did Arthur would call before I could reach him, putting Sara at risk. I can't have that.* As if on cue, Mihael's phone rang. Alec carried on walking as Mihael stopped to answer it.

'Alec, wait!' He called. *A breakthrough?* Mihael had always called him Foster before.

Alec stopped; he was outside the DDR Museum. They were closing up for the night. Alec thought about Peter, and how his phone call this morning had interrupted the man's visit there. *Sorry, Peter for getting you mixed up in this.* Mihael caught up with him.

'What's that?' he asked, pointing at the building.

'It's a museum dedicated to how life was in the DDR.' Mihael had a confused look on his face, so Alec explained. 'The DDR was the Deutsche Demokratische Republik, after World War Two Germany was split into East and West. The DDR was the east, along with half of Berlin. The river there was the part of the border in the city, the other part was the Berlin Wall which you would have heard of.'

Mihael nodded, he looked interested in the history lesson, so Alec continued, 'Mihael is Slovenian, isn't it? Is that where you are from?'

'My father is from there. I was born and raised in Bulgaria.'

'I've been to Sofia a few times, it's a lovely city. I love all the street art, the paintings on buildings.' *Not really, it's a very poor imitation of Berlin.*

'I'm from Pernik, it's much nicer than Sofia, and every winter we have the Surva, the festival of masquerade. You'll have to... oh.' His face dropped and then became stern as he remembered his purpose.

Slowly, Alec, slowly. Alec patted his arm, 'I'm sure it's a great place, who knows, I may get the opportunity... in this life or the next.' Alec smiled as he mimicked Russell Crowe in *Gladiator*. Mihael returned the smile, but Alec could see he didn't get the reference. 'Where was I? Oh yes, the DDR museum. Inside the museum there are exhibits all about everyday life during the period, so people can see how people lived and worked. It's very interesting. Shall we continue? It's not too far to the building site now.'

'I think so, yes.'

They walked up the stairs and came out in front of the Radisson Blu hotel and the Karl-Liebknecht Strauss B2 highway. To their left, Alec could see the Berliner Fernsehturm, lit up in the clear night sky. *It's such a lovely view of the city from up there, especially at night.* They crossed the highway and headed right towards the Humboldtforum, or Berlin Palace, which in the process of being reconstructed after being demolished in 1950. This was where they were going to hole up in and where Alec was going to shoot from. They walked around the perimeter, past the Humboldt-Box, a futuristic museum about the Palace, its history and how it would look after the reconstruction. Alec thought the Samsung branding that adorned the museum and the palace reconstruction site was gaudy but appreciated that private enterprise was needed to fund the venture and was glad it wasn't coming out of the taxes he paid to the German government. He wasn't considered as part of the diplomatic corps which paid their taxes to the UK. It was a bone of contention among some officers as German income tax was slightly higher than the UK. The structure was protected from vandals and the public by an eight-foot-high black wooden fence all the way around.

'There's no way I can climb that,' Alec said.

'Yes, you can,' Mihael said. 'I'll help you.'

They walked to a darkened corner around the back of the structure, away from the main road. Mihael crouched down and cupped his hands.

'Come on, Alec. You can do it.'

'I'm not sure about this, Mihael,' Alec warned. He put his backpack on the ground and then placed his hands on the wooden fence; he put his foot in Mihael's hands and braced himself.

'3... 2...,' Mihael counted down. A memory of scrumping apples with his brother Mark flashed in Alec's head. His brother small foot in Alec's hands, *Mark must have been five or six*. The same countdown. Their frustrated attempts to scale their neighbour's fence, for the apples lying on the grass. They used to covert those apples, looking down from their bedroom window above.

'1... go!' Mihael finished.

He pushed Alec high; Alec's fingers grabbed for the top edge of the fence. He finally got purchase and pulled himself up, Mihael still pushing up his legs. The top of the fence was a foot-wide flat surface. Alec struggled but managed to get his leg up, and the other soon followed.

'I'm up, I can't believe it!' There was exhilaration and exhaustion in his voice. 'Pass me up the bags.'

Alec laid across the top of the fence, his feet dangling over the over the side. Mihael passed up the bags and briefcase. Alec gently lowered them the other side.

'Now you Mihael,' Alec lowered his hand and felt the strong grip in return. He counted down and at "Go" pulled with all his might.

Mihael's feet scrabbled for purchase, slipping on the slick painted surface. His fingers reached the top and Alec grabbed the wrist with his free hand and pulled even harder. His face reddened from the strain and he felt his back beginning to go. Mihael managed to get a leg up on the top and gradually brought the other one up. They both collapsed on their backs, breathing in draughts of the chilled night air.

25

Alec and Mihael made it to the top floor of the palace. The palace was a concrete shell that looked like a multi-storey car park. Plain pillars and functional concrete staircases. There was dim lighting on each floor. *Possibly to assist the security patrols, if there are any.* They stopped to dress in their camping clothes and for a light meal. There was scaffolding covering the outside of the building, from the ground to the roof. Some sections of scaffolding were covered by an awning, plain on the inside, Samsung branding on the outside. Alec decided that they would stay on the scaffolding, between the building and the awning. *That should give us some protection from the arctic wind outside, and also from any patrols inside the building.*

They made their way round to the section of the palace facing the cathedral. With the penknife Alec made a small hole in the awning to ensure they were lined up with the entrance to the cathedral, Alec calculated that they were approximately one hundred and twenty metres from where the Prime Minister would exit their vehicle. *I could probably hit that with a catapult, let alone a sniper rifle. With a sniper rifle, it'll be like I'm standing next to them.* They set up their self-inflating base mats and got into their sleeping bags to protect them from the cold. The sky was overcast, and Alec hoped it didn't rain during the night. *That would make an already miserable situation far worse.* Once they were settled Alec asked Mihael questions about his time in Turkey and what home life was like in Bulgaria. At one stage Mihael showed him pictures of his girlfriend, and Alec knew that Mihael was starting to see Alec as a person rather than a target. *Slow and steady, gain his trust, make friends. When it comes to the end, he may hesitate, hell, he may even let me go. I'll need any advantage I can get.*

They talked, ate and drank the still warm coffee from the flasks. Newbury interrupted proceedings at random times checking up on them. Alec noticed Mihael was taking longer to answer the phone each time. When they weren't talking, Alec was thinking about Sara and the times they had spent together. How she always looked happy to see him and her excitement with each new place, exhibition, and show that Alec took her to when she came to Berlin. He always looked for fun, different things for them to do and see. Last time he took her to an art and music show in a cellar at Rosenthalerstraße, called Monsterkabinett. She loved going through the courtyards covered with street art and graffiti, she took countless photos, even getting selfies of them in front of some of them. Alec paid for tickets from the excitable host at the entrance to the show. They then went to the Eschschloraque bar next door while they waited for the show to begin; the bar was littered with strange creatures and artworks. When it was showtime, they descended the narrow staircase to the cellar, and the English-speaking host took them into the darkness where they experienced a bizarre mix of robotics, monsters and techno. Sara absolutely loved it and had told him she wanted to go again.

The night passed as it does, Alec looked for opportunities to contact Claudia to tell her where Sara was, however, Mihael didn't let him stray. He followed Alec during toilet breaks and during their own security patrols when they checked to see if they were being watched. Alec tried to keep the frustration out of his voice. He didn't want to spoil the groundwork he had laid. *If I'm still alive, I have a chance.* He kept telling himself.

At one stage he dozed off, snug in the layers of clothing and the warmth of the sleeping bag. He was woken by Mihael and was surprised that it was daylight.

'What time is it?' He asked.

'Just after eight, we have two hours before the Prime Minister gets here. You were shouting in your sleep.'

'Probably, I get regular nightmares, have done for many years now. Sorry. Did you get any sleep?'

'No, I can't until this is done.'

'Why don't you get your head down for a while, I'll keep watch. It'll be alright, I'll wake you if Arthur calls.'

'Thanks, I'll be ok though. Not long to go now.' *Damn.*

They sat in silence as Alec woke up fully. He peeked through the hole in the awning and could see people milling around on the Lustgarten grass, taking photos of the cathedral and Altes Museum beside it. On the roof of the museum, he could see security services setting up for the visit. He remembered from the briefing that they would be doing the same on the roof of the palace. *Hopefully, Arthur hasn't organised security patrols of the lower floors. That's one advantage of having him in charge of both events – The PMs and the shooting – there should be gaps for exploiting.*

With an hour to go, Newbury called, and Alec asked if he could speak to his old friend. Mihael passed him the phone.

'Arthur, before I do this I need to know Sara is still alive. I need proof of life.' he said.

'I'm in the middle of things here. I can't just drop everything and head over there.'

'Arthur, I'm not asking, if you want me to do this, I need to speak to her.'

'For god's sake Alec,' He cursed. 'Okay, I'll head over there now and call you back.'

Newbury hung up, and Alec passed the phone back to Mihael.

'I need to speak to her one last time.' He explained.

'I understand,' Mihael said. Alec thought he spotted some sympathy coming from his companion.

'Thanks, Mihael.'

While Alec waited for Newbury's call, to keep himself occupied he packed away the camping equipment into his backpack. He removed the layers of clothing he had added.

'This will give me more movement when it comes to shoot,' he exclaimed to Mihael. *And it gives me more movement if I need to get away.*

With a half-hour until the Prime Minister arrived Newbury called. Mihael answered the phone and passed it to Alec.

'Uncle Alec?' Sara's voice was timid and scared.

'Yep, I'm here, how are you doing? Have you been hurt?'

'No, I'm okay. They tied me to a chair and left me here in the dark, but I'm not hurt. What's going on? They wouldn't tell me, and then Uncle Arthur came. He wouldn't release me.'

'Arthur has decided to kill the Prime Minister, and he wants me to do it. The only way he could make me would be to threaten to hurt you. So, I've told him I'll do it, and

215

he said he'd let you go. I'm sorry, Sara, I really am. It'll be over soon.'

'You should choose your friends with more care, Uncle Alec.'

'I know that now. I love you, Sara. I'll see you soon.' Tears came to his eyes and his voice caught in his throat.

'I love you too.' And she was gone.

'There, you happy now?' Newbury said. 'Make sure you don't miss.'

He hung up the phone. Alec passed it back to Mihael as he wiped his eyes on his sleeve. 'I need to be alone for a while. Get my head together. I can't shoot in this state.'

Michal nodded and motioned for Alec to go on. Alec entered the building and headed for a far corner and sat behind a pillar. He checked to see if Mihael had followed. Nothing. *Yes! He finally trusts me.* He quickly pulled the phone out of his jacket pocket and saw numerous missed calls from Claudia. He had known she had tried to call him as his pocket gently vibrated each time. This was why he didn't give up the jacket for a warmer one from the store. Fortunately, in Newbury's office, he had muted the phone's speaker to stop the annoying fanfare when the phone was switched on. He dialled Claudia's number.

'Alec, where the hell have you been?' She said.

'Claudia, there's no time. Arthur is behind this all. He has Sara; they are at the safe house on Thrasoltstraße. Get there as fast as you can. I have to kill the Prime Minister if you don't get there in time or he'll kill her.'

'Alec-'

He cut her off, 'There's no time I have to get back. I won't be able to answer the phone so text me when you have her. I love you.'

He hung up the phone and put it back in his pocket. He

heard footsteps and then Mihael's voice.

'Alec? Where are you?'

Alec stood up and came out from behind the pillar. He wiped his eyes. He tried hard to keep the hope from his voice. 'I'm here. I'm okay now. Let's get things set up.'

Alec was laid on top of Mihael's sleeping bag, to protect him from the cold, wooden scaffolding boards. He looked through the scope of the rifle and tracked various people as they moved around the entrance of the cathedral. He recognised a few from the office. *There's Harper speaking to marksmen on the roof of the Altes Museum.* Old Museum. It houses the *Antikensammlung.* Collection of Classical Antiquities. Which are stone sculptures, vases, craft objects and jewellery from the 10th Century to the 1st Century BCE, or as Alec knew it BC.

'Not long now,' Mihael said.

'Nope.'

Mihael was looking through his own peephole in the awning, to Alec's right. Beside him on the floor of the scaffold was his pistol with silencer. Alec was satisfied to see this. His hard work gaining Mihael's trust had paid off. *If he was a professional that gun would have been aimed at my head.*

Because of how close they were Alec needed Mihael to spot for him. Alec's view through the scope was narrow and focused; Mihael had a view of the Lustgarten, the entrance and the roads leading to the cathedral. Alec wasn't sure if the Prime Minister would be coming along the Karl-Liebknecht Strauss B2 or through the side street Bodestraße. The B2 was the direct route, and he knew from the meetings was the planned route. However, a last-minute change or traffic could have altered that.

Mihael's phone rang, he went to answer it, but stopped and said, 'I see their car, it's coming along the main road West to East.' He ignored the phone.

Alec adjusted the aim and tracked the vehicle. It came to a stop outside of the cathedral. The passenger door opened, and a bodyguard got out. Alec could see the beige earpiece and the wire hanging down his neck into the receiver probably attached to his belt. He went around the back of the vehicle and opened the rear door. Alec's finger moved from the trigger guard to the trigger. He took a deep breath and stilled his body. The Prime Minister stepped out of the car. Alec could see them clearly through the scope, a wide smile on their face. *For Sara.* His finger tightened on the trigger, and then he felt his pocket vibrate.

26

'Why haven't you shot yet?' Mihael asked. 'They're in the open.'

'The bodyguard is in the way,' Alec lied. He reached down into his jacket pocket with his left hand. Slowly. His fingers grasped the barrel of his gun. 'I'm still tracking. I'll get them don't worry. It won't be long now.'

He gently pulled the gun out by his fingertips. As he turned it around, he prayed Mihael wouldn't notice. When he had the stock firmly in his hand, his right hand dropped off the rifle and Alec lifted his body to bring his left hand around so he could shoot. Mihael turned his head towards Alec and his eyes widened when he saw the gun. He reached down for his own gun but decided he didn't have enough time. He jumped onto Alec, his knees landing on the back of Alec's thighs, his hands groping for the gun. Alec tried to shake him off, but he couldn't get any momentum lying on his stomach. The gun fell out of Alec's hands and slid off the scaffolding, clattering against the metal poles as it fell. Alec managed to draw his knees up under him and started bucking like a rodeo horse. He heard a clang as Mihael's head struck a steel scaffolding pole. Alec pushed harder, and suddenly Mihael's weight was off his back. He heard a cry and lifted his head. Mihael was hanging by one hand to the scaffolding rail, the other to the board, his legs and body dangling.

'Help me, Alec,' Mihael begged. 'Please.'

Alec stood and looked at him. There were tears streaming down Mihael's face. His eyes were wide. Alec shook his head.

'I hope Jaromir kicks the shit out of you in the afterlife.' Alec stamped on the hand holding the board and prised Mihael's fingers from the rail. He fell to the ground, screaming all the way.

Alec pulled out his phone and called Claudia. 'Have you got her?' He asked.

'Yes, she's safe. We missed Arthur though, I saw him running, but he'd gone before I could get him. Are you ok?'

'Yeah, I'm fine. Thanks to you. The waiter is dead though. I'll get Arthur, you keep Sara safe for me.'

'I will. Alec?'

'Yes?'

'I love you too.' She hung up.

Alec saw Mihael's phone on the scaffolding board. He picked it up and pocketed it. . *I'll leave the rifle, it's not needed anymore.* He looked for Mihael's gun but couldn't see it.

He heard a shout from above and looked up. He saw a security guard pointing at him. He ran into the main building and through the empty shell to the stairwell. He could hear heavy boots descending. He raced down the stairs, slamming into the walls to change direction. *How many floors are there?* A shot rang out and then another. Cement dust and chips were flying everywhere. Alec reached the ground level and headed for the entrance to the building site. *I won't be able to climb the fence myself; I'll have to take my chances at the gate.*

He got to the gate and saw a crowd of tourists waiting to

enter. He remembered reading about tours of the palace, which took place each day from ten o'clock. He had thought of taking Sara but decided it would be too boring. He heard shouts behind him and felt his left arm go numb and then burn. He then heard the crack of a rifle echo around. *The marksmen on the roof.*

He pulled open the gate and the tourists started shuffling in. He pushed through the crowd, ignoring their cries of protest. He broke through the mass of people and sprinted in a zig-zag fashion to prevent another shot. *Schloßplatz or Karl-Liebknecht Strauss? Head towards the cathedral and all the security there or away from it? Easy decision.* He reached Schloßplatz, lungs burning and legs like jelly. He stopped for a moment against a building out of sight of the palace and the building site. His breathing was heavy, and the thumping of his heart worried him. *Can't have a heart attack now.* He thought about where the nearest U-bahn station was. *Hausvogteiplatz is the closest. Can I reach there before I'm caught? I'm going to have to.* He ran along Schloßplatz as it merged onto Werderscher Markt. He glanced behind him and could see pursuers chasing him; he turned left at the next turning and then right onto Jägerstraße. He ran past the open ground and saw a man sitting on a bench, *Die Spiegel* newspaper in hand, watching Alec as he ran. Alec resisted the urge to give him a wave and continued past the Chipps vegetarian restaurant on the corner. He could feel blood dripping down his arm. *Keep going, old man.*

He turned left onto Oberwallstraße, he heard sirens in the distance, getting closer. *Not far now.* A shot from behind struck the car windscreen in front of him, the glass shattered. Alec put all his might into one final push, knowing the station was just around the corner. Another shot, this one hit the wall next to him. He turned right onto Hausvogteiplatz and saw the entrance in front of him. *I hope a train is coming.* He bounded down the steps to the platform level and saw a train pull in and stop. The doors opened, and he jumped into the nearest carriage. The doors took what felt like a lifetime to close, and the train pulled away. Alec was breathing rapidly, and his heart pounded in his chest. He collapsed onto a seat in exhaustion. He wanted to curl up into a ball. The train's tannoy system announced the next stop: Spittelmarkt. Alec realised he was on the U2 line and heading East. *I need time to think about where Arthur will be. He won't be east, he hates that side of the city, always has done. He said it depresses him. I need to stop and have a think.*

The train pulled in to Spittelmarkt station, and Alec got off. His legs were still shaky. He walked up the steps to the street level, pulling himself along using the handrail. He came out on Wallstraße, and could hear sirens faintly in the distance. He walked into the Schäfer's Brot café just down from the station entrance. He ordered a cup of tea and a pastry and sat at one of the tables with a view out of the window. *Spending five minutes now thinking is worth an hour or more chasing around.* Alec sipped his tea and then added four sachets of sugar. *I better sort out my arm first though.*

He left the table and went to the café's bathroom. There he removed his jacket and hung it on the peg on the back of the door. His suit jacket arm had a great tear in it. He removed it and hung it with the jacket. The shirt sleeve was sodden with blood. He took off the shirt and looked at the wound. *Not as bad as I thought, they only winged me.* He smiled at the thought. With toilet roll and water from the sink he cleaned his arm as best as he could, he winced each time he went near the inch-long gouge the bullet had made in his upper arm. When done he wadded some tissue into a ball and stuck it in his mouth, he chewed it around until it was malleable and then packed the wound with it. *I'll probably get infected, the mouth is full of bacteria, but it'll be better than losing more blood and passing out.* He wrapped the arm with more toilet paper to hold the wadding in place. He then dried the shirt sleeve with the electric hand dryer. It stiffened in the heat, turned into cardboard. Once it was dry Alec bent it this way and that to bring some flexibility back to the fabric. He got dressed and cleaned up the toilet area of blood. *I don't want anyone to contact the Police.* He left the bathroom and returned to the table.

Arthur wouldn't have planned for failure. It's not something he's ever been good at. He'll have to regroup, think about a plan of action. He's probably sitting in a café just like this thinking of his next move. Alec took a bite of the pastry. His stomach growled at him in anger. He called over the waitress and asked for a ham roll. *Arthur will need to go back to his place in Neustaaken which is west of the city. He'll need his passport and some cash. He wouldn't have a stash in the city. He's been out of the field far longer than I have. Once he has been home he'll want to get away, Tegel is the nearest airport to him, but he'll have to show his passport and will assume that I would have told about him. He wouldn't risk being caught at airport security. So, he'll get a train. Where to?*

Alec's sandwich came, and he started eating it. *The closest train station to him is the Berlin-Staaken station, but that would only take him to Rathenow or Wustermark, he'll want to get out of Germany. Amsterdam, Prague, or Basel? They are the Intercity destinations. That leaves*

Berlin-Spandau station or Hauptbahnhof stations. Intercity services travel from both. Berlin-Spandau is the closest to him, Hauptbahnhof is the largest one. Will he look for speed of exit or anonymity? Alec mulled over the problem. He finished his sandwich and his cup of tea.

He should expect us to assume he'd head straight to a different country, using the border like a teenager in a horror film uses a bathroom door to block themselves from the killer. The subtle method would be to head towards Cologne, from there he can go to Brussels, Paris and Luxemburg and then onwards. That's how I would do it. It still leaves the question of which station he'd depart from. It'll take me about forty-five minutes to get to Berlin-Spandau, using the U-bahn and twenty minutes or so to Hauptbahnhof. Maybe I can push him one way or the other.

He took out Mihael's phone and dialled Newbury's number.

'Mihael, what happened? Did you kill Foster?' Newbury asked as soon as the call connected. Alec remained silent.

'Mihael answer me! The Prime Minister is still alive, so you aren't getting your money.'

'Mihael's a little busy right now,' Alec said. 'I thought we should have a chat.'

'Alec?' Arthur's voice sounded uncharacteristically unsure. Alec liked the sound of it.

'Not who you were expecting old friend?'

'What happened to Mihael?' Alec ignored the question.

'The Police and the company are heading to your apartment and to the nearest stations to you as we speak. I wanted you to hear from me that your plan failed. Claudia has told them everything. They know it wasn't the

Russians, just the actions of a bitter old man who will never see another sunrise.' *That should stop him running to Berlin-Spandau.*

'We can come to a deal, can't we? We have a lot of history together. I've always been there for you. For Stephanie, Mark, and Sophie. I was there for you. I kept you in your job as you lost the plot and tried to drink yourself into oblivion. I have money. You can have it. Please, Alec, let me go.'

'You tried to start a war. You kidnapped and threatened Sara. You threatened Claudia. You wanted me to die,' Alec's voice was ice cold. 'Your little friend was no match for me; he took a header off the palace, they're probably still trying to scoop up his brains. I'm coming for you now. You better run and run fast.'

Alec hung up the phone; he put it in his pocket and took out his wallet. He placed thirty euros on the table, tucked under his plate, more than enough to cover the bill and service. He went down the steps of the U-bahn station and waited for the next train, he was in no hurry. He knew Arthur would drive to Hauptbahnhof, the trains were out of bounds and Arthur would never even consider the bus. A taxi would take forty minutes or more even if Arthur could get one immediately. *Arthur would get in his beloved imported Jaguar XF and drive.* A train arrived, and Alec took the U2 line heading towards Pankow. He stayed on the train three stops until Alexanderplatz, where he alighted and took the S7 S-Bahn train to Hauptbahnhof, or Berlin Central Station.

Alec had a brainwave, he took out his phone and called Claudia. She answered on the first ring.

'Alec, are you ok?' Her voice was breathless.

'A little nick to the arm, but I'm fine. I'm heading to

Hauptbahnhof, I think Arthur's coming here to get a train to Cologne. I was calling to see if you can get the boffins to track Arthur's phone to confirm it. See if he learnt anything from my mistakes the past few days.'

'I'm already ahead of you. They are tracking him as we speak. He is currently on the B2 and should get in at the same time as you.' *Shit, he must have driven faster than I thought he would.*

'You're tracking me too? Of course, you are. Do you want a Head of Section job after this? Mine will be up for grabs.'

'Shut up Alec, you aren't going anywhere. I've told everyone that you foiled a plot to assassinate the PM and are on your way to apprehend the ringleader. You might even get a medal.'

'I could kiss you.' *Damn right, I will.*

'I expect more than that. Someone mentioned going shopping I seem to remember.'

'I'll buy you the biggest, the gaudiest ring a lowly intelligence officer can afford.'

'Head of Section, please remember that I wouldn't lower my standards to be with anyone less than that.'

'Of course not, my darling, maybe I should start looking for promotion opportunities to keep you in the luxuries you deserve.'

'There is a Head of Berlin job recently vacated. Nudge, nudge.'

'Only temporarily at the moment. I plan to make it permanent.'

'You be careful, I'll be along soon to clean up after you.'

'Where's Sara? Is she ok?'

'She's shaken up, but Peter is looking after her. They're

at mine; I figured that was the safest place for them.'

'Good idea. Peter stayed an extra day?'

'He said something about you owing him the best kebab in Berlin. I'm not sure he wanted to leave Sara though. I kept seeing him looking at her.'

'And you left them alone!'

'Settle down Dad, not everyone is like you, always thinking about sex.'

'Well… thinking about the other night, I pity them.'

'Alec!' He could hear her blush.

'The station's coming up, I better go.'

'You be careful, he's bigger than you.'

'And older.' Alec said, as though the three years would make that much of a difference.

'Just be careful. I love you.'

'You too… bye for now, beautiful.' He hung up.

The train came into the station and slowly halted. Alec was the first one off and went straight to the electronic station departures board. *Platform 7, that's on the lowest floor. How long have I got? Four minutes, shit!* Alec was on Platform 16 on the upper floor. He sprinted to the platform exit and bounded down the stairs, pushing past passengers coming up.

27

Alec made it to the entrance to Platform 7 with a minute to spare and a lot of angry people in his wake. He spotted the tall figure of Newbury get on the train further down the platform. He entered the First-Class carriage. *Of course.* The door close alarm started, and Alec ran to the nearest carriage and jumped on just as the doors closed.

The train started off with a jerk and Alec made his way through the carriages. He was breathing heavily from his sprint through the station and coupled with his earlier exertions escaping from the palace, he was struggling. He decided to take his time, *it's not as though Arthur is going anywhere. It's a four-hour train journey. By taking my time, it'll give him a chance to relax, think he's got away.* Alec sat down at a free chair and let his body recover.

After twenty minutes, his pulse was strong and steady, the blood rushing around his head had diminished, and his breathing was no longer ragged. Alec decided to call Claudia to let her know what was happening.

'Hi Alec, what's this? The third or fourth time you've called me today? How's the trip?' Claudia said. Alec could hear a lot of noise in the background.

'The third, I think. I miss the sound of your voice, obviously. It's a lovely smooth train journey. Where are you?'

'We got to the station a minute or two after the train departed. We're now travelling to Wolfsburg to catch it at the next stop. Have you seen Arthur yet?'

'Are you flying? It's very loud your end.'

'That'll be the helicopter, it's not the quietest.'

'I can imagine. I saw Arthur get on the train, and then I had to jump on before the doors closed. I'm just lulling him into a false sense of security before going to see him. I'm looking forward to dashing his hopes and bashing his skull.'

'I may have said this but be careful. You can always wait until Wolfsburg. Harper has already informed the train station and German police that we are tracking a known terrorist. The train won't go any further than the station. Oh, you owe Harper a drink by the way. I had to tell him we suspected him instead of Arthur. He was quite put out at the thought.'

'I suppose he would be. I may have been blinded by my dislike of the man and the trust of a so-called friend.'

'What is done is done. We can't change it. We just have to move on and make right what went wrong.' *Is she talking about us or Arthur? I suppose it's the same either way.*

'You're right, as always. I'm going to go and have a chat with Arthur. I'll be careful, don't worry. I can't wait to see you.'

'Make sure you are, I don't want a dead lover. Not my kind of thing.'

They said their goodbyes and Alec hung up the call. *It's strange, this feeling of teamwork and counting on others.* In the early days of his career, he'd been alone in the field and had got used to the feeling, relying on himself, not having to worry about anyone else. As time went by and he became more senior, he still preferred the solitary role, the undercover lone agent. The promotion to Head of

Section took this away from him, and he didn't like being behind the action. He now had the chance to learn from his past and take the sensible, team decision. *That's not going to happen. There are thirty minutes or so until the first stop. It's time.* Alec stood and started walking through the train. He reached the beginning of the First-Class section, a narrow corridor down the left-hand-side of the carriage, eight individual compartments on the right. Each compartment had a clear glass sliding door, and Alec could see the occupants inside. The downside was that they could see him too. He longed for the olden days where the compartments had curtains that could be drawn across the windows giving privacy inside. A flash of memory struck him of enjoying that privacy with Claudia, many years ago, when they took the train for a romantic break in Prague. The curtains were drawn for the entire trip. He smiled at the thought, and his smile faded as he got his head back in the game.

He slowly walked down the corridor looking into each compartment as he passed. *No Arthur... No Arthur.* He came to the last compartment in the carriage and peeked into it. *Yes!* Newbury was sitting against the window, his back to Alec. He was watching the world speed by, gathering his thoughts. Alec put his hand on the door handle, took a deep breath and slid the door open.

'Arthur? Arthur Newbury? What a coincidence us being on the same train, how the devil are you?' Alec exclaimed with false camaraderie. He closed the door behind him, not taking his eyes off Newbury. 'You can stay seated, Arthur. The jig is up, the fat lady has sung, and you're going down for a very long time.'

'Cut the crap, Alec, I should have known you'd turn up.

You're like a bad penny.'

'Don't you want to know how I knew you'd be on this train? It's quite clever.'

Newbury stayed silent. His body was very still, but his eyes were darting all around, like a cornered animal.

'No?' Alec made his voice sound disappointed. 'It's not as ingenious as starting World War Three because I can't be with the woman I want, but it's pretty good.'

'Leave Julia out of this.'

'Oh, I would, but you brought Sara and Claudia into it. I'm just lowering the conversation to your level.'

Newbury didn't respond to that. Alec was struck by how much larger Newbury was compared to him. Alec was giving up six inches in height, at least thirty pounds and Alec recalled the punch he received in the office the day before, and that in his youth Newbury had been a boxer, regularly taking part in intra-service bouts. *Maybe I should have waited for back-up. Too late now, just have to roll with it. What's it they say in the movies when against a stronger, bigger opponent? Make them angry, so they make a mistake? Time for some lies then.*

'Speaking of Julia, did you know she came to see me when she found out about you and that tart from the office?'

Newbury looked up at Alec, a question on his lips.

'Yeah, she wanted to know if I knew about the affair, how long it had been going on and how serious you two were. She was very upset, you know. She really loved you.'

'Go on,' Newbury said. Alec could see his cheeks reddening.

'Well we had a few drinks; I comforted her and told her the truth about you. Then we kissed. I don't know who started it. It could have been her, it may have been me,' Alec could see Newbury's fists clenching and unclenching. The knuckles white. Alec braced himself for the attack and continued, 'the next thing I knew we were undressing each other, pure raw passion, her hands all over me. She's a wild one, that woman. Her new fella must be having the time of his life.' Newbury lowered his head slightly, got ready to charge. 'Anyway, I can see why you'd give up the world for her. She *tasted* delicious.' Alec deliberately licked his lips as though remembering the time and taste.

Newbury leapt from the chair and charged at Alec. It was the opportunity Alec had been waiting for, as Newbury closed the small gap between them Alec raised his arm and slammed his elbow into Newbury's face. The impact pushed Alec back against the door. Newbury fell backwards. Alec followed up the strike with a kick to Newbury's unprotected groin. Newbury doubled up with an "ooomph" escaping from his lips. *Shit, it worked.* Alec stepped forward and aimed a punch at the side of Newbury's head. Newbury, however, was waiting for the move and blocked it with his forearm. Alec lost his balance from both the momentum of the punch and the train taking a corner at speed. He staggered forward and cracked his head against the window. Newbury, now behind Alec, launched a series of blows to Alec's back, each one felt to Alec like a jackhammer, with his back the pavement. *I have to move.* He pushed himself backwards using his leg on the seat. Newbury grabbed him around the throat with his arm and squeezed. Alec stamped his feet hoping to catch one of Newbury's feet. He kicked backwards trying to rake his heels down Newbury's shins. Newbury kept his legs out of Alec's reach, bent Alec backwards putting more and more pressure on Alec's neck and throat. Alec clawed at Newbury's arms and hands, they didn't move. Alec's vision narrowed, the edges turned black. He couldn't breathe. He knew he didn't have long. He closed his eyes. *I can't end like this, this is pathetic. Think of Claudia and Sara.* Their faces came to his mind. He saw them fade away in the darkness.

Alec did the only thing he could think to do. He placed his feet on the chair cushions, one either side of the aisle, he pushed with his legs, lifting his body and legs as high as they could go and then dropped placing all his weight in the lower part of his body. It felt like his head was going to be torn off, but the energy of the drop was too much for Newbury to hold. His grip on Alec's neck broke, and Alec dropped to the ground. He gasped for air, taking big gulps. His right hand slid down to his pocket looking for anything that could be used a weapon. He pulled out Mihael's phone, wrapped in his fist. He thrust it blindly over his head, He felt, then heard a crunch and then a thud. He rolled around to face Newbury and scampered back against the side of the compartment as far away as he could. He looked up and saw Newbury with one hand over his mouth, the other on the back of his head, shock and pain in his eyes.

Alec struggled to his feet; Newbury brought both arms out in a boxer's stance, one hand guarding his face, the other ready to jab. His mouth a bloody mess. *The phone must have caught him. POW! Right in the kisser!* Alec laughed at the inappropriateness of the thought. Newbury snarled and dropped the guard and launched himself at Alec, he led with the jabbing hand. Alec dropped to his knees, his feet planted against the side of the carriage and pushed himself forward. Alec felt Newbury's fist glance off the side of his head with a sting. Alec continued the motion and felt the top of his head hit Newbury's face. Newbury cried out, he was forced backwards, and his legs went from under him, and he collapsed to the floor. Alec landed on top of him. Alec started punching Newbury's already bloody face, the nose snapped, the eyes shut, tears and blood dripped from the closed lids. He felt Newbury go limp underneath him. He punched a few more times to ensure it wasn't a fake. He stopped; his breathing hard, his damaged throat restricted his swallowing. He used the chairs either side to lift him up, and he slumped onto one of them exhausted, his shaking hands were bloodied and sore. His face felt like it had been run over. He stayed that way for a few minutes until the sliding door opened, and a voice started to ask, in German, to see his ticket. The question died as soon as they saw the man on the floor and Alec, bloodied, on the chair.

'Sorry.' Alec said. 'I'm *schwarzfahren*,' Travelling without a ticket. 'I'll have to accept the fine.' He burst into a fit of laughter and tears.

28

The train pulled into Wolfsburg Hauptbahnhof station and ground to a halt. A tannoy announcement advised passengers that the train would be stopping there due to a mechanical problem and they were to get on the next one. Alec stayed in the compartment with the subdued and restrained Newbury. The train conductor, once Alec had told him what had happened, had provided some ropes for Alec to tie Newbury up. Alec had his eyes closed, head leaning against the window when the door opened. He opened his eyes and was greeted by Harper, Claudia and four officers holding guns. He recognised them from the embassy but didn't know their names.

'Hi, honey. There's a present for you on the floor. Sorry, it's not wrapped.' He said, his voice croaked. He was feeling lightheaded from the painkillers and two whiskies the conductor gave him to wash them down with.

The officers dragged Newbury out of the compartment. Claudia sat next to Alec and hugged him; he winced at the pain but accepted the hug without complaint.

'Well done, Foster,' Harper said. 'You did really well, saved the Prime Minister, stopped World War Three and also answered one of the questions that always comes up at office parties.'

'What question is that?' Alec asked.

'Well, who would win in a fight between you and Arthur, of course. I always said you'd win, you're scrappy and willing to break the rules. Arthur didn't stand a chance.'

Alec smiled, 'Richard, why haven't we ever gone drinking together? I think I like you.'

'Maybe we will. I'm going to make sure Arthur is apprised of his rights. I'm sure you read them to him, and he resisted, but it is good practice to have them on record. I'll see you around.' He left the compartment, leaving Claudia and Alec alone.

'I thought he'd never go.' Alec said, as he broke the hug and brought Claudia's face to his. They kissed deeply and passionately. Alec forgot about the pain.

***

The taxi stopped on Mommsenstraße, outside Claudia's apartment building. Claudia got out first and went round to Alec's door. She opened it and helped him out of the vehicle. Alec shuffled round in the seat and dropped his legs out of the door. Claudia gave him her shoulder to lean on. Together they walked and hobbled to the apartment building door. The taxi drove off, splashing into puddles from the recent downpour as it went.

'It seems strange we were only here yesterday morning. It's like a lifetime ago.' Alec said.

'We should have stayed in bed.'

'Sadly, that was not an option. The dreams wouldn't let me.' Alec prodded his head with his free hand.

'I suppose the guilt of letting the PM die could have put a dampener on things.'

Alec's hand moved to her breast, he gave it a little squeeze, 'Probably not, to be fair.'

'Alec, oh my god! You can barely walk, and you're

having dirty thoughts. Also, we're on the street, what would my neighbours think. This is an upmarket neighbourhood.'

'You're the one who said we should have stayed in bed. Besides, I was just checking they were still there. I missed them.' He kissed her on the cheek.

'Well, keep your naughty thoughts and your filthy hands to yourself. Your niece is upstairs, and Peter. They won't want to see you groping a middle-aged woman.'

'The sexiest middle-aged woman anyone has ever seen.' Alec said.

Claudia hit him gently in the stomach, 'you're supposed to say, "You're not middle-aged, my beautiful darling." I guess there is time to fix you, you've spent far too much time on your own.'

'I wouldn't argue with that.'

'That's a good start.' She kissed him and then opened the door to the building.

'Oh crap! I forgot about the stairs.' Alec cried.

They reached the top of stairs after much sweat, tears and cursing. Alec must have said the word "lift" at least twenty times.

'You should have tried doing that with a buggy and a screaming infant three or four times a day. Mind you they didn't scream as much as you just did.' Claudia said with a sweet smile on her face.

Alec grumbled under his breath as Claudia rang the buzzer to the apartment. Alec recalled the harsh sound from the night this all started.

'Hello?' Sara's voice spoke over the intercom.

'Hi, Sara, its Claudia and your Uncle… Just checking you and Peter were decent before we came in.'

'Aunty!' Sara exclaimed in shock. Alec's eyes widened in surprise.

'I'll take that as you are okay for us to come in then.'

'Of course, oh my god.'

Claudia put her key in the lock and twisted. She pushed the door open.

'You're a wicked woman, Claude,' Alec said with a smile.

'Of course, also you'd probably have a heart attack if we went in and they were on the sofa *in flagrante delicto*. I can't be having that.'

'That's true, I almost had one going up those stairs.'

They went into the apartment, Alec kicked off his shoes beside the door and closed the door behind him.

'Uncle Alec!' Sara came running up to him, her brown hair flowing behind her. She went to give him a hug and caught herself. She kissed him on the cheek. 'How are you, Uncle? You look like hell.'

'You should see the other guy.' He quipped. He waved his hand in front of his face. 'Big Mess. No one takes my niece and gets away with it.'

'Thanks, Uncle.'

Alec shrugged off his jacket and hung it on the coat hook, 'The state of it, I'd probably be better off burning it.' The jacket had a hole in the upper arm of the sleeve where Alec had been shot. It was caked with mud, dust and Newbury's blood.

'I agree, go on Alec, go and lay down on the sofa, I'll get rid of this and then get you a drink.' Claudia said. She removed Alec's wallet and phone from the pockets and handed them to him, opened the front door and left with the jacket.

'It served me well; I'll have to get another one.' *Or*

238

maybe that trenchcoat?

'This way Uncle, lean on me.' Sara proffered her arm.

Alec took it, and gave her a cuddle as well, 'It's great to see you again, Sara. I'm sorry for what happened; I'm so relieved you're okay.'

'I'm fine, Uncle Alec, really. Peter has been a great help.' Alec's eyes narrowed.

They went into the living room; Peter was sitting on the sofa. He stood up when they entered and moved out of the way. 'Hi Stefan – sorry, Alec, it's good to see you again. You look even worse than you did on Tuesday. You should take greater care of yourself.' He smiled.

'Thanks, Peter. I'm sorry for dragging you into this mess. I honestly didn't realise this would happen.'

'It's okay, being shot at is good for the heart. Makes you think about things. Look at what's important and what's not.'

'That's for sure,' Alec said as he lowered himself onto the sofa. 'I'm sure there are better ways of doing it though.' He saw that Sara had stood next to Peter, quite closely.

'Quite possibly.'

Claudia entered the room with a cup of tea and placed it on the table next to the sofa. 'May I get you anything else, darling?' She asked.

'No dear, thank you though,' Alec replied. Claudia sat on the sofa next to him, her hand on his knee.

'So, Uncle Alec, are you going to tell me about you and Aunty Claudia?' Sara asked.

'Aunty Claudia? Makes me sound ancient.' Claudia said.

'No one could ever call you ancient, she's always called you guys Aunty Claudia, Uncle Roger, Aunty Julia and Uncle Art…' The name faded away. 'She used to say we were like family,'

'Well, you were, even when Uncle Alec was at his loneliest. I wasn't worried being away from him because he'd always have his Berlin family to keep an eye on him.'

'Lonely? Me? I don't think I ever get lonely. The voices keep me company.' Alec laughed.

'Are you sure you're not concussed?' Claudia asked.

After a while, Alec began to feel itchy and could smell himself. He decided he'd have to do something about it.

'I'm going to go back to the flat, have a shower and put on some of my own clothes.' He told them.

'Are you sure?' Claudia asked. 'There's no problem you using Chris' or Roger's clothes.'

'I'd prefer my own. Thank you though.'

'I'll come with you Uncle Alec,' Sara said.

'Thanks, Sara, I'll be okay. I can't wrap myself up in cotton wool. I'll go home and get showered and changed then meet you all on Mehringdamm at nine. I owe Peter a kebab after all.'

'That's one of the reasons I'm still here.' Peter said.

'Only one? I can't think of anything else,' Alec said, with his eyebrow raised. A blush spread across both Peter's and Sara's cheeks.

'Alec, be nice,' Claudia said.

'Yes, dear.'

'You're going to get a taxi. I'm not having you on public transport in your condition. You'll probably fall asleep again and end up in Poland.'

'Okay, you're probably right, and I don't really fancy the walk to and from the stations, to be honest.'

Claudia ordered him a taxi, and Alec said his goodbyes

and made his way slowly downstairs, *still no lift I see.* He felt better moving around, although it hurt, sitting still hurt more. He left the building and waited for the taxi. The earlier rain had turned to snow; small flurries danced in the air, Alec drew his suit jacket closer to his body to ward off the cold.

29

The taxi driver took Alec the slightly longer way home, down the B2 and through Tiergarten, before heading south at the Victory Column roundabout. The golden statue of Victoria, nicknamed *Goldelse* by Berliners, at the top of the column was obscured by the heavy snow. Large chunks of it hitting the windscreen before being swept away by the wipers. *I'm glad I got a taxi. I don't fancy walking in this tonight.* Alec tracked the journey in his mind, partly to ensure the driver wasn't ripping him off. The taxi turned left onto Von-der-Heydt-Straße and followed the path of the Landwehr canal east. It turned onto Lindenstraße, and then onto Alte Jakobstraße. *Not long now.* Alec was looking forward to being home, the familiar comforts and surroundings called to him. The driver turned right onto Neuenburger Straße. Alec saw the housing estate opposite his flat, it's faded paintwork drab and flaking. *It's far more run down than Claudia's neighbourhood, but it suits me fine.*

'Just here driver, thank you.' Alec said.

The taxi drew to a stop; Alec reached over and gave the driver twenty-five Euros.

'Keep the change.' Alec said with a smile. He exited the vehicle and walked up to his building, a grey snow-clad four-storey building with a café-slash-bakery next-door. The snow was coming down hard and was settling on the ground. Alec was careful to ensure his footing was sound.

Don't want to slip; I don't think I'd ever get up. He opened the door to the building and went inside. *After all the grief I gave Claudia about the stairs in her building, I didn't even think that mine has no lift either. I may have to apologise. Not straight-away though.* He started the long climb.

Alec opened his front door and kicked the small pile of built up mail out of the way. He groped for the light switch he knew was to his right, lifting his arm caused echoes in his back. He grimaced. His fingers found the switch and flipped it. Light filled the hallway, and Alec entered. He noted the dry and musky air, *I really should give this place a thorough clean before inviting Claudia round.* He closed the door behind him and hung the suit jacket on a coat peg hanging on the wall, next to his grubby and torn trenchcoat. He looked at the mail on the floor. *I'm not going to be able to pick that up.* He moved the pile around with his foot to try to see if any of the items looked important. *Just bills and junk mail by the looks of it.*

He walked into the kitchen and without turning the light on went to the fridge and opened it. The light illuminated the clean and organised work surfaces behind him. He took out a small plate of frankfurters wrapped in cling film, he broke open the wrapping and sniffed them. There was no smell apart from the smoky meat aroma. He put the plate in the microwave and turned it on. He, then, moved over to the sink, took a glass from the draining board and filled it with water. He took a sip, the water giving his throat some welcome relief. The microwave "dinged" and Alec removed the plate and picked up a sausage. He took a bite. He had difficulty swallowing because of his throat, so he drank some water to wash the sausage down. He put the remainder of the frankfurter he was holding back onto the plate and left the kitchen.

He moved to the living room and turned on his stereo system. He knew there was a CD already in the tray, so he pressed play and spun the dial to increase the volume. The opening electronic chords of "Major Tom" by Peter Schilling boomed out of the speakers. Alec turned the dial back a bit, in respect of the neighbours downstairs. He smiled recalling the look on Sara's face two Christmases' ago as he unwrapped her present, she had an amused smile and delight in her eyes. The handwritten songs titles and artists on the cover, the album titled "Uncle Alec's Cheesy 80s Music."

'I don't have a CD player,' he said, puzzled.

'Open up the other present on the other side of the tree,' she said. 'It time for you to get rid of those dusty records and embrace the 1980s, next year I may get you an iPod Classic so you can enter the 2000s.'

He went to the bathroom, humming along to the music and peeled off his clothes. His shirt had blood on the collar, sleeve and body area, some his, some others. He bundled them into a ball and threw them in the corner to deal with later. He avoided looking in the mirror at his injuries. *I'll check them over after the shower*. He ran the shower, waiting for a minute before entering to allow the temperature to get to the right level. The water stung the top of his head, he shuffled forward, so it was beating on his neck and back. The heat of the water eased his aching muscles. He let the water flow over the wound on his arm, the sting felt good. The toilet paper bandage disintegrated, and Alec used his foot to nudge the scraps that fell to the shower floor into a corner so he could fish them out later when he could bend. After he felt clean enough. He stepped out of the shower and dried himself gingerly with a towel. *Now for the mirror.* The first thing he looked at was his face. *Wrinkles, laughter lines, weird dyed brown hair, better than my weird normal grey hair.* He took in the bruising around his eyes, still deep in the tissue and yet to express itself fully. The bullet graze on his cheek from the bar was a nasty red mark, his throat was bruised and raw. He looked lower down, his chest and torso were thankfully clear of injuries. As were his legs. His feet ached, and he had blisters on each foot, at the heel from all the walking and running he had done over the past few days. Each blister had swollen, filled with liquid, just begging to be popped. *A visit to a chiropodist is needed I think.* He looked at the wound on his arm, the skin surrounding the gouge was turning red and looked very angry. Alec opened his medicine cabinet and took out the bottle of Octenisept antiseptic spray. He liberally sprayed it on the wound, it immediately started to burn. Alec gripped the sides of the sink until it passed. *That hurt more than the shot.* He dabbed around the wound with tissue paper, drying the skin. He removed some sterile dressing from the cabinet and surgical tape. He applied the dressing, taping it in place. *Now for the bit I was dreading.*

Alec turned around and looked behind him into the mirror. His neck limited his movement. The bruising from Tuesday had developed and started turning a sickly yellow and green colour around the main deep purple strike zone. *Mihael's friend really did a number on me. I hope the Russians treat him likewise.* The new bruises from Newbury were showing as pink and red blotches, swollen patches of pain across both sets of ribs. *It could have been much, much worse.* Alec consoled himself. He wrapped the towel around his waist and left the bathroom.

New Order's "Bizarre Love Triangle" was playing in the living room. Alec started singing softly along with it as he went into his bedroom, he turned on the light and left the door open to hear the music, and started getting dressed. He dressed in his normal suit and trousers combination, clean shirt, no tie. *I'm not really a jeans and t-shirt guy.* He had trouble putting the socks on, bending was an issue, so he decided to go without them. He took out an old pair of slip-on leather shoes from the depths of his wardrobe and slid them on, trampling the backs down. *I'll fight with these later.* He kicked the shoes off his feet and into the hallway. After dressing, he went to the suit jacket hanging by the front door and took out his wallet and phone from the pocket and placed them into the one he was wearing. Alec returned to the living room, turned on the light, turned off the stereo, interrupting Alphaville's "Forever Young" and sat in his armchair. He was grateful for the old-fashioned upright nature of the chair, and the lumbar support. *Far better than the modern leather recliner that Sara wanted me to get last time she was here. This is a proper reading chair.* He turned on the television using the remote control resting on the table and started flicking through the channels looking to see if any of today's excitement had made the news.

Alec woke with a start, his sleep broken by the vibrations of the phone in his pocket. He took it out of his pocket and saw it was Claudia. He answered it.

'Hi sleepyhead, just a wake-up call as it's almost time to leave to meet us.'

'What? I wasn't asleep. I've had a shower and am dressed and fully refreshed and raring for a night on the town.'

'Okay you liar, you were practically sleeping on the

sofa when you were here, I had to keep nudging you every time your eyelids dropped while you were talking to Sara and Peter. At least you didn't start snoring.'

'There may have been a rough few nights, with little sleep.'

'Poor baby, we'll go out and then make our excuses and have an early night tonight, let the lovebirds enjoy Berlin alone. Anyway, I miss having you near me.'

'I was thinking about you while I was showering.'

'Really?' She purred.

'Yes, I would have loved someone there to clean my back.'

'Alec, you jerk! I was being all nice to you, and you do that. I don't think we can be together anymore.' Alec could tell she was trying not to laugh. Her voice pitch had changed, and her breathing was more conscious.

'I'm sorry my darling, truly, utterly and sincerely.'

'Alright, don't milk it. I'm going to go now, don't go back to sleep. I can't wait to see you.'

'Me neither.'

They said their goodbyes and Alec smiled as he hung up. *She is certainly going to keep me on my toes. I'm not sure if that's a good thing at my age.* He decided to leave for Mehringdamm now, to ensure he wouldn't fall back asleep and because he knew it would take him forever to get to the bus stop on Lindenstraße in his condition and in the snow. He stood up, his bare foot treading on the remote control that had fallen off his lap while he slept. He kicked it across the room in surprise and anger. *I'm not bending down for it.* He left the tv on in disgust and went into the hallway to put on his shoes. He slid his feet into them carefully, and gently lifted the foot so he could hook the back with his finger. Reaching down put pressure on his back, but he gritted his teeth and did it anyway. A little sweat and a lot of effort the shoes were on. He took his old trenchcoat down from the hook, *it'll have to do until I get a replacement,* and put it on. He checked he had his phone and his wallet in his suit jacket and opened the door.

Standing in front of the door, on the landing was a man. He was wearing a suit and tie, Alec could see the outline of a shoulder holster beneath the jacket. A scar on the left cheek. It took Alec a moment to place the face. *Outside the Golden Dolls club in the rain.*

'Captain Olegovich? What are you doing here? Weren't you told I didn't kill Jaromir?' Alec said, confused.

'Oh, I was told.' He swung his right hand and the baton he was holding extended and struck Alec on the side of his head, by the temple. Alec's world went bright and then dark, then he didn't feel anything as he fell in a heap on the floor.

30

'Wake up, you old bastard.' Olegovich snarled. He slapped Foster round the face. *That felt good.* He repeated the action. *Not too much, you don't know how much he can take.* Foster stirred but didn't wake. Olegovich reached for the bucket of icy water on the rough concrete floor. He threw it over Foster and then threw the bucket at him too. The thin metal made a satisfying clunk as it struck the unconscious man's head. *Nothing.* The water dripped from the man and the simple wooden chair he was tied to, onto the bare concrete floor.

Olegovich stood up from his crouch and walked to the window. He moved the edge of the blackout blind and looked down. He could see the cars speeding along Friedenstraße, their headlights blazing a trail through the snowy air, the lights reflecting the white and giving the landscape an eerie night-time brightness. He looked beyond the road and saw the cemetery opposite, dark and forbidding.

'You'll be there soon.' He said to his guest.

Still nothing. Olegovich could see the man was still alive, his chest was rising and falling. He just wished he'd wake up so he could have some fun. He looked at Foster. He'd already had bruising under his eyes, and when Olegovich had removed the man's shirt, he was dismayed to see the massive amounts of swelling and bruises on his back. *Someone kicked the shit out you. That's a shame. I wanted to be the one who did that.*

Olegovich sat down in the chair facing Foster and waited.

Foster started to come around an hour later. Olegovich sat forward in his chair in anticipation of the realisation that would come. Foster opened his eyes, squinting from the glare of the floodlight pointed at him. His breath was vapour, and he was shivering in the ice-box apartment. Olegovich could see the arms and chest muscles quivering to stay warm, legs shaking. The look on Foster's face was priceless. Pure confusion and pain.

'Where am I? What happened?' He said. Olegovich remained silent and waited.

He saw Foster's eyes widen as he remembered opening his door. *He looked so surprised.*

'Olegovich what's going on? Why? I didn't kill Polyakov.'

Stay silent, wait for the anger to take hold.

'Talk to me goddamn it!' Foster attempted to rise. The plastic ties held his hands to the arms of the chair. Olegovich could see every muscle straining to release him from the bonds. He couldn't move more than an inch. Foster tried kicking his legs at Olegovich, the kicks fell way short.

Wait.

'I didn't kill him. Let me go.' Foster tried rocking his body, starting with his head but couldn't gain any momentum. He gave up trying and sat back. He looked at Olegovich and waited.

Now. Olegovich slashed the baton against Foster's bare thighs. Once. Twice. He saw dark blood break through the risen welts. *This isn't satisfying enough.* Olegovich

250

transferred the baton to his left hand. He threw a punch with his right. It connected with Foster's cheek. *Better.* Another punch to the same place. Foster's head cracked back, and he screamed. *Yes!*

'You can scream all you want in here. We own the whole building and the ones either side. No one, but me, will hear you. Go ahead, I won't stop you. I want to hear you scream and beg and cry.'

He launched another punch hard in Foster's face. He aimed at the nose, aimed for a break. Something to get Foster's attention. But at the last second Foster lowered his head and Olegovich struck the forehead. He felt a knuckle pop and roared in pain. He slapped Foster with the baton in his other hand, but he knew it wasn't as strong as he wanted it to be and Foster had made a point. *He might be old, but he's smart. Be warier. Take your time. He's not going anywhere. Even if he dies of pneumonia in this cold room, he'll still be dead.* His hand began to swell. He moved and stood behind Foster to hide his discomfort. He looked down at his right hand, and the knuckles at the base of his little and ring fingers had sunk into the hand. He tried flexing the hand to make a fist, but his hand wouldn't close, and it hurt too much, in his mind it felt like the gears of his hand had crunched, the bones grinding against each other. He resisted the urge to vomit at the thought. Not a squeamish man, the feeling of arthritic bones grating away to nothing brought to mind a vision of his father attempting to tie his own laces, the agony writ large upon his face. His fingers no longer obeying their master. The shouting and the beatings as he bent down to help his father. Withered and useless. *Strong enough to wound my heart, though.*

Olegovich shook his hand to clear the memories and

251

the pain. He waited until he felt in control enough to speak without betraying his condition.

'There is a file on you in the SVR. I have read it. Not particularly impressive for someone so high up in his organisation.'

Foster didn't say a word. Olegovich could see he was listening as he had fractionally turned his head to hear what was said better.

'A decent, but not spectacular career. Ten years ago promotion to Head of Russia in Berlin. Second only to Newbury. Then nothing. A lonely, alcoholic, old man, despised by his colleagues.' Olegovich noticed Foster tense when he mentioned Newbury. *What's there I wonder? Jealously? Resentment?*

'I know you didn't kill Polyakov. I'm amazed anyone thought you would have. That would involve some balls. Some passion.' *Time to scare him, get that heart pounding.* 'We caught the man who did. He's currently in hospital getting his face repaired. He tried to keep silent, but soon sang when he realised how much trouble he was in. Just like you will do.' Olegovich swung the baton, and it struck Foster on the upper arm where the bandage was. *Not as much power in the strike as I would have liked.*

Foster cried out and started cursing. Olegovich struck him again in the same spot. Foster tried to move away but couldn't free himself from the restraints. Olegovich could hear the tears in his cries. Then he heard a laugh. *What?*

'You dumb bastard. The weight-lifting giant didn't kill Polyakov. His partner, Mihael-something did. A rodent-looking fella with a long nose and a hairband. For all your threats and baton-twirling, he held out on you.' Foster mocked him with more laughter. Olegovich could feel his anger rising, he struggled to contain it. *Not yet, you can't let him get to you. He'll pay.* Foster continued, 'Mihael is out of your reach too, Mr Not-so-Scary. He took a swan dive off the Humboldt Palace and found out he couldn't fly. I'd say he was a typical KGB officer, none too bright and easily swayed. But, he escaped your notice, what does that say about you? You're not so impressive. Tell me what is this all about?'

Olegovich was rocked by what Foster had said. *Kochanov lied to me? Foster doesn't sound like he's lying. His tone is making that clear. I heard about the man and the shooting at the palace it was all over the news. I didn't make the connection. Was Foster there?* Olegovich composed himself and walked back round to face Foster. *I want to see his face when I tell him.*

Olegovich sat down and looked at Foster. There was an air of defiance about him. *The arrogant fool. I'll wipe that smirk off his face.*

'I'll tell you what this is all about,' Olegovich said. *Finally it's time.* 'You killed my father, and I am going to make you scream over and over again. I am going to destroy you so much that even your dead brother won't recognise you when you join him.' Olegovich watched Foster's face change. His mouth opened, his eyes opened wider, the colour drained from his face. *I've waited a long time for this.*

253

31

Alec felt confused and angry. *His father? I don't even know the man. What the hell?... How dare he mention Mark.*

'I don't know who your father was,' Alec said. He looked directly at Olegovich trying to see a resemblance to someone from his past. *Nothing.*

The baton swung against his thigh, it slapped with a sting rather than the force Alec was expecting. *His weaker hand? I must have hurt him when he punched me.*

'You know who he was!' Olegovich screamed. Flecks of spit left his mouth.

'I really don't,' Alec said.

'How can you not know who he was? He was my father, you killed him.'

That doesn't help. I haven't killed a lot of men, I admit. But no one, apart from Mihael, that I knew their names. Some Russian guy? A voice the back of his mind started speaking to him, he couldn't place it.

'I don't know. Honestly. Who was he?'

Olegovich looked at him, Alec could see the hatred in his eyes.

'My father's name was Oleg Konstantinovich.'

Well, that makes sense, based on the patronymic. The patronymic is the Russian naming system of the middle name or patronymic, "ovich" meaning "son of". *I'm still none the wiser to who he was though.*

'He was a *Praporshchik*,' a warrant officer. In the GRU. He was stationed in Berlin. He'd been here for almost three years, he left the service in 1990.' The voice in Alec's head was shouting for attention now. 'It was in August of 1989 that you killed him. Gunned him down in a café, when you were with that traitorous whore.'

Oh shit. That useless piece of crap was this guy's dad? Alec's thoughts went back to that day, the GRU non-commissioned officer. Alec wanted to think about Stefanie, but he resisted the urge. *Now's not the time.*

'You remember!' Olegovich said, his voice triumphant. 'Now you know why you must die.'

'Wait,' Alec said. 'You said he left the service in 1990. I shot him the year before. He lived, I didn't kill him.'

'He didn't die until in 2007, but your bullet killed him. He had to retire. Give up the job he loved so much. He was in agony until he died. You robbed him of a life. You robbed me of a father.' He swung the baton at Alec, again and again, punctuating each statement with a swing on the baton.

Each one caught Alec on the upper right arm, the other one to the wounded one. Alec noted that he still favoured his weaker hand, the baton swings stung rather than hurt, but Alec acted like the strikes were more than slaps, he screamed in mock-pain with each blow. Alec noticed that although the chair didn't move when he rocked side-to-side, it did when he went from front to back. *I can work with that. I wonder if I can do an 'Arthur' on him? It won't take much to make him snap. He looks close enough already.* Alec thought about it while Olegovich hit him again with the baton. *He's twenty years younger than me and in far better shape, damaged hand notwithstanding. And you're tied to this chair, remember.* The strikes to the

255

arm were becoming a nuisance, he could feel his arm deaden due to the repeated blows. *Get him talking. Give yourself time. Claudia is probably looking for you.* He looked around the room for his clothes. *Over there.* He spied them bundled up in the corner, next to the dripping tap in the wall. *That suit was Saville Row, my best one.* He thought irrelevantly.

'So that is what this is about, because of me, you couldn't spend quality time with your father?'

'You destroyed his life. I will destroy yours.'

'Would it help if I said I was sorry?' *Sorry I didn't finish him in the café.*

'Your apologies would mean nothing to me. You have no idea what it was like for him, or me.'

'So, tell me. This'll be your only chance. Make me see what my actions caused. I know you've been thinking about this moment for years, all the things you wanted to say when you finally got the opportunity. Well, now's your chance, let it all out.' *Not too much, Alec. He's not like Mihael, this one has a brain. Reaching Captain at thirty-one isn't easy.* He looked down at the floor. 'Please?'

'So, you can give penance for your sins before you die? The Sacred Mystery of Confession. Your file didn't mention you were religious.' Olegovich referred to the Eastern Orthodox Church practice of repenting sins before death.

Is he religious? It could give us common ground, a small mistruth to create a bond, give me an opening. 'It's not something that really goes with the modern world of spying. I was raised Catholic and attended Mass every Sunday when growing up.' *In the words of the 45th US President: "Fake News".* 'Let's say I'm a closet believer, like many of your countrymen were before the war, theirs not through choice. You have to know your sins before you can repent them. Go on, tell me. It may give you some catharsis, some release.'

Olegovich raised the baton again, but his hand stayed. 'You're going to die tonight.'

'We're all going to die one day, only God knows when.'

'There is no getting out of this for you. You are going to die in a lot of pain and a lot of blood.'

'T- t- then there's no harm in you telling me what it was like, how you felt.' Alec put on the stammer in his voice. *Ever the optimist thinking you can lie, charm, and cheat your way out of this.* He argued with himself. *It's better than going out with a whimper.*

Alec saw Olegovich's eyes flare at the stuttering words and a wicked smile appeared on the Russian's face. *He likes the fear.* Olegovich swung the baton again. Alec made himself flinch and try to hide away from the blow. This one caught him on the side of his head. It was stronger than the previous ones. Another blow, this time to his forearm, another to his thigh. Each blow becoming stronger. *Alec, what are you playing at?* A strike to Alec's cheek opened the skin. He felt blood trickle down onto his chest. Again. The trickle became a splatter. Again. The splatter became a flood, covering his chest, stomach, and into the waistband of his boxers.

'Tell me goddamnit!' Alec screamed.

Olegovich stopped. Alec's breathing was heavy, his back slick with sweat. His front with blood. His cheek on fire. Olegovich grabbed Alec's face, lifting it up to the light. He looked into Alec's eyes. Satisfied with what he saw there he dropped his hand.

'I think I will. I don't want this to end quite so soon.'

He stopped, stood up and walked over to the window. He moved the blind and looked out as he composed his thoughts.

'My father came back from Berlin a wreck of a man. He was doing his duty, and it left him with nothing. Your bullet punctured his lung. There were complications with the operation. Left him on oxygen. He had a stroke. He was crippled down the left-hand side. He had to depend on my mother for everything. Unable to wash or dress himself. Then my mother died when I was ten...' Olegovich paused, he looked at Alec. Tears fell from his eyes. 'I became his carer. Do you know what it is like to have to clean up your father when he messes himself? The shame and embarrassment on his face. Having to be washed by his only child.

'We had no money; his pension was small. What we did have he spent on medicine and drink. His frustration at life and how it had turned out. Your name screamed over and over again. Alec Foster and his fucking whore. Alec Foster the British scum. The years of depression and anger. I was the only one there. The only one he could reach. The focus of the beatings. Have you ever had a crippled man try to beat you and being unable to? You have to pretend the blows hurt, the words sting. You beg them to stop. Just so they don't have to face the humiliation of being unable to even hurt you. I promised him I would get our revenge on you, and here you are. I hope he is looking down at us with a smile on his face.'

He stopped. The tears had gone, replaced with the zeal of purpose. *He will come at me now, and it won't stop until I'm dead. I'm out of options... Unless...*

'Your father was a joke. What was he? A warrant

officer? At his age? If he was any good, he'd have been at best a junior lieutenant. It wasn't me that kept him back. That was all on him. You call the woman a whore? She was a goddess. Your father probably saw her every day as he stood at his guard post job. He wouldn't be trusted to do anything else. He probably dreamt about her when he was fucking your mum. He wouldn't have had the guts to speak to her. She was so far removed from him, in terms of both rank and class. She looked like a movie star whereas he looked like he permanently stood at a bar. Serge-pisshead drowning his hate in cheap vodka then going home to beat his wife and kid and then masturbate to a woman who didn't know he even existed.

'Your father saw a woman he could never have, talking to a man wearing clothes he'd never afford. It wasn't duty, it was jealousy. He was a lousy shot. He had the drop on us, and only one bullet hit the mark, the others took out a window and a chunk of the ceiling. I'm surprised he didn't shoot himself in the foot. I shot him. He killed the woman I loved. I still picture him lying there amongst the broken china and upturned tables. Lying there in a puddle of his own blood and piss, he might well have shit himself too. He fucking stunk. So yes, I remember your father. I remember the bloodshot eyes, the shaking hands, and the piss stained trousers. I remember thinking how unfair it was that this pathetic man could extinguish the life of one of the brightest lights I had ever seen. I wish for both our sakes I had shot him over and over again. Just so his foul presence on this world had ended sooner. I am sorry, you know. Sorry that sack of shit wasn't man enough to end his own life, instead he hung on poisoning yours. I'm glad he's dead. I just wish it was sooner.'

The blood had drained out of Olegovich's face. His

eyes were wide open in shock.

'I'm going to kill you.' He charged at Alec. *Here we go.*

Olegovich hit Alec with his right hand, all the years of frustration and hate built up into one punch. The force knocked Alec back, the chair toppled. Olegovich screamed in pain and grasped his hand. He fell to his knees in agony. The fall backwards knocked the wind out of Alec, he gasped for air. *You're used to this now, the air will come, don't panic. Get yourself out of this chair.* The wooden chair back cracked when it landed. Alec started straining against it. He heard the wood splinter underneath him, he strained harder, and the chair arms came away from the back of the chair. Still struggling to breathe he rolled over and got to his knees. He arms were still attached to the chair arms, but it was a big improvement. He snapped off a chair leg and stood up. The oxygen had started to enter his lungs. Alec took a large lungful of air and lunged at Olegovich.

Alec slammed the chair leg into the side of Olegovich's head, knocking him to the floor. He regained his senses quicker than Alec thought he would and rolled away just as Alec struck again. Olegovich jumped to his feet, shaking his head. He positioned his feet in a forward martial arts stance, shoulder width apart, with the left foot forward, and waited for Alec's next move. *My only chance is that his reactions are slower because of the blow to the head, need to get this over with quick.* Alec moved forward cautiously holding the chair leg like a dagger. *It's not long enough to give me a reach advantage. I'll have to use it smartly. It's not much of a weapon, but it's all I have.* He feinted to go right, Olegovich followed the move. Alec moved back left and stabbed with the chair leg, it struck Olegovich on the damaged hand, and he howled in pain.

Alec followed it up with a punch to the gut, the chair leg leading. The wood impaled the Russian's stomach and lodged in the man's gut. Alec tried to pull it free, but Olegovich had grabbed his hand. They were face to face now, and Olegovich crashed a headbutt into Alec's face. Alec fell back, his nose broken. With Olegovich still holding his hand, he twisted in the fall onto his front. He flinched at the wet coldness of the concrete floor. Olegovich let go of the hand and jumped onto his back, knees first. Alec felt his ribs crack under the pressure and screamed. Olegovich pinned Alec to the ground with his body weight. He grabbed Alec's hair and slammed his face into the floor.

'Now you die.' *I'm sorry Claudia, I failed you. Sara, I'm sorry.*

He raised Alec's head and pushed down again with a cry of, 'For you, father!'

Alec was past seeing, his vision was black, his face deep red. He heard a crash from the door and then two bangs, the movement of his head stopped, and the weight above him slid off. He pressed his head against the concrete and allowed the darkness to carry him away.

32

Alec heard a page being turned in a book beside him. He slowly opened his eyes; the bright light made his pupils contract. He squinted, allowing only the bare minimum to penetrate. He turned his head towards the sound and coughed gently. *Don't want to spook anyone.* He could feel the cough in his ribs.

He heard a squeal and the squeak of the vinyl chair covering as the person sitting there moved. A thud as the book hit the floor.

'Uncle Alec!'

Alec smiled and then his eyes closed, and he drifted back to sleep.

'…he moved.' Alec heard Sara say.

'Of course, dear. He's been through a lot. It'll take him a while to come back to us.' *Their voices sound heavenly, like a pair of angels.* Alec tried raising a hand to get their attention, but he could feel its refusal. *I'm not paralysed, am I?* A bolt of fear shot through him. He forced his eyes to open. He ignored the pain from the sudden light. Two figures stood before him, he could make out their familiar figures, silhouetted against the brightness.

'…' He said. A hiss with no words, his swollen tongue preventing their formation. His lips dry and frozen in place.

'Alec?' Claudia.

'Uncle Alec?' Sara.

'…' He blinked a few times to clear his eyes. He licked his lips with no saliva. *A drink?* The women smothered him in their tears, he could feel his own running down his cheeks joining with theirs, then down his neck onto the sheets. They stayed like that for as long as they needed. Sara broke off first, then Claudia, with a kiss to his forehead. Alec's eyes had adjusted to the light, and he looked at the two women in his life with fresh, albeit red-rimmed, eyes. Sara, her brown hair up in her travelling pony-tail style, her blue eyes clear and sparkling. Claudia had her blonde hair in a similar style, Alec enjoyed the look it gave to the shape of her face. Her blue eyes were bloodshot, a knot of concern between her eyebrows.

'Can I get you anything Uncle Alec?'

'…' *Water.* He coughed.

'A drink?' He nodded his head.

'I'll be back in a sec,' she rushed off out of his field of vision.

'It's good to have you back, my darling.'

'…' *You are a vision.* He smiled. Alec decided that wasn't enough and waggled his eyebrows. He could feel tightness all around his face.

'Oh, Alec!' Claudia's voice broke.

Sara returned with a cup of water and a straw. She put the straw to his lips.

'The doctor said you could have only a little bit.'

Alec sucked on the straw and felt the cool relief of water hitting the inside of his lips, his gums, his tongue. He fought the impulse to suck harder and slowly wetted all areas of his mouth.

'T…t…thanks,' he said. His voice a scratchy whisper.

'It's good to have you back, Uncle Alec. I was so

worried.'

'I'm sorry.'

'Don't be silly,' she scolded him with a smile.

He looked at Claudia, 'my arms. Can't move 'em.'

She looked down at the bed. 'They're strapped down. Try wiggling your fingers.'

Alec strained and attempted the movement.

'They're moving. Can you feel anything?'

'I can.' The relief he felt was almost as great as the shame of his panic. He could feel his cheeks burning.

Claudia looked at him, 'you don't have to be embarrassed. It's an easy mistake to make. You have three broken ribs, they are strapped up, that might make it hard to breathe-''-Just seeing you does that,' Alec said.

'Nice line, Uncle Alec. Very smooth,' Sara said.

'May I continue?' Claudia said, sounding put-out but looking pleased with what he had said. 'Your ribs are strapped up; your arms were as well to stop you moving in your sleep and damaging the ribs further. The bullet wound on your arm has become infected, the doctor found pieces of toilet roll in there. I'm not going to ask. Your back is very badly bruised, as are your arms and legs. Your face...' Her voice caught, she coughed. 'Your face, well, your nose is broken and splinted to straighten it out, you have deep cuts on your cheeks that might scar, but the doctors said there are things they can do to try to minimise that.'

'That'll be from the baton he was waving around. So, you're saying I look a mess. But, at least I'm not paralysed.'

'More water Uncle?'

Sara brought the cup to his mouth again. He drank carefully.

'I'm so glad you're ok, Uncle.'

'I'm not sure how ok I am, but at least I'm here with my two most favourite people in the world.'

'You're so soppy sometimes. Especially for a grumpy old man.' She reached down for a gentle hug and then sat back on the chair.

'Sara, could you give Claudia and me some time? We need to talk about what happened.'

'Of course, Uncle Alec. I'll let you and Aunty Claudia "Talk".' She held her hands up and performed an air quote gesture. She laughed as she stood up, noticed her book on the floor and picked it up. 'I'll go and read this in the visiting room. The chairs there are comfier there anyway.'

'I'll come and get you when we're finished,' Claudia said.

'Thanks, Aunty.' She left the room.

'So, my dear, what happened? I remember Olegovich smashing my face into the floor, but after that there's nothing.'

Claudia sat on the bed next to him, she reached for his hand and intertwined her fingers with his.

'When you didn't turn up at Mustapha's kebab, we went to your flat thinking you'd fallen asleep. Your front door was partially open, and there was blood on the landing. Peter and Sara waited, and I went inside to see if you were still there. I was so scared something had happened to you. I couldn't breathe. I checked all the rooms, the tv was left on in the living room, but obviously, you weren't there. So, I called Control and got them to trace your phone.'

'You're going to have to stop doing that, you know. It's a terrible invasion of my privacy.'

'Shut up, darling,' she smiled. 'Anyway, they traced

you to the apartment building on Friedenstraße. They were very surprised when their system flagged the building was owned by the Russians. Our security team picked me up, and we headed to the building. Only one of the apartments had its lights on so we forced entry to the main entrance and headed up there. The security team burst the door open, and we entered. Immediately we saw you were out cold, covered in blood. I thought you were dead. Oh my god, you looked awful. Olegovich went to slam your head into the floor, and I shot him. I checked you for a pulse and… here we are.' Tears ran down her face.

'You saved my life. You know that, don't you? Without you there he would have killed me. I'll never forget that.' *I wish I could move my arms. I want to hold her so badly.*

'Why was he trying to kill you? Wasn't he told you didn't kill Jaromir?'

'It was nothing to do with Jaromir. I killed his pathetic father, years ago. He was avenging him.'

'You killed his father?'

'Yeah,' Alec frowned. 'He was the Russian that killed Stefanie in '89, I told you about that the other day. How long have I been in here anyway?'

'Four days.'

Alec whistled, 'I've never had so much sleep. Thanks to you it wasn't permanent. Where was I? Oh yes, Oleg Konstantinovich was his name. I never knew it. He died in 2007. Olegovich was convinced it was because I shot his father eighteen years previously. He blamed me for his shitty upbringing and shitty father.'

'How do you feel about that?'

'I don't think I'll lose any sleep over it. Stefanie was special. Almost as special as you. She didn't deserve to die at his hands. How about you? You're the one that killed

Olegovich.'

'I feel fine, it was either him or you,' she shrugged. 'It was no contest.'

'I was expecting you to tell me it was a hard choice, that you agonised over it before tossing a coin.'

'I'm not in a teasing mood,' she smiled. 'I think it must be the odour coming from you, I'm not sure you were cleaned off before they put you in that bed.' She waved her hand in front of her nose.

'Well, luckily for me you're here to give me a sponge bath.'

Claudia laughed and shook her head. 'If you're well enough to think about stuff like that I think you're well enough to do it yourself.'

'Spoilsport.'

Claudia stuck her tongue out at him. The door to the room opened, and a doctor and nurse entered.

'*Herr* Foster, it is good to see you awake finally. We are going to run some tests to determine the extent of your injuries.'

'I'll go and join Sara, we'll be back in a bit,' Claudia said. She squeezed Alec's hand. 'It's so good to have you back with us.' She bent down and kissed his forehead. She stood up, gave his hand another squeeze and left the room. Alec followed her with his eyes. A tear came to the corner of his eye, hung around for a few seconds and then trickled down his cheek. *You are a lucky man, Alec, don't ever forget that.*

'So, *Herr Doktor*, how long am I going to be stuck here?'

***

267

'Have you got what I asked?' Alec asked Claudia as she came into the hospital room. Her hair was damp, and there were rain streaks on her coat. Alec was sitting in the chair beside the bed. *The Gone-Away World* book from his apartment in his hands. Sara had picked it up for him, along with some of his clothes, before she had left to go back to England.

'Yes, I've got it.' She held up her handbag. 'Are you sure you want to do this alone? You've been in here for two weeks now. You haven't been anywhere apart from a walk to the bathroom and the occasional jaunt down the corridor to the hospital shop.' She sat on the arm of his chair. Alec wrapped an arm around her narrow waist.

'I'm sure. It's not that I don't want you there. I don't want to go anywhere without you. She's part of Stefan's world. I'm not sure the fact I've been lying to her for twenty years would go down very well. Especially if I turn up with a supermodel on my arm.'

'You old smoothie.' She smiled. 'So, you're keeping Stefan going?'

'Yeah, he's like an old friend now, I've had enough of letting them go. Did Sara get away alright?'

'Yes, I dropped her and Peter off at "Alex" as you guys call it. They are very much in love you know. Peter is a lovely young man.'

'Has he decided what he's going to do? I think he's gone off the idea of corporate lawyering. His heart was never fully in it.'

'He did mention something about maybe looking at joining the service in some capacity, especially now he can get the hero who saved the Prime Minister's life and solved the murder of one of the Heads of the SVR to recommend him.'

'What me? I think he over-estimates any influence I may have.'

'You'd be surprised, you've been stuck in here since the incident. There is talk about you taking Arthur's spot. He won't be needing it.'

'It's a shame they took away the death penalty for treason.'

'What about the job?'

'We'll see, I may have to decline and visit the distilleries of Europe. There's a woman who would be a better candidate anyway. Smart and clever, it's hard to be both, you know. Popular within the whole Berlin office, has all the right connections, well, apart from a strange affection towards a trampy partner, and is smoking hot too.'

Claudia blushed. 'I was going to go with you on your imbibing tour, remember.'

'Like I said, we'll see. If I'm the hero you said people are saying, I'll have some influence over both your careers. I'm too old for a promotion, and if you remember I didn't handle the last one very well.'

'Well, that's true. You were awful.'

'Thanks, Your Royal Bluntness,' he laughed. 'We'll talk about it later. Shall I meet you at yours or do you want to go to mine?'

'I've seen the state of your place. Do you even own a vacuum?'

'So, yours it is, then. I'll be there around ten. If I'm late, you have my permission to track my phone.'

'I wasn't going to ask. I think I'll be keeping tabs on you until you're back to full strength and even then…'

Alec took her hand, 'It's over now. Nothing will come between us again.'

Claudia bent her head down and kissed him soundly. 'I hope so. You better go now, it'll take you a while to get there with your cane.'

'I was thinking of leaving it. I'm not that old that I need a cane.'

'You do need it. It's just temporary to give you and your back support after all the abuse it took recently. Think of it as a sword, you can be Errol Flynn swashbuckling your way through the Berlin public transport system.'

'That does sound attractive. I think I'll be Inigo Montoya from *The Princess Bride* instead though.' The famous line from the film came to Alec's mind: "Hello, my name is Inigo Montoya. You killed my father. Prepare to die." *Maybe not.*

Alec moved closer to the edge of the chair, and Claudia stood up to give him room. He placed his hands on the arms of the chair to support himself as he stood up. He reached for the cane beside the chair and his book and placed them on the bed. He walked over to the coat hooks and took down his recently laundered trenchcoat. The act of lifting his arms was far less painful than it had been a few days before. Claudia came over and helped him into it. She straightened his tie and fussed with his hair. She went over to the bed and collected his cane and book and handed them to him. Alec slipped the book into the coat pocket and gave the cane a few swings.

'*En garde!*' He put himself in a fencing pose and prodded Claudia gently with the tip of the cane. She shook her head.

'One of these days you'll grow up.'

'Not if I have my way. Shall we go my fair maiden?' He bowed stiffly and held his arm out for her to take.

They walked arm in arm through the hospital, Alec's free hand getting used to the cane. The rubberised tip making the occasional squeak on the highly polished floor. They took the Große Hamburger Straße exit. The rain had ceased, the cobbled pavement was slick with water.

'Watch your step,' Claudia warned. 'What station do you want to go to?'

'You need the Hackescher Markt station, the S7. So, I'll drop you off there and get the tram from Monbijouplatz to Alex and then hop on the U2 to Nollendorfplatz.'

'How do you know this off the top of your head? It's incredible really.'

'Some people collect stamps or shoes, I collect public transportation routes. It's served me well in the past and especially recently.'

'That's true. I can't believe you ran from the Cathedral to Hausvogteiplatz station. I walked it the other day to see how far it was. I didn't think you had it in you.'

'Me neither, to be honest.'

They walked south along Große Hamburger Straße past the Jewish Memorial Cemetery and the Magicum – Berlin's magic museum – opposite, down to the Sixties diner on the corner with Oranienburger Straße, they followed the road round to the right, to Monbijouplatz.

'Is that your tram stop?' Claudia asked.

'Yeah, I'll walk you to the station though, it's just down here.'

They walked down Monbijouplatz, with the Monbijou Park to their right, the trees bare and forbidding with the grey blanket over the sky and chill air. A couple of minutes later they walked under the bridge supporting train tracks, the thunderous rumble of a train passing above them echoed around them. They came out onto Kleine

Präsidentenstraße. Alec could see the Berliner Dom ahead of them. *Didn't I come this way with Mihael?* He felt no pity for the man. *He killed Jaromir, kidnapped Sara and was going to kill me. He got what he deserved.*

'The hero returns to the place of his victory.' Claudia said.

'I was just thinking that, but not the hero or the victory part. It seems so long ago. We go to the left, away from the cathedral.'

They went along Henriette-Herz-Platz. It felt strange retracing the steps he took with Mihael, past the eateries under the station. He held Claudia tighter as they passed the BBQ Kitchen restaurant. They soon came to the entrance of the Hackescher Markt station. They stopped outside, Claudia gave Alec a hug, and they kissed passionately.

'I'll see you soon,' Alec said.

'You better.' She turned to walk away, stopped and reached into her handbag. 'You'll need this won't you?' She took out a beige envelope wrapped in a brick shape. She handed it to him. He put it in his pocket, the other one to his book.

'Thanks, I forgot about that.'

'I do worry about you. Old age making you lose your marbles, the bangs to your head wouldn't have helped.'

'I love you too.' Alec kissed her on her cheek. She smiled and turned. She walked into the station, twice looking back at him standing there; he watched her go and resisting the urge to join her. *As much as it pains me when we part, I do like watching her leave. I must do this though.*

33

Alec turned to walk back to the Monbijouplatz tram stop but changed his mind. *Alexanderplatz is only ten minutes away. I'll walk it. I hate backtracking on myself.* Alec continued along Henriette-Herz-Platz, turned left onto An der Spandauer Brücke, ducked under the bridge this side of the station and turned right onto Dircksenstraße. He followed the curve of the road as it ran parallel to the train tracks. Passed the restaurants all along the road, under the tracks. *Doesn't the noise of the train or the vibrations disturb the ambience?* He could see the Fernsehturm tower poking out over the tracks, watching over East Berlin. The station was very close to the tower. He remembered taking Sara up to the viewing platform on one of her first trips to Berlin. She loved the view from up there so much they went back that night to see the city lit up. The road straightened, and he could see Alexanderplatz station in the near distance. He quickly crossed Karl-Libenicht Straße and walked, cane prodding the ground to the station. *This is where Peter was when I spoke to him on the phone.* Alec turned around and looked behind him. *Mihael and the weightlifter's car would have been parked there.* A chill swept through him at the thought of Sara's kidnapping. *Mihael paid for it though.*

He entered the station and headed to the U-bahn platform. He found it easily enough and stood at the platform and waited for the train. It didn't take long. He pressed the button to open the doors and hobbled on. He sat near the door. The doors closed after their warning alarm and the train moved off. He passed all the stations he had the night Jaromir was killed. He didn't fall asleep this time.

The train stopped at Bülowstraße, and Alec gathered his thoughts and put them away in a corner of his mind. The doors closed, and the train continued, passed the buildings with house-sized murals on them. *I think I like street art. It's better than graffiti, I'm not sure I understand it though.* The sky was darker now, streetlights had switched on. The train slowed as it came up to Nollendorfplatz, and then stopped. Alec stood up, holding the edge of the seat partition for support. He leaned on his cane with his other hand. He stepped off the train as the doors began to beep and headed down the platform to the right. He walked with unaccustomed hesitancy. Hesitant about being knocked on his arse and hesitant about what was coming. He walked down the stairs to the ground floor, holding the bannister as he went, trying not to trip other travellers with his cane. He exited the station to the left.

He looked for Brigette as he came out, she wasn't where he'd seen her before. *I may be too early.* He walked around the station, past where it seemed like a city's worth of bicycles were stored. *There.* She was standing with a group of other women, some young, some a little older. He heard her dirty laugh and smiled. He tottered over to her, his cane occasionally catching on the uneven block paving.

'Hello, you *Geiler alter Mann*,' horny old man, she said with a touch of distaste in her voice. 'I'll be with you in a moment. I don't think you'll be able to handle me though. Maybe one of the younger girls will be better.'

'I don't think I could have handled you when I was

younger,' Alec said. 'Sometimes I wish I had tried.'

Brigette's eyes widened, 'Stefan? Is that you?' Her voice changed to one of excitement. It reminded Alec of how she sounded all those years ago. He smiled at her and made an awkward little bow.

'I promised I'd be back to take you for coffee.'

'I can't believe it.' She crossed the gap between them and gave him a hug and a kiss on the mouth. He winced when she tightened the clinch. She must have felt him tense. She released the embrace and looked at him.

'Oh my god, are you ok?'

'Is there somewhere around here that does a decent cup? I'll tell you all about it.'

Brigette took him to Miss Honeypenny on Winterfeldtstraße, a sports bar. Alec smiled at the name. *Is she hinting that she knows I'm a spy?* They walked past the empty tables out front into the bar, it wasn't much busier. They sat at a table away from the bar and away from the outside. Brigette sat facing the wall, leaving the opposite seat with the view of the bar for Alec. *She remembers after all this time?*

'I'll have a coffee and a brandy,' Brigette said.

'I'll have the same, that'll warm us up.' Alec hobbled over to bar. He ordered the drinks and pointed at the table. The bartender nodded, and Alec returned to the table and sat down.

'I didn't think I'd see you again,' Brigette said

'I did promise. After the help you gave me I couldn't go back on it.'

'I didn't do anything. Did you catch up with Makary?'

'Yeah, he was DJing at the club like you said. Thank you. I had to agree to a night out with him, but he helped me.'

'So, what happened to you?'

'If you remember I said I was in trouble.'

'Yes.'

'Well,' he waved his hand in front of his face. 'It found me.'

The bartender brought over the drinks. The coffee was steaming, the brandy welcoming. Alec lifted the brandy and toasted, 'To renewed friendships.' They clinked their glasses and took a drink. The liquid burned Alec's throat and made him cough. Brigette laughed.

'That's not the Stefan I remember.'

'It's been a while since I had a drink. Where was I? Oh yes, trouble. Did you hear about an attempt on the British Prime Minister a couple of weeks ago, and maybe a Russian being shot in a bar?'

'Yes, didn't a man fall from the top of the palace onto spiked railings and the police found a rifle there or something. I didn't hear about a Russian being shot. Wait, a couple of weeks ago? There was a city-wide manhunt for a man, the picture on the newspapers wasn't very clear, but I thought he looked familiar.'

'The man from the palace kidnapped my niece, he also killed my friend, from the Russian embassy and tried to kill me. He didn't fall. I made sure he couldn't do it again. The picture was me. The police thought I killed my friend.'

'So, you stopped the man from killing the Prime Minister, rescued your niece, how is she doing by the way? I remember when she was born; you couldn't stop talking about her. It was like she was your own child. You rescued her and avenged your friend's murder. Wow, that's hot.' She smiled. 'Why hasn't there been any mention of this on the television. You're an action hero, like James Bond, or the German equivalent at least. You could make a fortune selling your story to Hollywood.' Her eyes were sparkling.

'Work wouldn't like it. We're supposed to keep a low profile. I'm glad the photo in the papers was so bad. I would have been forced out of my job otherwise. Oh, Sara's doing good. She's met a man, Peter. He's English, a little older than her, but seems like a really decent man. So that's good.'

'I'm glad for her. You talked so much about her, when we met up, it's like she's my own niece. I could have sworn you were getting broody. So, how's your love life? Any children? Married?' She rested her arms on the table, and her face was cradled by her hands, she looked into his eyes. Alec had the thought that there was something behind the question, something deeper than the usual how-are-you-doing chat between friends. *Be kind.*

'No, no children. I missed that boat. Because of something that happened I couldn't let myself believe I deserved a second chance at love, so I pushed away from the two of the three women I have loved.'

Brigette sat there, her mouth open wide at his words. *I hope I haven't made her believe there's a chance for us. That wasn't my intention. If Claudia hadn't happened, then maybe it could have been.*

'One of them was Stefanie, she's in the picture you have from the other night. She died in my arms, shot because of me. Shot because of a difference in political ideologies.'

'The other two?' She asked.

'Well… you're one of the two. I did love you, you know. If I had been stronger things could have been different, they should have been. I'm sorry. I was an emotional wreck. I do still love you, but it's not the same. I would do anything for you, I hope you know that. But that leads me on to the other one…'

Alec could see the disappointment clear on her face, then saw it change to forced indifference. *Shit. I'm sorry Brigette. I'm not good at this.*

'Who is she?'

'Her name is Claudia, we were together a long time ago, after Stefanie. We ended it as she wanted commitment and I couldn't allow myself to give it. She married my friend and has two amazing kids, they're grown up now. My friend died, about a year before my brother and his wife did. Cancer. That fucked me up: them all dying so quickly together. I retreated into a bottle and away from the world, until Jaromir, my Russian friend, was killed. Somehow, Claudia and I got back together, and things are good between us. I'm sorry Brigette. I never wanted to hurt you, and I mean it I'll always be here for you like you were the other night for me.'

'I hope you and Claudia are very happy.' She wiped a traitorous tear from the corner of her eye. Alec reached over and held her other hand. She swiped it away. Took a deep breath and stood up. She reached into her handbag and took out the picture of Stefanie. 'I suppose you want this back.' She dropped it on the table and walked out of the bar. Alec collected the photo, put it in his jacket's inside pocket. He laid twenty Euros on the table and rushed as fast as he could in his state after her. Out of the bar, he looked both ways for her but couldn't see her. *Shit!* He started walking to the right and then back to the left. He couldn't decide which way she could have gone. He held his head in his hands and ran his fingers through his hair in frustration. *You idiot!* He kicked one of the chairs. It scraped across the pavement on metal legs and toppled with a clash. He stood there for what seemed like ages, then picked the chair up and put it back. As he did so, he saw her on the other side of the street, partially hidden by a tree. He smiled and crossed the road. *Thank you.*

'I thought you had gone.'

'You didn't have to take it out on that poor chair.'

'It was asking for it. Shouldn't have got in my way. I'm sorry I'm no good at talking about emotions and feelings. Even having any is new ground for me. I meant what I said though. I do love you and always will. It just never was the right time for us.' He took the beige brick out of his pocket. 'This is what you said I owe you, I don't think it covers it, but it's yours. My number is inside. If you ever need me, I'll come running. I promise. However, I'm not planning on leaving it another ten years before I see you again, if you don't mind, I'd like to keep you in my life. You are one of my dearest friends, and at my age, you need as many as you can get.'

'Of course, I'll still be in your life. You are stupid you know. You'll have to introduce me to Claudia, I'll judge if you're worthy of her.' She took the envelope from him and dropped it in her bag. 'I'm going to go now, maybe spend some of this. I love you, Stefan, don't be a stranger.' She kissed him deeply, he felt her tongue force its way into his mouth, could taste the brandy on it. She abruptly broke the kiss off. 'Just so you'll know what you could have had.' She walked off towards Viktoria-Luise-Platz, her head held high. He watched her go. *Damn. I won't tell that part to Claudia.*

Alec returned to Nollendorfplatz and took the U1 train to Uhlandstraße. He sat in thought, rocking to the motion of the train, oblivious to the other passengers thinking of the events of the call from Jaromir, that night and the following ones, thinking what he could have done differently. It was what he had been doing in the hospital when visiting times were over, and he was alone. He thought about Jaromir, Brigette, Makary, Roger, Claudia, Newbury, Peter, Sara, Mihael, and Olegovich. *I'm damn lucky to still be here.* It was the conclusion he reached each time.

The train stopped in Uhlandstraße and Alec got off and headed up the stairs onto Kurfürstendamm, he walked down past Douglas perfume shop, The House of Villeroy & Boch store, and when he reached the Steiff toy store turned right onto Knesebeckstraße then left onto Mommsenstraße. *Almost home.*

He came to Claudia's building and entered the lobby. He walked up the stairs to her floor. It took him a long time, but the cane helped his stability. *She's always right.* He pressed the intercom with its harsh buzzer, and she opened the door to him with a wide smile and embraced him.

'I'm glad you're home, how did it go?'

'Better than expected. We've made plans to elope, I'm only here to collect my stuff.' Alec saw Claudia's face drop, and he realised that she had been worried, not about his safety but his past. 'I'm only kidding. Don't you remember me saying I'm never letting you go ever again.'

She kissed him passionately, taking his breath away. When they finished his knees were trembling, his heart was pounding.

'I thought you were worried about what your neighbours would say.' He said once he was able to speak.

'Fuck 'em,' she said. 'I'm never letting you go again either.' She pulled him into the apartment and closed the door.

That night, Alec woke from his sleep. He felt there was something amiss. He got out of bed, careful not to disturb Claudia. He put on Roger's robe and opened the bedroom door. *Nothing.* He went into the hallway and closed the door behind him. He looked in the kitchen, the children's rooms and the living room. *Nothing. There's no one here.* He sat on the sofa in the dark and tried to think. It came to him, eventually. There had been no faces in his sleep, no mist, no blood, no accusations, no guilt. He hadn't had the dream; the nightmares had stayed away. *Well, isn't that something.* He stood up and crept back into the bedroom, he got back into bed as carefully as he had left it. He slowly backed himself up against Claudia's naked form, enjoying the warmth of her skin against his, the feel of her breathing. He closed his eyes and drifted off to sleep with a smile on his face.

The End

Acknowledgements

First, I would like to thank my wife, Helen for all her support, and patience. I'm sorry for all the late nights, and for continuously talking about my book. She was also the one who pushed me to submit my opening to Pen to Print. So, it's all her fault, really.

I'm going to give a big shoutout to my boys, Ethan, Logan, and Brandon, because I know the older two will get a kick out it (and hopefully the little one will when he learns to read). Hey little dudes, stop fighting, you've got each other for life, be nice and always be there for each other.

Thanks to Lena Smith and Zoinul Abidin at LBBD for organising the Pen to Print Book Challenge, and giving me this opportunity to shine, and thank you to David Walshaw and the team at New Generation Publishing for doing all the boring tasks, such as typesetting, eBook conversion etc.

A huge thank you to Barbara Nadel for letting me take up her precious time to mentor me, giving me great advice and support, and for the arduous challenge of editing my very rough words into a decent shape. Buy her books 😊.

Thank you to Lesley and Peter for their all help, comments, and time to make sure the first chapter was good enough to submit.

I've tried to make the book as accurate as possible, and actually went to the Becketts Kopf Bar and the Klo Bar during my research trip to Berlin. They are both very different places, but are both high on atmosphere and customer satisfaction. If you get a chance go to Mustafa's Gemüse Kebap on Mehringdamm do so. It is out of this world. Unfortunately I don't have Alec's unlimited 'company' resources so I couldn't try out the Goldhorn Beefclub restaurant, maybe another time. I didn't go to the Golden Dolls strip club either, I'm not as seedy as Alec, but supposedly it is the best one in the city.

The Bob Dylan quote in the epigraph, comes from an interview he did with AARP magazine in 2015. The article is available online and is a great read. I had written the story first and thought of a title 'A Young Man's Game' and was searching the internet to see if it had been used before when I came across the quote and thought it fitted perfectly with Alec Foster's struggles in the book.

The Inigo Montoya quote is from The Princess Bride by William Gibson, and also the film of the same name. The book is highly enjoyable and the film is one of my favourites.

I would also like to thank you for reading this. I hope you enjoyed it as much as I enjoyed writing it. Please leave reviews wherever you can and feel free to add me on Twitter @paulblakeauthor and say 'Hi'.

Paul Blake, London, 2018

Lightning Source UK Ltd.
Milton Keynes UK
UKHW01f1958240718
326227UK00001B/14/P